"Where are

Tuk shook his hea[...]
are no longer wh[...]

Annja felt the pillows. The fabric they [...]
was smooth and silky to the touch. She looked around
the room and saw that the same type of material
covered the walls. Light came from somewhere, but
it was subdued and reflected inward from an outside
source. The room seemed designed to transition people
from wherever they'd been into this place. Waking up
to a harsh lightbulb probably wasn't the best way to do
that, so the lighting was dim, but Annja could still see
everything.

"How long have you been awake?" she asked.

"A few minutes, no more," Tuk said. "I'm afraid that when
you told me to stop breathing, I did exactly the opposite
and took a huge breath, which no doubt hastened my
own demise as it were."

Annja grinned. "You can't be faulted for that."

Tuk leaned closer. "You know, that is the second time
I have seen that sword of yours. How is it possible for
that to somehow conceal itself on your body and not be
noticeable?"

Annja laughed. "If I tried to explain it to you, you'd only
have more questions. And they'd probably be questions
I couldn't answer. Not because I don't want to. But
because I don't know the answers myself."

Tuk leaned back. "I see. But you have it here still?"

Annja closed her eyes and saw the sword hovering in
the otherwise. "It's here," she said.

Titles in this series:

ROGUE Angel

Alex Archer

FALSE HORIZON

A GOLD EAGLE BOOK FROM

WORLDWIDE®

TORONTO • NEW YORK • LONDON
AMSTERDAM • PARIS • SYDNEY • HAMBURG
STOCKHOLM • ATHENS • TOKYO • MILAN
MADRID • WARSAW • BUDAPEST • AUCKLAND

Recycling programs
for this product may
not exist in your area.

First edition March 2011

ISBN-13: 978-0-373-62148-4

FALSE HORIZON

Special thanks and acknowledgment to
Jon Merz for his contribution to this work.

Printed in U.S.A.

The
LEGEND

...THE ENGLISH COMMANDER TOOK
JOAN'S SWORD AND RAISED IT HIGH.

The broadsword, plain and unadorned,
gleamed in the firelight. He put the tip against
the ground and his foot at the center of the blade.
The broadsword shattered, fragments falling
into the mud. The crowd surged forward,
peasant and soldier, and snatched the shards
from the trampled mud. The commander tossed
the hilt deep into the crowd.
Smoke almost obscured Joan, but she continued
praying till the end, until finally the flames climbed
her body and she sagged against the restraints.

Joan of Arc died that fateful day in France,
but her legend and sword are reborn....

1

Nepal was one of the places in the world where Annja Creed felt that the line between fantasy and reality grew very thin. It's relatively modern city, Katmandu, still nestled enclaves of the old world—when the lines between Buddhist, Taoist and Hindu religions intersected and the Mongols of the north fell down upon their southern neighbors. And the most imposing, the massive Himalayan mountain range shadowed the entire region with its sheer magnitude and incredible stillness and tranquility.

In Katmandu, motorbikes raced around while rickshaws still peppered the streets pulled by wiry little men intent on earning enough money to feed their families. Dust filled the air and gasoline fumes tainted every breath.

Masses of eyes watched every happening on the crowded streets. While Nepal was ostensibly a monarchy, it also shared a border with Tibet and China beyond that. As such, intelligence services from around the globe plied their cloak-and-dagger trade in the shadows and overhangs of the city. Paid informants kept track of their various targets and Annja knew it would be almost impossible to lose any surveillance she might pick up.

Not that she expected to be followed.

Her purpose for being in the capital city was one of pure adventure and not some underhanded government operation. And she felt excited about the prospect of finding the target of her quest.

She'd journeyed from her home in New York at the behest of Professor Mike Tingley, head of the Ancient Religions department at Charlesgate University. He'd emailed Annja and asked her if she might be interested in accompanying him on his trip. When Annja saw where he was headed, she immediately made plans for a personal leave from hosting her cable television show, *Chasing History's Monsters,* and started planning in earnest.

The flight over from New York City to the first waypoint in Osaka, Japan, took twelve hours. Annja used the time to research as much about their quest as was possible. In the Osaka airport, she bought a bowl of soba noodle soup at one of the stands and watched as tourists buzzed past her. She never tired of visiting foreign countries and exploring their cultures.

The connecting flight put her in Katmandu the next day. As Annja deplaned, the sights and sounds of the region rushed back to greet her. With her visa properly stamped, she hailed a taxi.

"Thamel," she requested.

The driver shook his head. "I can't drive in Thamel. Streets too narrow. You need to take a rickshaw."

Annja handed him a twenty-dollar bill. "Take me as far as you can and I'll get along the rest of the way."

The driver eyed the twenty and shook his head. "Dollar not good anymore. America economy bad."

Annja frowned and pulled out another twenty. "How about this?"

The driver pocketed the money and nodded. "Now it's good." He shifted the taxi into Drive and bolted out of the parking space outside the airport terminal.

Annja opened her window and took in the smells of Katmandu. The combination of diesel fumes and sewage made her nose crinkle but only for a moment. She remembered the scent and knew it was only a matter of time before she grew used to it.

Nothing's changed, she thought. The city still looks the same.

Twenty minutes after leaving the airport, the driver braked by a corner congested with people. "As far as I go. Thamel's a few blocks farther down."

Annja thanked him, then hopped out and dragged her bag with her. In all the years that she'd been traipsing across the globe, she'd mastered the science of packing light. She had a few key articles of clothing that could be combined into an endless array of outfits. That, plus her laptop computer and a credit card for quick purchases, helped her feel at ease with just a backpack.

She walked down the street as the sounds of the city bombarded her ears. Honking seemed to be its own form of communication. From the deep blasts of the truck horns trying to muscle their way through the city to the nasally *beep-beeps* of motorbikes threading through paths barely wide enough to accommodate them, the air felt thick with driver frustration.

Annja smiled as she reached the outskirts of Thamel and entered the quieter enclave. Traffic was significantly lighter. Rickshaws pulled past her and she waved two of them off. Small motorbikes zipped by, some of the drivers pausing to stare at her. Annja shook her head. She knew she was probably quite exotic-looking to the people of Nepal with her height, her long thick chestnut hair and amber-green eyes. She didn't feel beautiful, especially not after the long flight, but people had commented on her looks enough that she accepted that many considered her to be very attractive, even if she wasn't comfortable with it. She wanted a hot shower and a good night's sleep. But first, she had to meet with Mike.

In his last email, he'd told Annja where to find him. He wanted to meet in the place they'd enjoyed so much the last time Annja had been here, a small American eatery called Blue Note.

It was the one place in Katmandu that Mike could find his favorite meal of all time—a cheeseburger and a cold beer.

Annja spotted the faded blue sign swinging back and forth in the dusty air and smiled. The owner refused to slap a fresh coat of paint on the building, preferring to keep an understated profile.

At the door Annja paused and then pushed her way inside. Instantly, she heard Ella Fitzgerald belting out an old song. She saw the gaggle of American faces turn toward her. She could pick out the mountaineers among them. They were eagerly poring over maps and studying the best routes that would take them in sight of Mount Everest.

But the Blue Note also attracted its fair share of surly characters, as well. She spotted two unshaven hulks of muscle eyeballing her from across the bar. Then she saw Mike's hand waving her over and she grinned.

Mike Tingley looked more like a linebacker than a professor of obscure religions. He'd gone to college on a football scholarship and had refused to stop exercising as his years advanced. Almost forty-five, Mike could easily bench over three hundred pounds and his presence was more than enough to belay any hostility.

He rose as Annja came over to his table. "I see you made

it safely." He hugged her and then stepped back. "You look amazing."

Annja grinned and punched him in the arm. "Cut it out. You know I just crawled off a plane after almost a full day in the air."

Mike gestured for her to sit. "Grab a chair. I'm sure you've got questions."

"Do you have the answers, though?" she asked.

He grinned. "First things first. You want a burger?"

Annja looked at Mike's plate. Judging by the few remnants, he had already inhaled his favorite meal. "If I order one, do you promise to leave it alone?"

"I've already had my fill. You know I can't resist this place." He waved a waiter over and ordered for Annja. When the waiter returned a moment later with their beer, Mike raised his glass.

"Here's to you, Annja. I appreciate you making the trip over. Really."

Annja clinked glasses with him and then took a long sip. She put the glass down and smiled. "I'm happy to be here again. It's been too long since we've worked together. Thanks for asking me to come along."

Mike leaned forward. "So? What do you think of my plan?"

"At first I wasn't sure what to think," Annja said. "I mean what you're proposing has been mulled over and even searched for for so long that most people consider it a pure fantasy. Or that it must have been destroyed many, many centuries ago."

"And that's what makes this so exciting," Mike said. "Because I'm positive that everyone else has been searching in the entirely wrong part of this country for it. Everyone's been wrong."

"Except for you," Annja said. "Imagine that."

"Well," Mike said. "I might be wrong, too. I guess we won't know for sure until we actually get out there and find it."

"What made you think you could even find the place, anyway?"

"It's been a hobby of mine ever since I read the book that first described it in detail."

"But *Lost Horizon* was a work of fiction. No one really believed that, did they?" Annja asked.

Mike nodded. "Plenty of people did. And plenty of them thought they were going to find it. As recently as a few years ago, there were still exploration teams making concerted efforts to locate it. But no one has ever succeeded."

"Until now."

Mike raised his glass. "You're always the optimist, Annja. That's what I love about you."

"Plus, I'm the only friend of yours who's crazy enough to actually fly across the globe to be a part of this."

"There's that, too," Mike said with a laugh. "But if nothing else, at least we'll have a fun time of it."

Annja sighed and leaned back in her chair. "Shangri-La. It's incredible to think that in this day and age a place supposedly so mystical and fantastic could even exist."

"Well, *what* it is, is open to speculation. I never really bought in to the notion that it was some incredible utopia. It's more the idea of the place that draws me in. That prospect of finding an untouched bit of geography that has been able to keep itself from becoming as molested as the rest of the planet—that's a pretty potent lure for me."

"And what happens if we do find it? What then?"

Mike shrugged. "I'm in academia. You know the golden rule."

"Publish or die."

"Exactly."

"But won't that mean exposing the place to the horrors of modern society?" Annja said.

Mike frowned. "I suppose it would. But I guess it depends on what we uncover when we find it."

"*If* we find it," Annja said.

"Hey, what happened to all that optimism?"

The waiter returned with Annja's burger and she bit into the thick patty, finding it just as juicy as it looked. She chewed slowly, savoring the rush of saliva in her mouth.

Mike watched her intently. "Good, huh?"

Annja nodded and around mouthfuls asked, "How many did you eat?"

"Only two," Mike said. "Doctor's orders."

Annja frowned and wiped her mouth. "What's that mean?"

Mike shrugged. "Seems my diet is starting to catch up with me. My cholesterol is too high."

"A lot of people suffer from high cholesterol. Can't you go on statins or something? What are all those pharmaceutical ads I keep seeing during my dinnertime back in the States?"

Mike smiled. "I'm on the statins, yeah. But even with them, I've got to make some major changes to my diet or else I'm history."

"Mike, you're as strong as an ox," Annja said.

"And nursing a cholesterol count of nearly three hundred," Mike said. "Fitness isn't all of the picture, apparently."

Annja frowned. "Then I guess you'd better store up on the burgers while we're here, huh?"

Mike took another sip of beer. "If you can help me find Shangri-La, then that will be better than any amount of these delicious, incredible burgers."

Annja took another bite. "You've got all the help you need.

You know that. Just let me enjoy my food and you can tell me all about what we're going to be doing."

Mike finished off his beer and leaned back. "My first order of business is ordering another burger."

Annja stopped eating. "I thought you said you'd had your fill."

"Well, yeah, but that was five minutes ago. I'm hungry again."

Annja started to laugh, but then caught a flash of movement out of the corner of her eye. The surly twosome who had eyeballed her when she'd entered the bar were maneuvering closer to where she sat.

Annja allowed her eyes to pass over them as she casually scanned the bar. Nothing about them sparked any memories. Not that that meant anything. She had been around the world enough and on too many adventures to know everyone she might have angered. The list of people who wanted her dead was probably a long one.

But she hadn't told anyone the details of her trip. And she thought the idea that someone would know she was coming was a bit far-fetched. So if the two guys eyeing her weren't there for her, then were they there for Mike?

"Say, Mike…"

"Yeah?"

"You aren't in any trouble, by any chance, are you?"

"Me? No. Why?" he asked.

Annja put down the rest of her burger and wiped her hands. The two men were headed straight for their table. "Because we're about to have guests."

2

From deep within the recesses of the crumbling brick facade across the street, a small Nepali man known as Tuk watched the restaurant with little more than a bored expression that echoed the blandness he felt inside. He was being well paid to watch the strange and beautiful woman he'd followed from the airport, but he knew nothing as to the reason. But Tuk had learned a few important things in his life as an orphan outcast, one of which was simple—when a foreigner offers you money to watch and do little else, it is smart to accept the generous offer.

Tuk scented the air and caught a whiff of cigarette smoke on the wind, hidden just a little by the pervasive gas fumes. His eyes moved in their sockets but did little else. As far as Tuk knew, no one could see him, ensconced as he was in the depth of shadows amid the twilight.

His stature made him perfectly suited for the role of surveillance. He was thin, almost wiry, yet possessed strength in his frame. He moved quickly and could easily pass through crowds like a soft breeze and no one would ever be the wiser.

Tuk had come to Katmandu as a child. He had little memory of his life before that. All he knew was that he had no one. He assumed his family had either abandoned him or they'd been killed in an avalanche, perhaps.

Tuk had wandered down the river valleys and shallow hills of the mountain ranges until his feet carried him to the outskirts of Katmandu. From there, he managed to scrape out an existence, although it was only such by the barest of measure.

As the desperate so often do, he developed a keen eye for opportunities. In his youth he worked to become an expert guide on the city streets for foreigners who came to this land seeking to ascend to the heavens. As he grew older, Tuk's ability to navigate unseen led him to another class of foreigner with little interest in the mountains themselves, aside from what lay across their snowy peaks.

By the time Tuk finally understood that he held a certain amount of value to the various intelligence services that employed him, he was already deep within the community as a tracker. At first, representatives from several organizations had offered him full-time appointments, but Tuk had shrugged them off. He thought his best chance of prospering lay not in the fold of one nation's spies, but in the community as a whole. He would hire himself out to whoever could afford his fee, which grew with each passing year.

As the years advanced, however, Tuk found himself being replaced with the advent of sophisticated electronic tracking systems. Gradually, his former clients opted for their tiny microchips and circuit boards over the wiry man they'd relied on for so long.

And Tuk found his fortunes fading away. But not entirely. Every now and again, someone would still seek him out. But his espionage days were over. His new clients were less patient people. Drug runners, arms dealers and other like folk used Tuk because it was cheaper than buying the technology to do the work.

And Tuk, ever the adaptable sort, was forced to lower his own personal standards and accept the work.

He hated it for the most part. Just being in contact with the clients made him feel dirty and his soul unclean. Tuk would only tolerate their presence for so long—enough time to get the details of the job and the payment for his services at the completion.

He'd had to give up the respect he'd once enjoyed from the spies. In him, they'd seen a fellow craftsman. Tuk had worked hard to nurture his talent and they understood that. Despite the fact that he worked for no country but himself, they'd all treated him like one of their own. And Tuk had enjoyed that feeling of belonging.

The men he worked for now cared little about his talent unless it produced results. More so, they treated Tuk like an insignificant mosquito that they barely found tolerable. They all had insulting nicknames for him and tossed his payment at him whenever they were finished.

Tuk was seriously considering leaving Katmandu and moving out into the countryside. He had a little money left, stashed away in a variety of hiding places in the city so utterly obscure that he was certain no one knew where they were. He could use that money to set himself up in a small house. Perhaps he would become a farmer.

He imagined life, looking out at the vastness of the enormous mountains each day, would be calm and enjoyable. Even as he had toiled in the narrow streets of Katmandu, Tuk had always felt drawn to the countryside. He'd come from somewhere out there. And he knew deep in his heart that someday he would return.

The previous day had started like any other. He left the tiny apartment he rented and made his way to find breakfast. He'd only traveled ten yards from his home when his instincts sparked up and he knew that someone was watching him.

At first, he was worried that one of the drug runners was going to kill him. But he disregarded that notion. Ever since he had started dealing with criminals, he'd taken extreme caution in how he worked his way back home each night. He used routes that doubled back on themselves. Tuk was sure that none of them would be able to track him.

But after another few blocks, he thought that maybe someone from his earlier life was stalking him. The prospect of that puzzled and thrilled him at the same time. He was puzzled because, in all his years, he'd never done anything to betray the confidences of whomever he worked for. He'd never done anything to warrant someone wanting to kill him.

And in that confidence, Tuk felt his heart soar. Perhaps, just perhaps, they were coming back to him for work. Maybe their fancy gadgets couldn't do what Tuk could do. Sure, he was older now, but he still had vitality flowing in his veins. He could still complete their assignments with ease.

At the food cart, Tuk ordered his meal and then turned, casually gazing up the street. He saw nothing suspicious.

He frowned and cursed himself silently for being such a hopeful fool. He was getting old, he thought. And his desire for his former life had made him think that a return was possible when it was not.

Those spies, he told himself, are long gone. And they're not coming back.

"Excuse me."

Tuk nearly leaped out of his own skin at the sound of the low voice. He turned and was immediately struck by the size of the man standing next to him. He loomed large over the entire food cart and Tuk was completely in the man's shadow.

But while there was no doubt that the man was both imposing and ominous, there seemed no threat directed at Tuk. If anything, Tuk felt that the man might even respect him a little. It was a theory quickly turned to fact when the man spoke again.

"Are you Tuk?"

The inflection of voice told Tuk all he needed to know. The man knew him not from his dealing with thugs, but from his intelligence work. Tuk smiled. "Yes. I am he."

"I would like to ask for your assistance in a small matter I have to deal with," the man said. "And I will pay you very well for your services, say twice the rate you used to obtain from the British?"

Tuk smiled. "That would make me very happy indeed."

The man nodded. "I was certain it would." He gestured to the street. "Walk with me and I shall tell you of the matter."

Tuk fell into step beside the stranger and they moved off down the street. Tuk found himself marveling at the manner in which the giant man moved. Not so much like a steamroller or some other juggernaut, but with the practiced, careful step of a dancer. The man's grace belied his immense size and Tuk knew this was no ordinary spy.

"She will come from America. A young woman in her twenties. Dark hair that flows down past her shoulders. She is lithe. Quick. And in battle, she is a most formidable opponent." The man showed him a picture of a beautiful woman.

"I won't fight her," Tuk said.

"I should hope you won't," the man replied. "But have little doubt that if she spots you, then she will make every effort to find out why you are following her. And she can be most persuasive."

Tuk smiled. "She will not see me."

"Indeed. And that is exactly the reason I have come to you, my friend. I know of your reputation. I know of your skill. This is not a matter to be entrusted to a faceless bit of technology, but rather to an expert such as yourself."

"I will follow her from the moment she leaves the plane until such time as you wish me to stop," Tuk said. "And never will she be the wiser."

"Excellent. Excellent." The man handed Tuk a small envelope. "Take half of the payment now for your trouble."

"Trouble?"

The man chuckled. "You are used to never being seen and yet here you are walking down the street with me. And I tend to attract attention despite my best efforts. I am therefore ruining your usual cloak of invisibility. For that, I sincerely apologize."

"You are not troubling me in the least," Tuk said. He appreciated the man's deferential attitude. "Had you not employed me, I might again find myself needing to find a job with a lower class of person. One I do not wish to seek out, but circumstances have dictated that I do just that in order to survive."

The man nodded. "The realities of life do not tolerate the whims of our hearts, do they?"

"Not often."

"Take this assignment and I will triple your payment. I know the pain of working with idiots. I wouldn't wish it upon anyone."

"Your generosity is most appreciated."

"As is your discretion," the man said. "And your talent."

"What would you have me do once I pick up the trail?"

"Nothing. You do absolutely nothing except follow her. For you to attempt otherwise would be suicidal."

There was nothing boastful or arrogant about the manner

in which the large man spoke. It was simply matter-of-fact. And Tuk had little reason to doubt the man's words.

"As you wish."

"She will most likely head to Thamel."

"What makes you say that?"

"That is where all foreigners tend to go, isn't it? And this woman is adept at blending in with the surrounding scenery."

Tuk nodded. "I won't let that fact enable any assumptions on my part."

"I know this."

They reached the end of the street and throngs of foot traffic swelled around them. The large man turned to Tuk and smiled. "Thank you for your help."

"How will I know where to find you?"

"Take this." The large man reached into his pocket and pulled out a small phone. Tuk recognized it as a disposable unit like thousands of others sold all over Katmandu. It was anonymous and therefore useful to the very drug runners Tuk despised.

"Press and hold the two and it will ring to my phone. Tell me where you are and I will be there. The phone is set to vibrate. If I call you and you do not answer, I will assume you are unable to talk at that moment for fear of giving your position away. However, I will expect a return call as soon as you are able."

"Understood."

"Then we are in business."

Tuk frowned. "One last question, if I may?"

"Yes?"

"How did you find me?"

The man smiled. "You are a rarity in this part of the world, my friend. But not so in other places. In every city and town there are those who know it better than anyone else. I only needed to take my time and you revealed yourself when the universe judged the time right."

Tuk smiled. "I'm glad to be of service."

"As am I."

"I know better than to ask your name," Tuk said. "But what about the woman? What is she called?"

The man started to walk away, paused and looked back at Tuk. "Her name is Annja Creed."

Tuk said the name to himself several times, trying it on for size. When he glanced back, the large man was gone.

Outside the Blue Note, Tuk wondered what exactly such a woman might be doing in order to attract the intense scrutiny of the man who now employed him. She seemed ordinary enough, albeit skilled at movement through crowds. Tuk had trailed her on a motorbike from the airport, and when she'd given up the taxi, he had parked and followed her on foot.

The phone buzzed in the pocket of his worn pants. Tuk reached in and pulled out the phone. "Yes?"

"You have her?"

"It is as you said. She is in Thamel. At a restaurant called the Blue Note."

"Keep watching her."

"You're coming here?"

"Not yet. But I will soon."

The line disconnected and Tuk was left to wonder some more about the woman called Annja Creed.

3

Inside the Blue Note, Annja was oblivious to the little Nepali man stationed outside with orders to report on her movements. She had other things to consider just then, like exactly how she was going to deal with the two men heading toward her table.

"Mike?"

But Mike only frowned. Annja glanced at him and then back at the hulking masses in front of her. They both stopped short of coming within range of a swift kick from Annja's boots. That meant they had a situational awareness Annja recognized, marking them as seasoned professionals.

"Hi, Mike," the one sporting a goatee said. "How ya been?"

Mike frowned. "I don't know you."

"Sure you do. You know our employer, Mr. Tsing. So if you know him, then you know us."

Annja looked at Mike. "Who is Mr. Tsing?"

"A miserable bastard, apparently," Mike said. He looked

back at the huge men. "Why are you bothering me about this now? I told Tsing I needed a few more weeks to pay him back."

"Pay him back?" Annja sighed. "What are you paying him back? What did you need money for?"

The goateed henchman smiled. "He wanted to buy a map. A fifty-thousand-dollar map."

Annja's eyes widened in alarm. "Fifty grand? What kind of map costs that much money?"

The goateed man pointed at her. "You see? That's exactly what Mr. Tsing would like to ask our friend Mike here."

"Since when does Tsing care what his money is used for as long as he gets repaid?" Mike asked.

"Since he found out you were blowing fifty large on a map," the man said. "Now, you can come along with us quietly and without any trouble. Or we can beat you senseless and then take you to Mr. Tsing. Makes no difference to us."

Annja smiled. "Suppose we don't feel like seeing Mr. Tsing just now? What about you guys go back to him and say you couldn't find Mike?"

"We already told him we had you two in sight. He's very interested in seeing Mike and apparently he's very interested in meeting you. Says he loves your show."

"How did you know who I was?" Annja asked.

"We have ways of finding out who is on airline manifests. It comes in handy for Mr. Tsing to know when he has business associates coming to town. Or other people that he's interested in meeting."

"Great. A fan," Annja mumbled. "That's just what I need right now." She looked at Mike. "When were you going to tell me about this?"

"I was hoping I wouldn't have to," Mike said. "Tsing told me I had all the time I needed to pay him back. This is as much a surprise to me as it is you."

"Fifty grand? That must be some map."

"It is."

The goateed thug cleared his throat. "Are you coming with us or do we have to drag you out of here?"

Annja eyed him. She could easily draw her sword and cut both men down before they could blink. But she wasn't sure that unsheathing her blade in a crowded restaurant was the best way of handling this. At least, not in view of everyone else in the joint. Maybe she would try her luck once they got outside and into some narrow alley. She imagined Mr. Tsing would infest some tiny haunt on the back side of Katmandu.

Mike nodded. "Fine, we'll go with you to see what Tsing has to say. I like this place too much to cause trouble in here, anyway."

"Smart," the man said. "I'm sure he won't keep you long. This is more of a social call than a collection call."

"What a relief," Mike said.

The two men led them out of the Blue Note. Annja looked around but saw little chance for action. Throngs of people swelled around them and the two henchmen bracketed Mike and Annja between them. The tide of the foot traffic carried them along.

Mike whispered in her ear. "Don't worry, I can handle Tsing."

"Can you?"

"Sure. He's a businessman. The last thing he wants is to spill any blood. He'd much rather make money."

"And the map?"

"I believe it shows the true route to finding Shangri-La."

"Where'd you get it?"

"An archivist for James Hilton."

Annja glanced at him. "You mean the same James Hilton who wrote *Lost Horizon?*"

"The same."

"But most people who read that book believed that Hilton based it on Hunza Valley in Pakistan," she said.

Mike nodded. "Yep, and others think it's actually in the Kunlun mountain range. But neither of those suppositions is correct."

"And this map shows the way?"

"It's true that Hilton visited Pakistan and particularly the Hunza Valley only a few years before *Lost Horizon* was published. But as for him basing the book on the area, that's rubbish. Hilton knew what he'd discovered and didn't wish for it to be torn apart by the curious."

Annja saw the henchmen were steering them down a street with less traffic. They were on the outskirts of Thamel now. Ahead of them, more modern buildings loomed. They passed cell phone shops and nice restaurants.

"So, Hilton…lied?" she asked.

"Yes," Mike said. "Throughout the early twentieth century and into the 1930s, there were many British explorers over in this region. It was a natural place to go to, given the British Empire's India connection. Hilton and others like him made trips up to this part of the world and were fascinated by what they saw and perceived as both mystical and wondrous places."

"So, if neither the Hunza Valley nor the Kunlun Mountains are the location, then where would it be?" Annja asked.

"That's what the map will tell us," Mike said. "But we need to get away from Tsing and his goons if we have any hope of discovering it."

"Seems like Tsing is going to have a problem with that."

"Who cares?"

Annja glanced at Mike. "I'm not exactly thrilled at the idea of spending this entire trip being hunted by the likes of these two. And Tsing doesn't sound like he's the forgiving type."

"He's not."

"So, suppose we see what he has to say before we decide to go about this in a different way?"

Mike smiled. "But if we decide to go that way?"

Annja winked. "Then it won't be a problem."

Mike nodded. "Good."

The goateed man called a halt to their march. "Hold up here," he said.

Annja paused and saw they were in front of a four-star hotel. From the circular roundabout, lush green plants shot skyward in front of the plate-glass windows. In front, several limousines pulled around.

Annja looked at their escort. "He lives in a hotel?"

"Top floor's a penthouse," the man responded. "But even still, we won't tolerate any monkeying around here. Mr. Tsing owns the hotel and doesn't want his guests disturbed."

"Ever the gracious host," Annja said.

"You'll find out soon enough." The man nudged her forward. "Walk into the lobby and head for the elevators. Remember we're right behind you."

Annja and Mike entered the hotel lobby. In any other part of the world, they might well have appeared underdressed given their immediate environment. But in Katmandu, they looked like any other well-heeled adventurous couple. And no one paid any attention.

Behind them, the henchmen came up close.

Annja and Mike stepped into the hotel elevators and waited as the men joined them. The goateed man stepped inside and slid a special key into the lock. Instantly, the doors slid shut, mirrored panels casting their reflections back. The huge men faced Annja and Mike.

"Won't be long now. Mr. Tsing has just finished another business meeting so I don't think you'll have to wait."

Annja felt the sudden sensation of her stomach dropping as

the elevator shot skyward. Numbers flashed and she realized they were going much higher than she expected.

At last the elevator dinged and the doors slid open. The goateed man nodded. "Out."

Annja and Mike stepped onto a plush red carpet that muffled their footsteps. The dim light made her squint to make out the massive pair of oak doors in front of her.

"Mr. Tsing has an aversion to bright lights," the man said. "He prefers the level of illumination always be kept dim to save his eyesight."

"You guys wear night vision in here?" Annja asked. "It's ridiculous how little I can see."

"It doesn't seem to bother Mr. Tsing," the goateed man said.

"Well, as long as there's that," Annja said. She looked at Mike. "Have you been here before?"

"Nope. My meetings with Tsing always took place at his restaurant."

The goateed man grunted. "Mr. Tsing uses the hotel for his most important meetings."

"Guess I didn't rate," Mike said.

"Apparently," Annja muttered.

The big henchman knocked once on the door, his knuckles creating a massive boom that echoed for a moment before dying in the artificial twilight. He looked back at Annja and Mike. "Behave yourselves when we go in."

Annja smiled. "I'll be on my best behavior."

He frowned and started to say something, but then stopped as the massive doors swung back on well-oiled hinges. Inside, the gloom was even deeper than in the hallway. Annja could smell incense wafting from inside.

A form appeared next to the door and she saw that it was a woman. "Enter."

The henchman led them into a large entry hall. Inside, the

windows were open to the night air. Far below, Annja caught glints of the lights of the city twinkling around them.

And then another form appeared before her. "Annja Creed."

She squinted and saw a thin rail of a man with heavy folds surrounding his eyes. But they gleamed with an almost imperceptibly acute sense of sight despite the relative darkness.

She smiled. "You must be Mr. Tsing."

He bowed low. "I am."

"Nice to meet you."

Tsing grabbed her hand and then Annja felt the leathery touch of his lips on the back of it. There was the briefest flicker of moisture and she realized that he'd licked her skin. Resisting the urge to recoil and kill the little cretin, Annja took a deep breath and exhaled slowly.

Tsing straightened and then turned to Mike. "Mike. How very nice to see you again."

"Rather soon, wouldn't you say?" Mike replied.

Tsing shrugged. "Well, we have much to discuss. After all, our former arrangement seems hardly fair given the fact that I had no knowledge of what you intended to do with the money I provided."

"What do you care what I do with it?"

Tsing glanced at Annja and then back at Mike. "I care very much what my money goes toward. Especially so if it appears I might make even more on a business proposition than what I first expected."

Mike shook his head. "We have an arrangement already. There's no need to discuss this any further."

Tsing held up a crooked finger and waggled it in front of their faces. "That's where you're wrong, Michael. The underlying tenet of my business—one that you sought out of your own free will, I might mention—is that as the primary shareholder in your life, I can make and remake any arrangements as I see fit."

Mike frowned. "And if I don't like the new parameters of the deal?"

Tsing smiled. "I truly hope it won't come to that."

There came a high-pitched wailing scream from somewhere outside, and in the next instant Annja saw a flash as the bulk of a body tumbled past the windows. The scream died away in the night air. In her mind, Annja could imagine the body hitting the street far below and shuddered at the vision.

Tsing watched them both closely. "I'm sorry you had to see that. Another of my business partners saw fit to dispute my attempts at a more equitable financing arrangement."

Annja frowned. "So you killed him."

Tsing smiled. "I believe it will be ruled a suicide." He clapped his hands. "But come in, let us sit down and see if we might avoid any such unpleasantries. I am very interested in hearing what you both have to say."

Tsing turned and led them deeper into the suite. Annja and Mike had little choice but to follow.

4

Tuk watched the hotel from beneath the overhang of a small electronics boutique that specialized in global positioning systems and cell phones. He had trailed Annja and the men with her to this hotel with very little effort. When they'd emerged from the Blue Note, it had been an elementary matter to ease into the traffic slipstream and follow them to this destination.

But Tuk was not happy.

As the party had exited the Blue Note, his weathered face had creased and then flushed. He knew the men who escorted Annja Creed. The heavyset man with the goatee was known as Burton and the other man was called Kurtz. They were two of the worst enforcers working for Katmandu's most illustrious crime syndicate run by Mr. Tsing.

Tuk had worked for Tsing in the past, when his personal circumstances had forced him to take jobs from such despicable people. Tsing's treatment of Tuk bordered on abusive, and after he had withheld part of Tuk's payment, the small man resolved never to work for him again, personal finances be damned.

Burton and Kurtz had especially insulted him by tossing him out of his last meeting with Tsing and threatening to kill him if he ever showed his face around there again.

Tuk thought about the miniature folding kukri he carried in his pocket and how he would dearly love to use the knife to end Tsing's life and that of both Burton and Kurtz, if he was given half a chance to do so. He never used to carry a weapon, preferring instead to rely upon his natural stealth abilities to remove him from harm. When he worked for spies, there was never much danger to him. But working with criminals meant constant danger so Tuk had taken to carrying a smaller version of the curved blade favored by the Gurkhas, the famed Nepali warriors who often served in the British Army.

Why was Annja Creed meeting with Tsing? And just who was the other man with her that Tuk did not recognize? If he read the body language right, and he felt that he did, then Annja and the other man were not going with Burton and Kurtz willingly. Tuk also thought it doubtful that in the short span of time since Annja had left the airport that she had somehow managed to run afoul of Tsing.

That meant the other man must have been responsible.

But how?

Tuk's brow furrowed as he thought about it. Tsing specialized in any manner of criminal enterprises, but drugs, prostitution and extortion were his favorites. Less lucrative was the loan sharking, but Tuk nodded to himself. Perhaps that was it. If the man was in debt to Tsing, then this would not end well.

Did that also mean that Annja Creed was in danger?

Tuk slid the small cell phone from his pocket and pressed the two on it. The phone dialed a number that did not display on the screen, which Tuk now shielded to keep it from revealing his presence. He put the phone to his ear and waited.

"Yes?"

"The woman—Annja Creed—is at the Fairbanks Hotel."

"All right."

"She was brought there under duress."

"What do you mean?"

Tuk recounted what he had seen and waited for the man on the other end to comment.

"You're certain of this?"

"I know Tsing," Tuk said. "He is a worthless criminal who enjoys seeing people suffer."

"You have history with him?"

"Yes."

"I would have thought it foolish for anyone to cross you," the man said.

Tuk inclined his head. "I appreciate your saying that, but it has happened ever since my lack of work with my former employers."

"Understood." The man paused. "And you say Tsing has the uppermost floor to himself?"

"It is my understanding that he lives there, yes."

"You've been inside?"

"Never."

"I need to know what is going on. Is it possible for you to get inside?"

Tuk frowned. This was going a bit further than he normally went. Surveillance was one thing. Actual infiltration was something else entirely. And it meant danger. Especially since Tsing, Burton and Kurtz all knew who he was. If they spotted him…

"I realize this is asking more than you are normally tasked with," the man said. "But I will make sure you are properly compensated for your efforts. If you can get inside and make sure that Annja Creed is safe, I will pay you an additional fifty percent of your fee."

Tuk's heart raced. With that much money he could easily leave this life behind and retire out in the countryside. It was too good not to take the chance. And if he happened to get a shot at Burton or Kurtz, perhaps he could exact a small measure of revenge on them.

As if reading his mind, however, the man continued to speak. "Make sure no one sees you. It is absolutely vital that Annja Creed not know you are watching her. She is incredibly intelligent. Any hint of your involvement will inevitably cause her to start reasoning out my existence in this matter. And at this moment, I cannot afford for her to know I am here. Do you understand?"

"Perfectly."

At that moment, Tuk heard a sudden scream and then a body crashed down across the street into a stand of trees. There was a sickening sound of impact and then nothing more. A few spectators started forward and then Tuk heard someone yell for an ambulance.

"What was that?" the voice on the phone said.

Tuk frowned. "If I know the man, and I do, it would appear that Tsing just had someone thrown off the roof of the hotel."

"A woman?"

Tuk shook his head. "No. It was a man."

"The same man who accompanied Annja Creed into the hotel."

Tuk bit his lip. "I don't know. It could have been, I suppose, but in the darkness I cannot tell."

"She could be in danger," the man said. "It's vital you determine whether she is or not. If you think her life is in jeopardy, you must call me back as soon as possible."

"I understand."

The line disconnected and Tuk slid across the street. Already in the distance, he could hear the approaching sirens.

As he came abreast of the circular drive leading up to the hotel entrance, he paused and then moved to where the body lay. In the midst of the curious onlookers, he drew no attention to himself.

Crumpled in a bloody mangled heap was the body of the man who had just fallen. Tuk looked him over and saw that the pants were not the same color as those worn by the man who had accompanied Annja Creed.

That was good news.

He turned back to the lobby. A steady stream of onlookers was rushing out to see what had caused so much commotion. Entering the lobby now would make him stand out. He waited a few minutes until he saw a bellhop dragging a luggage cart behind him.

That was his chance.

Tuk sidled up next to the cart and walked smoothly into the lobby as if he belonged there. He had often found that confidence helped with his virtual invisibility. The cart also helped hide him behind the garment bags.

Tsing occupied the penthouse and gaining access to that area required a special key in the elevator. Tuk had no such key. That meant he would be forced to take the stairs.

He entered the elevator and pressed the topmost-floor button, holding it down to cause the elevator to run express to his destination. He regarded himself in the mirrored doors and smiled. All that money! It would be his if he could just live long enough to see this assignment finished.

As the numbers flashed by, Tuk thought about the relative peace he would soon enjoy. Long walks would be the greatest exertion he would face, but otherwise, he would leave behind all the congestion and urban decay. And he would be immensely grateful for it.

At last, the top floor came up and the elevator dinged softly before the doors opened. Tuk looked out to either side, but saw no one else in the hallway. He stepped out and let the doors close behind him.

Down the hall he saw the exit sign for the stairwell and headed for it. He hoped that it would also go up to the penthouse and roof. Surely Tsing's men had used it to throw their unlucky prisoner over the top. Tuk would use it to gain access to the penthouse floor.

He pushed open the door carefully, and listened. As he had hoped, the stairs ran up as well as down. He stepped into the cool stairwell and quietly strode up the steps.

Two flights farther up, he saw an unmarked door and stopped. This was the penthouse level.

A small amount of space showed under the door and Tuk got down on his knees and bent his face until he could see under the crack. He paused and let his eyesight adjust to the darkness on the other side.

As far as he could tell, there was no one in the penthouse hallway.

Tuk raised himself and turned the doorknob slowly.

The door opened and Tuk slid through. He could smell the incense that Tsing always insisted be kept burning. Tuk's nostrils flared in disgust. He hated everything about Tsing, and his preference for incense and anything vaguely mystical was in direct contrast to his barbaric ways.

But one thing that Tsing insisted on helped Tuk and that was the low light. He faded into the shadows near a potted giant fern next to the massive oak doors and sidled up as close as he dared to the main entryway. This would make for a decent observation post.

How long would he need to stay, though? The man on the phone had told him to make sure Annja Creed was safe. But how could he do that if he was out here? Tuk listened at the door in vain. The heavy wood barred any sound from passing through it. And unlike the stairwell door, there was no such space at the bottom of the entry doors to the penthouse.

Tuk realized with a start that he would have to enter the penthouse itself.

He examined the door in front of him. There would be people inside. At least five, he reasoned. Tsing, Burton, Kurtz, Annja Creed and the other man. There might even be more.

Tuk took a breath and examined the lock. He could force his way in, he supposed, but that would simply alert everyone to his presence. And the man on the phone had been most insistent that he remain utterly invisible to Annja Creed.

Tuk wasn't sure how the woman would be able to piece together Tuk's presence with the man on the phone, but he knew enough not to question such things. If the man on the phone demanded that Tuk remain invisible, then that was exactly what Tuk would have to do.

But how?

He heard a vague sound and realized almost too late that someone was approaching the door. He slid back behind the large fronds and then heard the telltale click of a lock being disengaged.

The door swung open.

Tuk held his breath.

A solitary figure swept out toward the elevator bank. A woman dressed in a long mandarin-style dress with a slit running up its side revealed a brief flash of skin as she passed the giant fern.

The elevator doors slid open and she stepped inside. In the light of the elevator, Tuk could see the sharp lines of her Han ancestry. She had the look of lethal beauty about her.

The doors closed and Tuk stepped out from behind the fern just as he heard the doors to the penthouse swing shut. A soft gasp of air told him they must have had a delay to their closing to keep them from banging. Hydraulics? It didn't matter. What did matter was that the pause in their closing gave Tuk the opportunity he needed.

He stepped into the penthouse.

Instantly, he moved to the hall table and sank down to his knees. It was essential he give himself enough time to take in all the ambient sounds of his new environment. If he moved too soon, he would risk being surprised by someone he hadn't noticed.

But if he took too long, the woman might return at any moment and spot him.

Tuk's heart thundered in his chest.

His ears perked up. Conversation. It came from a number of voices farther on in the penthouse. Tuk strained all his senses.

With a quick gulp of air, Tuk moved deeper into the penthouse.

5

Tsing ushered Annja and Mike into a grand living room. Annja could make out a large wraparound leather sofa that faced windows looking out over the city of Katmandu. The pervasive scent of incense hung heavy over the entire penthouse and Annja quickly realized that the sickly sweet smell was too cloying for her.

"Please make yourselves comfortable," Tsing said. He reclined on the farthest portion of the couch and pulled his feet up under him. "I really don't want this to be an adversarial relationship. Everyone always makes out so much better when things are nice and civilized, don't you think?"

Annja raised her eyebrows. "Since when is tossing someone off a roof nice and civilized?"

"It's not," Tsing said. "And it's a reminder that as cordial as I'm being right now, that mood can quickly turn. You'd do well to remember that."

"Noted," Annja said. "Now what is this all about? Even if

Mike did borrow money from you, he certainly hasn't reneged on that deal, has he?"

"No," Tsing replied. "He has not. And, in fact, I fully expect him to repay me as he promised. But that's not really the issue."

Mike said nothing so Tsing continued. "What this is about is what he used my money to purchase. And I know full well what it was."

"What?" Annja asked.

"A map that shows the way to Shangri-La."

Mike frowned. "How did you find out?"

Tsing smiled. "You might say that I've had an almost obsessive interest in locating it for the majority of my life."

"Really?" Mike said.

"And I know what the rumors are and who has what for sale. As I said, my obsession with the place has led me to have quite the network of contacts."

Annja shook her head. "If that's the case, then why didn't you just buy the map yourself before Mike came to you?"

Tsing shrugged. "Sometimes people can be particular about who they happen to deal with. And I'm afraid that my reputation tends to precede me. I, of course, made overtures to purchase the map earlier. But the seller refused, saying that he would not do business with me."

"I'm surprised he didn't end up taking a dive off the roof," Annja said.

Tsing smiled. "Violence is always a means to an end. But there are often better alternatives. If he would not sell to me, then it was merely a matter of arranging for someone else to buy it. In this case, I made sure that your friend Mike here found out about it."

Mike frowned. "You baited me?"

"As much as my reputation precedes me, so, too, does yours. You are one of the few professors who have not gone along with the more outlandish theories of where Shangri-La truly is. I have known of you for some time now. I've bided my time. Waited. And when you learned about the map, I knew you would come here and seek to buy it."

"But how did you know I'd come to you?"

Tsing shrugged. "I know everything about your financial situation. There's little that cannot be accomplished with a few keystrokes these days. Even here in our rather remote portion of the world, we can still reach out and discover all we need to know. The map was too expensive for you. Yet after you laid eyes on it, I knew you would need financing for it. But you wouldn't seek help from conventional means. After all, what if it turned out to be a ruse? You would become the laughingstock of your peers. No, you did exactly what I expected you to do. You came to me."

"And you gave him the money," Annja said.

"Absolutely."

"Knowing full well that he would buy the map with it."

"Yes."

"And then you would have what you needed."

Tsing shook his head. "Well, not quite. You see, I am bound by some rather perturbing aspects of my condition. I suffer from a skin ailment that prohibits me from going out into bright light. I dare say that I would make for a poor explorer. As such, the map is not as useful to me as it would be to someone else."

Mike sighed. "You used me and now you want me to do your dirty work."

"I want you to use the map to find the fabled location and then report back to me here," Tsing said.

"What do you hope to gain from that?"

Tsing smiled. Annja noticed the utter whiteness of his polished teeth, even in the dim light. "I am part optimist and part fool believer. If the legends that surround Shangri-La are to be believed, then the place is a utopia of mystical qualities. I may, in fact, travel there by night and eventually find a cure for my condition."

Annja laughed. "I've known people who thought that they could find magical places before. And each time they've been sorely disappointed."

Tsing turned slightly to better face Annja. "And what brings you over here, Annja Creed? Is it just the promise of adventure with an old friend? Or is it something else?"

"What do you mean?"

"I mean nothing more than I asked." Tsing smiled broadly now. "I have long enjoyed watching you on that delightful show. You have so much more…presence than that other rather pitiable woman."

"Thanks. I like keeping my clothes on, if that's what you mean."

"But your reputation also precedes you, doesn't it?"

"I doubt it."

"I know, for example, that you are an inherently dangerous woman."

"Says who?"

"Says any number of witnesses to your rather adept fighting prowess. If rumors are to be believed, and I must admit I'm a bit of a sucker for such tales, then you have quite a formidable manner about you."

Annja frowned. What else did Tsing know about her? She wasn't comfortable with the direction the talk was heading. The last thing she needed was Tsing asking about her sword. Had he heard rumors about that, as well?

"This is quite a nice place you've got," she said. "How is it you came to afford it?"

Tsing waved his hand. "A trifling matter not worth much discussion. I simply happened to make a great deal of money and invested in the right places. That's all."

Annja raised an eyebrow. "And the government here? How is it you escape their attention?"

"As I mentioned before, violence is only one method to achieving a goal. It is useful at times, yes, but overall it's a deplorable thing to have to resort to. Often, better outcomes can be had if a little bit of leverage is applied."

Annja grinned. "And your proximity to Tibet probably doesn't hurt, either, huh?"

Tsing's eyes narrowed. "Are you driving at something?"

"Just a theory," Annja said.

"Care to share it?"

Annja smiled. "Not a chance." She nodded at Mike. "So, you want Mike and me to find this place using the map he bought."

"The map *I* bought," Tsing said. "The money used was mine. I am the map's rightful owner. You may consider it a loan right now, but it belongs to me."

"As you say," Annja said. "So we find this place and then what? We come back and tell you about it and that's it?"

"Yes."

"And Mike's debt of the fifty grand?"

"Forgiven."

"You're serious?"

Tsing nodded. "Absolutely. The map is mine and I paid for it. I want only what I cannot achieve on my own. You must locate the exact position of the fabled land and then come back to me. What I do from that point on is no longer any concern of yours. Any attempt to meddle with my affairs after that will be dealt with firmly, if you catch my meaning."

Mike grunted. "Perfectly."

"Excellent." Tsing clapped his hands. "And just to make sure there are no hard feelings about all of this, I will even loan you the use of one of my smaller planes. It will, I have no doubt, be of tremendous help to you in your search."

"I don't suppose it would do us any good to refuse your kind offer?" Annja asked.

Tsing smiled. "That would be tremendously disrespectful of you to do so. And really, I must insist that you use it. At least I know that you will be in good hands."

Mike glanced at Annja. She shrugged. "Seems as though we don't have any choice in the matter."

"You do have a choice," Tsing said, "but I'm afraid the other option isn't nearly as enticing as the one I've put before you now."

"What about Mike and his find? Does he get to tell the world that he found it?"

"And why would he want to do that?" Tsing asked. "Solely for the purpose of self-gratification? I daresay it would be much better for such a place to remain a fabled legend rather than to be overrun with mobs of tourists who would no doubt ruin the magnificence of the place."

"You're betting that it really is everything that the legends claim it to be," Mike said. "We might find it nothing more than a dried-up lake bed. It could have been demolished in an earthquake. There are any number of possibilities."

"And I'm counting on you to discover exactly what happened," Tsing said. "All I want is for you to report back to me as to what you find. If you do that and then leave it to me, then we will have concluded our business. Which I'm sure will make you a much happier man than you seem to be at the present time."

"The sooner we get started, the better," Mike said.

Tsing nodded. "Shall we have a drink to celebrate our new arrangement? I have the most delicious peach wine."

Annja held up her hand. "I had a beer earlier. Probably not the best idea to mix them."

Tsing frowned. "Mike?"

"I guess I'd better. I wouldn't want to be rude and refuse your kind offer."

Annja winced. Mike's tone was both condescending and rude. She saw both henchmen tense briefly before Tsing waved them back down.

"Bring the wine." He regarded Mike and then spoke simply. "I suppose you cannot be blamed for feeling a sense of betrayal, although you were a bit naive to think that it would be a simple matter dealing with me."

"I was stupid," Mike said. "I won't make the same mistake ever again. Trust me on that."

"I do. You don't strike me as someone who suffers failure easily. I would be remiss if I didn't warn you that trying to double-cross me would be foolish."

"I gave you my word and I'll stick to it," Mike said.

The goateed man brought in a bottle of wine and three glasses. Tsing poured for them all, despite Annja's earlier refusal. She knew she was expected to drink the wine, as well.

Tsing handed her a glass and then one to Mike. He raised his in a toast and smiled at them. "Here's to a successful adventure and an outcome we can all live with."

Mike frowned but raised his glass. Annja did the same. She put the glass to her lips and smelled the sweet wine. It didn't blend well with the cloying incense in the room. But she took a tentative sip.

Tsing watched her closely. "Do you like it?"

"It's…different."

"It's more of a dessert wine, I know, but I love it so. I can't imagine relegating it to such a minor role. I prefer it to stand on its own."

Mike finished his glass and set it down. "Pretty good," he said.

Tsing refilled his glass. "Have another."

Annja let more of the wine slide down her throat. It seemed marginally thicker than other wines she'd had in the past. She felt a warm glow come over her and despite herself, she realized she liked the flavor.

Tsing sipped his glass thoughtfully. "This particular vintage comes from a winery down in the southern part of the country. I happen to own it, of course."

"That must make for a nice discount on your personal supply," Annja said.

Tsing laughed. "Indeed it does."

Annja finished her wine. Tsing seemed almost too eager to refill her glass. Annja glanced over at Mike.

Mike had passed out.

She looked back at Tsing. He lifted his glass to her. "I must compliment you on what I perceive to be a rather incredible constitution. Considering your friend is already unconscious, I hardly expected you to last a full glass."

Annja's vision swam. "Why?"

Tsing waved her concerns away. "Do not worry. I'm merely taking steps to ensure that you will do as you've promised. You won't be harmed. And tomorrow, you'll be on your way to finding the mystical kingdom of Shangri-La. For now, sleep well."

6

Tuk could hear Tsing's voice issue his commands. "Let them sleep and then deliver them to the airfield. Get them into the plane. When they wake up, they'll be fine."

Tuk shrank away from the conversation. He had to get out of the penthouse before he was discovered. He slipped back toward the front door. Already Burton and Kurtz were moving around too much for Tuk's comfort. He'd done what he'd been asked to do and now it was time to get out of there and report back to the mysterious man who had hired him.

As he backed away, his instincts suddenly screamed at him and Tuk had barely enough time to shrink into a shadowy recess before the main door opened. The woman in the mandarin gown came gliding back into the penthouse.

She froze.

Her eyes swept around the darkened penthouse like lasers. Tuk averted his eyes from her. From experience he knew that even glancing at someone could often trigger that primal awareness of being watched.

But Tuk felt genuine fear. Something about the woman unnerved him. She was someone other than the house servant she appeared to be. He could sense power in her.

She moved forward, closer to where Tuk squatted, hidden by the darkness. His heart thundered inside his chest and he willed it to slow, fearing she might even hear it. What was it about her that filled him with fear?

She paused again and he heard her sniff the air. How could she smell anything over the heavy mist of incense? Tuk marveled at her sense. She was completely attuned to her environment and knew something was out of order.

She couldn't tell just then what it was.

But her senses served her well. And now she moved even closer to where Tuk was hiding. Her eyes seemed to pierce the darkness in front of her. Tuk imagined that she had some sort of robotic night vision optical sensors or something equally outlandish.

The line of cold sweat that broke out along his spine almost made him start to move. He didn't think he'd ever experienced this kind of fear before, and in all of his years working with the intelligence community he couldn't recall ever feeling anything like it.

She knew he was there.

Tuk felt certain of it. He heard something in the darkness and realized that she had clicked her terribly long fingernails together. They looked like claws in the twilight. Tuk had little doubt they could effectively shred anyone she wanted. He realized that she reminded him of a feral cat that knows it has its prey cornered.

Just then Burton came around the corner and headed straight at her. She blinked and, in that instant, Tuk knew he was safe. Her concentration broken, she seemed to suddenly mask herself again in the guise of a servant.

Burton regarded her. "Mr. Tsing wants you to clean up the wineglasses. Make sure you use hot water on them."

She bowed low, took one final look at Tuk's hiding place and then slipped away. Tuk watched her turn a corner and vanish.

Burton wandered into another room.

This was his chance.

Tuk eased over to the main door and cracked it open, passing out of it as quickly and noiselessly as he could manage. He heard the soft hiss as the door closed behind him and then he was fairly running to the stairwell, shooting down to the floors below the penthouse.

Once there, he hopped on the elevator and sank to the lobby. He walked out as easily as he'd entered and then took up a position outside of the hotel. He would be able to see Burton and Kurtz remove Annja Creed and the fellow known as Mike.

He removed the cell phone from his pocket again and pressed the number two. It was answered immediately.

"Were you successful?"

"Yes," he said.

"Tell me everything you heard and saw."

Tuk faithfully recounted the entire escapade, delving into detail about the conversation and then also about the mysterious woman in the apartment.

The man on the phone seemed especially intrigued about her. "You said she seemed to know you were there."

"Without a doubt. She knew I was there. In another moment she might have killed me, such was the feeling she gave me."

"But when the man you called Burton came around the corner, she assumed the guise of a servant woman again?"

"Yes."

"Very interesting."

"Terrifying," Tuk said.

"She is no doubt some type of plant on Tsing. Of that we can be certain. But for what reason?"

"I don't know," Tuk said.

"Where are you right at this moment?"

Tuk glanced around. He was again hidden in the shadows and certain no one would see him. The only way he could be discovered was if someone overheard him talking on the phone.

"I'm hidden across the street from the hotel entrance."

"You said Tsing's men will take them to the airfield?"

"Yes."

"Is there a back entrance to the hotel they might opt to use instead of the front?"

"There is," Tuk said. "But it leads only to an alley too small for a car to travel down. If they want to use a car to transport Annja Creed and her friend, they will need to come out the front entrance."

The man grunted. "They'll wait, then, until very late. When there's a skeleton crew on duty in the lobby. That way they'll be able to pass without too much interest in what they're doing."

"That is my guess, as well," Tuk said. "I will stay with them all the way."

"Good. I need to look a little bit further into this strange woman you spoke of just now. I want to know more about her and who she really is."

"May I ask what your feeling is about her?"

"I'm not sure yet. But it may be assumed that she is no mere servant girl. She is obviously positioned close to Tsing for some reason. But for what, I don't know."

"She scared me. And I've never felt fear like that."

"You did well," the man said on the phone. "You acquitted yourself admirably and performed excellently. I'm very pleased with the results of your reconnaissance. Now I must decide what to do about this new wrinkle."

"I do not envy you."

"Just continue to make certain that Annja Creed stays safe. If Tsing lives up to his word, then all should be fine. But I want you around just in case."

"And if it appears that Burton and Kurtz mean them harm?"

The man paused for the slightest moment. "I don't wish to tell you how to handle that situation if you are not comfortable with it. However, my primary concern is that Annja Creed remains safe. As such, any steps you think wise to ensure that may be taken."

Tuk grunted. "Understood." He calmly fingered the folded kukri in his pocket. Dispatching Burton and Kurtz would please him.

"Don't be in a hurry to exact vengeance on those who have wronged you, my friend. Act only if the situation calls for it. But if you must act, then do it swiftly and boldly. You must strike first and be without restraint in order to win the day."

"I will."

"Keep me informed of any developments." The line disconnected and Tuk was once more alone in the darkness.

A stiff breeze blew out of the northwest and circled around his body. Tuk thought about what he'd heard in the penthouse and marveled. Even he knew of the legend of Shangri-La. It was supposed to be a mystical place of untold beauty and wondrous lands. The people who lived there were supposedly a master race of supremely intelligent and wise, peaceful people who knew the secrets of the universe.

But did such a place really exist?

It seemed too incredible to be real. And yet, here was the most powerful criminal in Katmandu telling Annja Creed and her friend Mike that he firmly believed it did exist. And here was an apparently famous adventurer and a learned man saying they believed the same.

If they thought the legends true, then Tuk supposed all that remained was to find out if it truly did exist.

He wondered what it would be like to discover such a land. With so much of his own past steeped in doubt and question, Tuk found the idea of seeing a place like Shangri-La a tempting diversion.

Perhaps when he was done working for the man on the telephone, he would try to find the place on his own. He didn't have to become a farmer. He could wander the countryside and find his own path. And there was no telling where it might lead.

Nepal, after all, was a land of legends and myths. The swirling mix of religions and peoples made for all sorts of craziness. Tuk grinned as he thought about the creatures said to exist outside the boundaries of civilization.

The yeti still walked according to legends he heard told by traders who came down to Katmandu from up north. Tuk wasn't sure what to make of that particular story, but he had enough memory of being outside the city to know there were many parts of the country that seemed to defy the modern age. Who knew what existed in the crevices of the vast mountain ranges that jutted out of the earth?

Anything seemed possible, he decided, when standing in the middle of the night in the shadows of the hotel.

Tuk frowned. This wasn't like him. Seeing that woman upstairs had shaken him. He recognized that the fear had welled up from the bottom reaches of his soul. He'd never felt this before and the fact that he did now shook his confidence.

It was not good for what he was tasked with doing.

Tuk only hoped that he would not run into the woman again. He knew she would rend him from head to toe with those lethal fingernails.

He shuddered in the dark as another breeze blew over him. Judging from the position of the stars overhead, the hours had passed quickly.

Tuk leaned back and stretched himself like a cat. He heard several pops and felt his muscles lengthen as he flexed this way and that. A sudden urge in his bladder made him adjust himself and then urinate in the corner.

But always, he kept his eyes on the entrance of the hotel.

His vigilance was rewarded shortly after three o'clock in the morning. He saw a sudden movement and then Burton and Kurtz each emerged from the lobby. Burton had the woman and Kurtz walked with Mike.

A black car rolled up and Burton eased Annja into the backseat. Kurtz slid Mike into the backseat and then got himself in, as well. Burton walked around and opened the front passenger side. He took a quick glance around and then slid into the car.

Tuk stepped out and over to the motorbike rack nearby. In seconds, he'd freed one of the small bikes and started the engine just as Burton's car pulled out of the hotel driveway.

Tuk let them get ahead by two blocks before following.

He glanced back at the hotel and couldn't help but feel like someone was still watching him.

He frowned and turned his attention back to the car. They drove at a leisurely pace. There seemed no sense of urgency.

Tuk, as much as he despised Tsing, felt fairly certain that he didn't mean Annja and Mike harm. He merely wanted them handled in such a way so as to prove that he was in absolute command of things. And certainly drugging them and positioning them in the plane would convey such a message.

Tuk wondered if Mike even had the map they'd spoken of with him. They would need it, after all, if they were going to fly and try to locate Shangri-La.

The car turned right and then followed the main road out toward the airfield. Tuk recognized the area and knew they were getting closer to the plane. He would have to make sure they didn't spot him as they rolled inside the airfield perimeter.

Half a mile farther on, Tuk saw the taillights flash red as they braked and then turned left into the entryway. He eased the motorbike over to the side of the road and waited.

From his vantage point, Tuk could make out the car rolling toward a small airplane like the kind that ferried mountaineers all over the country.

Burton got out of the car first and checked their surroundings. Then he waved for Kurtz to exit the car. Together, they got Annja and Mike into the airplane. When they'd finished, Burton walked over to the trunk and removed several bags and stowed them in the plane, as well. When that was done, both he and Kurtz got back in the car and drove away.

Tuk rolled himself back into the shadows and let them drive past. He waited until he felt certain they were gone.

Then Tuk headed toward the plane, an idea already forming in his mind.

7

Annja woke up as the first rays of sunlight needled their way through the cockpit window of the de Havilland DHC-6 Twin Otter aircraft and roused her from the foggy drug-induced sleep. She looked around, realized where she was and then nudged Mike, who sat in the pilot's seat.

He groaned and then reached up to stretch his hands, bumping them instead on the roof of the cockpit.

"Careful," Annja said. "It's cramped in here."

Mike's eyes fluttered open. "What the hell?"

Annja grinned. "Apparently, Tsing wants to make sure we get started finding Shangri-La right away."

"I guess." Mike looked around. "The plane's a little large for what we need, but I guess it'll do."

"Can you fly this thing?" Annja asked.

Mike nodded. "Got my pilot's license about five years back. When I knew I'd be spending more time in this part of the world, it seemed like a good idea to have it. The more you can be self-reliant over here, the better off you are."

"Would have been better if you were financially self-reliant, too," Annja said.

Mike blanched. "Yeah, all right, I know I deserved that one. I'm sorry, Annja, all right? Really I am. I had no idea that Tsing was pulling my strings like this. As far as I knew, it was a simple loan."

"That has now turned into something else entirely."

"Apparently so."

Annja looked him over. She could see that Mike was not happy about having to work with Tsing. At the same time, she could see his sense of adventure exerting itself across his face. Mike's eyes ran over the instrument panel and he switched on the two turboprop engines. Instantly, the propeller blades started to turn.

"We're really going?" Annja asked.

Mike nodded. "We've got no choice in the matter. Tsing made it perfectly clear what would happen if we refused. And for my part, I may as well see whether this map is legitimate or not. After all of the trouble it's managed to get me into, I owe it to myself—and you—to see it through."

Annja looked around. Behind her, she could see several bags. "Looks like they gave us a bunch of supplies."

Mike grunted. "It's the least they could do." He smacked his lips. "But I could do with a bottle of water. Any chance they packed a cooler back there?"

Annja felt around and found one. She pulled out a cold bottle of water for herself and one for Mike. "Cheers."

Mike polished off the water quickly. "All right, let's get this thing airborne and see what we can find out there."

"What about the map?" she asked.

Mike eyed her. "What about it?"

"You have it with you?"

Mike tapped the side of his head. "Everything I need is stored safely inside the old cranium."

"You're joking," Annja said.

Mike laughed. "Actually, I am. I had the map on me the entire time."

"What if they'd taken it from you?"

Mike shrugged. "You heard Tsing. He can't go out in the daylight with that skin condition of his. Maybe he's a vampire or something."

"Stop it," Annja said, laughing.

Mike reached into a pocket of his cargo pants and pulled out a folded-up piece of paper. He handed it to Annja. "Check it out."

Annja unfolded the map and frowned. "Most of the explorers who searched for Shangri-La thought it was either close to Bhutan or over near the western border."

"They were wrong," Mike said. "According to the map, the real location lies smack-dab in the middle of the country, closer to the Tibetan border."

"You're sure about this, huh?"

"As much as I can be." Mike opened up the throttle some and the plane began to move. "Now I'd better make sure we have clearance to take off or else we'll never make it out of here."

Annja pulled her headset on and listened as he keyed his microphone and spoke to the air traffic control tower. In a short time, they had clearance and Mike urged the plane down the runway and then into the skies over Katmandu.

Annja looked out of her window as Mike took the plane into a steep climb to gain altitude and then settled on a course heading northwest.

"We'll vector around and then head for Jomsom. That's the closest airfield in the part of the country we're looking for."

"And from there? It looks like we're going to Mustang," Annja said, looking at the map.

Mike nodded. "The map says that Shangri-La lies

somewhere in that area. It's probably nestled in between some of the mountains up there. Once we're beyond Pokhara, we'll be flying into the canyon of the Kali Gandaki River. It's an amazing sight. The Annapurna range flanks us on one side and Dhaulagiri sits on the other. The mountains effectively sandwich the area, making it difficult to gain entrance to most of the upper reaches of that part of Nepal."

"Are you sure buzzing that region with this plane is such a good idea?" Annja asked.

Mike glanced at her. "What do you mean?"

"It's Mustang. I don't think I have to give you a refresher course in history, do I? The CIA used to use the region as a staging ground for Tibetan Khampa guerrillas who used to cross over the border and harass the Chinese soldiers stationed in Tibet."

"Yeah, but that was back in the sixties and seventies. That's all in the past."

"We also happen to be flying the kind of plane that is used for parachute infiltration of special-operations troops. The Chinese might get a little nervous about us buzzing the joint."

Mike sighed. "We're sort of limited in terms of our options here, Annja. From Jomsom, most people continue either on foot or horseback to reach the area we want to fly to. But for us, that would take too long. And we would have the perspective we need from the air to see down and into the mountain valleys. We have to be airborne or else we may as well be searching for the proverbial needle in the haystack."

Annja frowned. Something didn't feel right about using the plane to search, but Mike was correct. Without their eyes in the sky, they'd have no chance of spotting anything.

"I understand that you're concerned about our safety. I am, too. And we've also got the weather to contend with up here. Annapurna throws up some ferocious winds and Dhaulagiri is no slouch, either. We take an updraft or wind shear the wrong way and we're toast."

Annja looked at him. "You're not doing much to instill me with confidence in your flying abilities, pal."

Mike grinned. "Just being honest with you. Figure I owe you at least that much for putting up with me not telling you about Tsing earlier."

"Forget it. Let's concentrate on getting this done. We can handle Tsing another time and place."

Mike nodded. "All right. We'll make a quick stop at Jomsom for fuel and then take off again. We've got the entire day before us and we should be able to get some great perspectives on the area once we're north of Jomsom."

Annja stared out the window of the plane and marveled at the landscape below them. Overhead, bright blue skies streaked with wispy clouds flanked the snow-topped peaks of the Himalayan mountain ranges. The roof of the world, Annja thought, never looked so utterly amazing.

"I suppose it's easy to see why so many people pictured this as being home to Shangri-La," she said a few moments later. "It's incredible up here in this part of the world."

Mike smiled as he pointed out a variety of landmarks. "The Nazis thought that Shangri-La was home to a superior race of Nordic people like them. In 1938 they sent an expedition to Tibet led by a guy named Schafer. They never found anything, of course, but it didn't stop Hitler from imagining that there might be a link to this part of the world."

Annja sighed. "I know a lot of areas up here claim title to Shangri-La, but that's mostly for tourism, right?"

"Sure. There's even an airline named after it that operates in this region. They had a serious crash in October '08. Sixteen tourists and two crew were killed two miles short of the runway at Jomsom. Terrible accident."

"Which we won't be reliving today," Annja said.

Mike smiled. "No chance. Look." He pointed out ahead of them. "Dhaulagiri, up close and personal."

Annja looked out the front windshield and saw the giant mountain ahead of them. "It's eight thousand meters, right?"

"Yep." Mike nosed the plane down toward the river valley. "We're on final approach to Jomsom now. I'll need to talk to air traffic control for a moment."

She listened to Mike informing Jomsom control that they were coming in. He nodded and then turned to Annja. "Ready for our first landing?"

"Sure."

Mike guided the plane down and in at a steep descent. As the runway loomed before them, Annja could see that the river valley wasn't that wide at all. The fact there was an airstrip up here was a miracle in itself.

Mike flared the flaps and then tucked the plane down on the runway with a slight bump. They raced along and Mike pressed the brakes, easing them to a stop. Gradually, he pulled the plane in and parked it next to another DHC-6 and then shut down the engines.

"All right, let's get this baby gassed up and get back up there. I don't want to lose any time."

He pulled off the headset and hopped out of the plane. Annja unbuckled herself and eased out of the seat and climbed onto the tarmac. She stretched and felt marvelous moving around again. She hadn't realized how cramped the interior of the plane was until just then.

Mike came walking back, directing a ground crew toward the plane. They dutifully led a hose to the gas tanks and started pumping.

Mike tossed Annja a can of soda. "Last gasp of civilization in these parts. From here on up north into Mustang, it gets downright spooky."

"Spooky?"

"Well, there's little up here to remind you of home. Pony caravans carry all the goods and, like I said earlier, most people are on foot or horseback. This is the frontier. Hell, parts of the region we'll be flying over are off-limits to us on the ground. We'd need someone from the government to tag along."

"Why is that?"

Mike took a gulp of the soda and then belched appreciably. "Who knows? Maybe the government knows where Shangri-La is and is just protecting it. Or maybe it's because some of the less intelligent tourists would blunder over the border into Tibet if someone wasn't around to stop them. No sense having an international incident if you can avoid it."

Annja took a sip of her soda. "Makes sense."

Mike watched the ground crew finish pumping the plane full of gas and then paid them from a bundle of cash he had in his pocket. He glanced at Annja and shrugged. "Mr. Tsing thought of everything. You all set to get back to it?"

"Yep."

Annja climbed into the cockpit and strapped herself in. Mike climbed in a moment later and looked at the back of the plane.

Annja glanced at him. "Everything okay?"

"I guess."

"What?"

Mike shrugged. "Probably just my mind playing tricks on me. That damned wine took me for a whirl last night."

"What is it, Mike?"

"Thought I saw movement in the back of the plane." He shook his head. "Nothing to it. You were climbing in when it happened and you must have jostled the plane. That's all." He switched on the propellers and smiled. "Let's get out of here."

Annja slid her headset back on and then felt the lurch as the plane started to move again. Mike keyed the microphone and spoke again to air traffic control. In seconds they hurtled down the tiny runway and shot back up into the sky. Annja leaned back in her seat, enjoying the rush of gaining altitude so fast.

Mike climbed and then banked around, continuing on their original northwesterly course. He leveled the plane off and then set a course that would take them farther into the Mustang region.

Annja wondered what the future held in store for them.

8

"The curious thing about Mustang is how the entire region pokes up into Tibet," Mike said. "It almost looks like a thorn in the side."

"Hence, the reason it made such a great staging area for the Khampa guerrillas," Annja said. "They didn't have to travel as far or retreat as much to get back to safety. It made sense to stage there."

Mike piloted the plane and brought them over a particular vista. Annja looked down and saw green fields. "That looks rather lush for the area."

"Concentrated irrigation," Mike said. "It's not indicative of the entrance to the garden of Eden." He smiled. "I know the temptation to call it such, but the farmers up here have adapted quite well to the parameters of their environment." He pointed ahead of them toward where the mountain called Dhaulagiri rose up like a towering majesty. "I want to fly a little higher. See if maybe we can spot something from up there."

Annja looked at the peak. She could see storm clouds clustering around it. "Are you sure that's such a good idea? That doesn't look too inviting."

Mike nodded. "We'll be all right as long as we don't get too close. The most important thing is to get as high as we can in order to observe more than we can see skirting this level. We keep doing this, all we're accomplishing is burning fuel."

"If you say so." Annja leaned back as Mike brought the stick back toward them and the plane responding by climbing. Annja could see snowfields out of the cockpit window. The wind suddenly buffeted the plane. Annja winced. Turbulence was something she didn't care for.

"It's a little choppy up here," Mike said.

"You don't say."

Out of the window, Annja thought she saw something glint across one of the snowfields. She frowned and squinted again. "Did you see that?"

"What?"

She shook her head. "I'm not sure. I could have sworn I saw something down there across that last field we buzzed."

"Like what?"

"A glint of something. Maybe metallic. Maybe someone was signaling us?"

Mike shook his head. "We're pretty close to the border of Tibet here. I doubt very much there's a party down there trying to signal us. Doesn't seem likely."

"I saw something."

Mike glanced at the instrument panel. "I can take another pass if you want me to check it out."

"Might be worth a look."

Mike nodded. "Hang on." He banked the plane and Annja saw the vista shift to the left. Mike kept the heading on course and then leveled off. "Over there?"

The snowfield loomed in front of them, about halfway up the side of Dhaulagiri.

"Yeah, just down there," Annja said, pointing.

Mike eased the stick forward and the plane descended a little. "All right, here we go."

Annja heard the engines whine as the plane dipped and buzzed the snowfield. They were probably a thousand feet over the top of the field when she saw it again. "There!"

Mike turned his head and frowned. "That looks like—"

"Mike!"

But Mike had already seen the sudden flash and jerked the stick hard to the left. Annja looked back and saw the flare as a rocket went streaking past the right wing. "What the hell!"

"Someone's shooting at us," Mike said. He drew the plane back to the right and then angled it so it was in a steep climb. "Hang on!"

Annja clutched at the armrests on her seat as Mike jerked the plane all over the sky, trying to make it a smaller target. Annja strained to look over the back of her seat and see behind them. But the mass of bags in the rear section made it impossible.

"I can't see!" she shouted.

Mike banked the plane now. They'd climbed in altitude and he swung the plane to the left. "We should have an angle on them in a second," he said.

But as they came around again, Annja saw nothing to cause concern. "I don't see anything."

"Neither do I, but someone very obviously shot a missile at us." Mike keyed the microphone and cleared his throat to speak to air traffic control. Annja listened as he relayed what had happened and notified the tower that they were returning to Jomsom. He switched off and turned to Annja. "It's too risky for us to be out here. If someone's got missiles and they're shooting at us—"

"But why would they?" she asked.

Mike shook his head. "Damned if I know. But we can't risk our lives trying to figure it out. The best thing to do is land and see if we can get some information from somewhere about this. Maybe Tsing can help us."

"Tsing? Why would he—?"

"Because he wants to find this place as badly as we do. And if someone is causing us problems, then they're causing Tsing problems, too. He won't tolerate that. And I'm sure he can bring some muscle to bear on it."

Annja frowned. "Seems like we're getting deeper into debt with him if we do that."

"You've got a better suggestion?"

Annja sighed. "I guess not."

Mike nodded. "I know it's not ideal. But we've got to use what we have. And if Tsing is desperate to find Shangri-La and can figure out who wants to blow us out of the sky, then that's all the better. Like you said, we can handle Tsing later on. What I don't want to handle right now is a missile while I'm flying over one of the largest mountains in the world."

"I understand," Annja said. "And you're right. We should land and get out of danger. I just don't understand why anyone would want to shoot at us."

"It's worthless trying to figure it out now. We don't know anything about who it might be. We're wasting time up here."

He banked the plane again and brought them on a course away from Dhaulagiri, back toward Jomsom. "Won't be long now," he said.

In the next moment, Annja heard a sudden explosion off the right side of the plane. The plane jumped from the impact of the rocket as it struck the right wing. Alarms sounded from the cockpit instrumentation. Mike shouted for Annja to hold on.

They were already rapidly losing altitude. The plane started spinning and plummeting toward the earth. Annja looked at what was left of the right wing and saw it was on fire. Black smoke poured out, swirling about them as they spun and fell through the sky.

"I can't control it!" Mike shouted. "We're going down!"

Annja grabbed the microphone and switched it on. "Mayday, mayday, mayday, this is—"

She could barely hear herself talking. The alarms were so loud. Looking out of the cockpit through the dense black smoke she caught brief glimpses of white snow. And then of Dhaulagiri looming in front of them again. The plane almost seemed to be climbing, but that couldn't be possible. She glanced at Mike and saw him straining to pull the stick this way and that, trying to fight the plane to a softer landing than the one Annja expected them to receive.

The plane toppled through the sky; the altimeter needle spun like a pinwheel and the numbers shot past. Annja tore her eyes away and braced for impact.

When it came, the plane slammed into the side of the mountain with a deafening sound of metal being crushed and torn apart. The cockpit window shattered and cold snow and ice filled the plane.

The plane seemed to keep sliding for a distance and then, at last, it came to a merciful halt.

Annja heard herself screaming.

And then saw nothing but blackness.

WHEN ANNJA CAME TO, daylight had already started to dip below the horizon and night was rushing back to claim its birthright. Annja groaned and twisted in her seat. She was wet from the snow and ice that had surrounded her and melted from her body heat. She fought to release the harness around her, scrabbling to dig through the snow to reach the release.

As she shifted, she felt a sharp punch of pain in her side and took a gasping breath.

She felt her ribs gingerly. One, maybe two, on her left side felt badly bruised or broken. She ignored the pain and struggled to release the harness.

She looked at Mike. His head was thrown back against the pilot's seat. His eyes were closed. Annja reached out for his neck and put her fingers against his throat. She felt a thready pulse there and exhaled in a rush.

They were alive.

But they both needed help in a bad way. Annja reached for the microphone, but as soon as she tried to key it, she heard nothing. The plane had lost communications in the impact.

Annja took stock. She could move her legs and arms. Aside from the ribs, she seemed okay. Her head had a lump near her temple. She'd probably bashed it on the cockpit as the plane hit and that's what caused her to black out.

But otherwise, she was fine.

She brushed some of the snow away from her window and peered out. From what she could see, the plane had hit the side of Dhaulagiri and then slid across and came to rest on a fairly level piece of ground. The right wing, which had been shot off by the second missile, no longer smoked and she saw why. It lay covered in snow and that had helped extinguish any remaining smoldering wires.

Annja frowned. That also meant that there'd be no smoke trail to help rescuers find them.

I need to get out of here, she thought. It was the only way she could get an accurate perspective on their situation.

Annja braced herself for the pain and then grunted as she clambered out of her seat. The pain in her side was tremendous, but she steeled herself and then clawed her way outside of the plane.

As she took her first step, she fell into waist-deep snow.

Instantly, she felt the cold smack her hard. Wind whipped around her and bits of snow and ice stung her skin.

She remembered that Mike had seemingly put some more altitude on even as the plane sank toward the earth. Annja looked around and reasoned that if Dhaulagiri was eight thousand meters high, then they were at least halfway up the mountain.

The air was thin and Annja's lungs struggled to fill themselves with oxygen. Each gasping breath brought more pain in Annja's side.

Then her ears caught a sound.

It was coming from the plane.

She frowned and started back toward it. Maybe Mike had regained consciousness.

But as she neared the cockpit, she could see that Mike was still out. She'd need to get a fire going soon if they had any hope of lasting the night.

She heard another sound. It was a moan. But it didn't come from Mike.

Annja steeled herself. Was the person who had shot them out of the sky coming back to finish the job he'd started?

If so, they were going to meet with a very unpleasant Annja Creed. She summoned the mystical sword she'd inherited from Joan of Arc. The sword gleamed in her hands.

"Who's there?" she demanded. "Show yourself!"

The wind whipped up around her. Annja fought off the icy sting and glared toward the plane.

She heard another moan. She struggled to get closer to the plane. As she did, the plane seemed to rock. Again, Annja glanced at Mike to make sure it wasn't him causing the motion.

It wasn't.

Someone else was inside the plane.

Annja's vision swam as she drew closer to the plane. How

in the world had someone else gotten on it? How was that possible? Did Tsing hide someone in there?

She swung her sword and cleaved an opening in the back of the wreckage. Like a piñata splitting open under the assault, the metal sheared under the power of the sword and spilled its contents into the snow.

Annja saw bags tumble out.

And then she saw a tiny man come falling out, as well. He was bloody and he looked terrified.

But he was alive.

Annja took a step toward him, felt another wave of pain wash through her and toppled over.

Back into darkness.

9

The simple fact of his predicament was that Tuk had never ridden on an airplane before. He'd seen plenty of them and he knew what they were and even the basic scientific principles behind them.

But he had never stepped onto one until he'd had the idea to stow away on the plane with Annja Creed and her friend Mike. Any fear he'd felt at the idea was quickly squelched by the promise of reward from the man on the phone. Tuk would again prove himself to the man and hopefully reap an even better reward.

He'd made himself as comfortable as possible after he'd crawled into the plane. His first order of business was to make sure that Annja and Mike were, in fact, still alive. He felt for their pulses and then settled down among the bags, cushioning himself and making sure that the cooler of beverages was closer to the pilot and copilot seats. The last thing he needed was one of them rummaging through the bags and discovering him hidden away.

Once he'd done that, he called the man on the cell phone.

"You're with them now?"

Tuk nodded. "I am in the airplane. They are still unconscious it would appear, but alive."

"Your plan is to go with them?"

Tuk smiled. "You requested I remain with them to make sure the woman stays safe. I intend to fulfill my end of the arrangement as best I am able."

"You're a marvel, my friend. Without a doubt the best I've ever worked with. Are you certain they won't know you're there?"

"They will not. I am secreted in the back with more of the baggage that Tsing's men left for them. I went through the bags. There is a lot of cold weather gear useful for trekking in the mountains. An assortment of other supplies are in the bags, as well."

"Mountain trekking? Interesting."

"The man known as Mike had a map on him."

The man paused. "The logical assumption would be that the map shows the location of Shangri-La on it."

"I have examined the map. It does not show anything but rather a series of routes that seem to focus on the middle of the country. Particularly, there are several routes through the Mustang region."

"Mustang?"

"Yes."

"What do you know of that area?"

"Not much. I know there are temples far to the north in Lo Monthang. But otherwise, very little is known about the region. Parts of it are even off-limits to many foreigners."

"Do you know why?"

"I've heard tell that the government is very sensitive to the fact that the Tibetan border is close. They don't want to risk offending the Chinese who occupy that region."

"That makes sense," the man said. "Still, I wonder…" His voice trailed off. Tuk left him to this thoughts and waited.

Finally, the man seemed to come to a decision. "You will stay with them when they fly up to the region?"

"I will."

"Excellent. I will be in touch. Let me know the moment you have any more information to share. You've done an incredible job."

Tuk beamed. "Thank you."

The line went dead and Tuk looked out of the back window. Dawn was starting to break across the eastern horizon. And from the front of the plane, he caught movement. The woman—Annja—was beginning to stir. The drug was wearing off and, very soon, they would both be awake.

Tuk tried to quell the sudden fear that stirred in the pit of his stomach. The prospect of flying now reared its head. Tuk did not fear many things in life, even given his diminutive stature.

But flying?

He shrank down among the bags and waited for the terror to begin.

WHEN MIKE BROUGHT the plane down at Jomsom, Tuk had a brief moment to take a breath. The flight up to the northwest had been terribly frightening. And yet, there had been something else that stirred within him—a sense of adventure and excitement. Tuk had labored so long for the spies of the world, that being on his own operation now thrilled him like nothing else had in his life. No wonder, he supposed, certain people actually flocked to the intelligence world.

He stretched his legs in the back of the plane and luxuriated in getting some blood flowing back into his limbs. He could overhear Annja and Mike talking outside of the plane and knew they would be back inside soon.

But he needed a drink.

Dare he risk it?

His parched lips begged for mercy and he crept forward in the plane like a shadow. With one hand on the cooler top, he reached in and removed a single bottle of water from within. He scurried back to his hiding place and drank the water. The cold liquid rejuvenated him and helped still his beating heart.

He let out an involuntary sigh of relief when Mike and Annja jumped back on to the plane. Mike caught the movement.

Tuk froze as Mike questioned Annja about it.

If they stopped to look in the back, he would be discovered!

His heart thundered in his chest. Perhaps there was a better way to make a living. Tuk knew that Annja and Mike wouldn't do him harm, but the prospect of discovery set his nerves on edge.

But Mike ignored his instinct and got the plane airborne. In the back of the plane, Tuk felt the water he'd just sucked down loll about his insides. Twice he had to bite back the surge of bile in his throat.

And the worst was yet to come.

After they'd climbed to a staggering height, Tuk felt his ears pop. The roar of the engines made his ears hurt and he buried his head down amid the bags. Then, without warning, Mike threw the plane all over the sky, twisting it this way and that. The engines whined in protest, but complied with Mike's directions.

Tuk and the bags in back, however, slid and tumbled everywhere. Tuk halfway expected Annja to turn and look back only to see Tuk's arms and legs akimbo as he sprawled from one side of the plane to the other while Mike engaged in his acrobatics.

But she didn't.

Gradually, Mike leveled the plane and Tuk gathered the bags about him again, trying his best to wedge them in around him so he could be reasonably secure. The last thing he wanted was to have to go through that again.

He caught snippets of conversation.

A missile?

Tuk gulped. Now he was facing the very real threat of being shot out of the sky, all because he'd had the brilliant idea to stow away on this plane.

He saw the dreamy visions of his retirement life evaporating before his eyes. This will teach me to get myself into these situations, he thought.

That was when he happened to look out the right side of the plane just as the second missile struck and exploded. Tuk jerked back reflexively as the explosion sheared the right wing off just short of the engine. Smoke and fire erupted and he heard the barrage of alarms sound inside the plane.

Annja and Mike shouted at each other. The plane started to spin and, from the sinking sensation, Tuk knew they were going down.

He grabbed at the cell phone in his pocket. Secrecy be damned, he had to let the man on the phone know what was happening. With his fingers a quivering mess, he managed to press the two and hold it long enough for the speed dial to kick in.

After what seemed an eternity, during which time Tuk had to close his eyes to keep from passing out, someone answered the phone.

"What's going on?"

"We've been shot down over the mountains! A missile!" Tuk whispered.

"Where are you?" The man's voice betrayed no real sense of emotion and Tuk realized that, as a professional, he knew exactly what he was supposed to do in this situation.

Tuk steeled himself. "We are north of Jomsom. The closest mountain is Dhaulagiri. I think we are going to crash there."

"Is anyone hurt at this moment?"

"Not that I can tell."

"All right, listen to me very carefully. You will most likely go unconscious when you crash. As soon as you regain consciousness, try the cell phone and see if you can reach me."

"I will."

"Stay with the plane if it's possible. I will find you. I promise."

Tuk gulped. "I am scared."

"You should be." The man paused. "I am coming for you right now. Stay alive and I will find you."

The line disconnected.

Tuk reached down to put the phone back in his pocket but then the plane impacted the side of the mountain. The cell phone skittered away from Tuk's grasp, sliding out and away from him across the aisle toward the cockpit.

"No!"

The airplane filled with the roar of the crash. Tuk heard the screech of twisting and tearing metal as the snow and ice crashed in through the cockpit window.

They were sliding across the snowfield. Tuk hoped they weren't going to career all the way to the edge and topple over into some giant chasm. If they did, no one would ever find them again.

Certainly not the man on the phone.

But even as Tuk screamed, he had hope in his heart that what the man on the phone said was true. That he was coming for them now.

Tuk clutched at the bags around him. They would be the only things that cushioned him in case some giant bit of rock chose to bite into the plane as it skidded over it. Tuk had no wish to be ripped open and he tried to maneuver his body onto the top of the bags as the plane continued to skid across the snowfield.

In the front of the plane, both Annja and Mike had already been knocked out. Snow flooded the passenger compartment and Tuk saw in horror that a growing wave of snow was headed right for him at the back of the plane.

He realized too late that his position on top of the bags was vulnerable and even as he tried to scamper back down to shield himself, the wave of snow picked him up and crashed his small head up against the roof of the passenger compartment.

Tuk saw stars and then darkness.

SOMETHING DRIPPED DOWN from his forehead.

Cold.

Tuk awoke and felt for his head. Blood? His hand came away clean. The snow had melted and woken him up.

He exhaled in a rush, realizing that he was still alive.

He could have cried at the moment, but then he saw that Annja no longer sat in her seat at the front of the plane.

Where was she?

Had someone taken her? Or had she been thrown free of the aircraft when they had crashed? If that was the case, she was likely dead.

But Tuk didn't think so. The snow and ice had wedged her in pretty well. The likelihood was that she had regained consciousness first, not looked in the back of the plane and seen Tuk, and only managed to free herself.

Tuk strained his ears and heard crunching sounds from

outside of the plane. Someone was walking around. Unsteady, but they were alive.

Tuk knew that the time had come to make his presence known. They would all be reliant on one another now if they had any hope of surviving. And he felt certain the man on the phone wouldn't mind.

Tuk frowned. But maybe not just yet. Maybe he would simply act the part of the stowaway. He could claim he'd gone out drinking and staggered inside the plane to sleep off his binge.

Yes. He would keep up appearances until told otherwise. Operational sanctity was his first priority. That and his personal survival.

But first, he had to get himself out of the plane—

Tuk jerked back as a massive sword blade suddenly sliced through the battered metal skin of the airplane, rending it apart. Tuk felt the bags beneath him suddenly start to spill out and with them went his body.

He toppled out of the airplane and landed at Annja's feet.

A sword? Where had she gotten that?

But Annja took another step forward, even as the first bits of surprise registered on her face at seeing Tuk. Then she fell over into the snow.

And Tuk scrambled forward to help.

10

Annja came back around and opened her eyes. She immediately felt the cold snow around her body and wondered what had happened. But then the memories flashed through her mind and she sat up instantly.

"Wait." A small hand held her down. "If you get up too quickly, you will vomit and dehydrate."

The face of the small man swam into view. Annja frowned and then remembered that he had somehow spilled out of the back of the airplane. "Who are you?" she asked.

"My name is Tuk."

Annja struggled. "Mike—?"

"The man with you is still unconscious. And he is still secured to the seat. I was unable to free him without assistance. Perhaps when you feel better, we might—"

"We'll do it now," Annja said. She slowly got to her feet and headed for the plane, followed by Tuk.

"I really think you ought to rest before we do this," he said.

Annja stopped and looked at him. He was tiny and looked more like a child than an adult. But she could see the creases and furrows in his face that come with the accumulation of life experience. She shook her head.

"If we leave him in there, he'll get hypothermia. We need to find some form of shelter and start a fire."

Tuk nodded. "Very well." He followed Annja around to Mike's side of the plane.

Annja looked inside. Mike's face looked peaceful but she was alarmed. She'd already regained consciousness twice and Mike had yet to move. Was it possible that he had a severe head injury? If he did, then they would need a medevac as soon as possible. But Annja had no idea how to go about getting one. The only hope she had right then was that Jomsom air traffic control had launched a search-and-rescue party for them.

"Help me wedge the door open," Annja said.

Tuk came alongside, and then as Annja held the door handle down he leaned and drove the door back with the force of his body. Annja looked at him and smiled. He might have been tiny but he had a lot of power in that body of his.

Together, they got the door open. Annja looked at Mike. As she twisted, she grunted as a sharp lancing pain shot through her ribs. They were tolerable, but would also need taping at some point.

First things first, she took Mike's pulse and found it stronger now than when they'd first crashed. That was a good sign. He was breathing well. But his cheeks were pale.

From the waist down he was covered with snow. Annja frowned. "We've got to get this away from his body. It's leeching the warmth right out of him."

Tuk nodded. "All right, let me help. You have an injury from the crash, it would appear."

Annja nodded. "You're no picture of perfection yourself, pal. You've got some blood on the top of your head."

Tuk frowned and reached up. His hand came away sticky and dark. "I hit the top of the cabin when we crashed. I am all right, though."

"Head injuries often look worse than they are," Annja said. "I've had enough of them myself."

Tuk stared at her and then looked back toward Mike. "Let me get him shoveled out of there." He bent low and started scooping the snow out from around Mike's body. Annja watched him work. He seemed to possess a store of energy.

But who was he?

"You want to tell me what you were doing in our plane?" she asked.

Tuk glanced at her. "I'm afraid my weakness for alcohol resulted in me stowing away there last night."

"Last night?"

"I was out drinking. I staggered past the airfield and realized I'd never make it home. The planes looked comfortable. I only intended to sleep off my hangover and then head back home." He shrugged. "However, that plan was soon cast to the wind when I awoke to find us all in the air."

"You could have said something."

Tuk shook his head. "I've never flown before. I decided it would be best to just let you get us wherever we were going. I took solace in the fact that we would eventually have to return to Katmandu. Once back, I would simply steal away with you and your friend, none the wiser."

"So much for that plan, huh?"

Tuk smiled and resumed digging out Mike. Annja saw his brow crease with concern. Then he started digging faster.

"What's wrong?"

Then she saw it. Bloody snow.

"No!"

Tuk nodded. "He must have an injury we cannot see." Tuk's hands came away bright red as the snow and ice melted and mixed with the blood. "It's vital we stop the bleeding as soon as we can."

Annja maneuvered her way around to the back of the plane where the bags and Tuk had spilled out. She rummaged through the bags and came up with a first aid kit. It wasn't anything exhaustive, but she found sterile gauze and pressure dressing inside.

She hoped it would work.

She moved back to Mike's side. Tuk had successfully gotten rid of most of the snow. Mike's lower torso was now exposed. As Annja came around, she saw what Tuk was staring at and frowned.

"It's his thigh," Tuk said. "It appears that a piece of metal pierced it from the plane's body. Probably when we crashed it came through and shredded part of his leg. He's lost a fair amount of blood."

Annja tore open the pressure dressing and handed it to him. "Get some on the wound."

Tuk dutifully took the dressing and pressed it into the wound.

The effect on Mike was almost instantaneous. His eyes shot open and he screamed. Annja put a hand on him and tried to calm him down. "Hold still, Mike. It's Annja. I'm here."

He stared at her. "Are you okay?"

She smiled. "Think so. Took a shot to my head, but that's nothing new there. I passed out twice, but I'm feeling pretty good now aside from some broken ribs."

"You sure?"

"That they're broken? Yeah. I've had them before." Annja frowned. "They're not fun, but they're manageable."

Mike nodded and then glanced at Tuk. "Who is this?"

Annja smiled. "Apparently, we had a stowaway on the plane."

"He was with us?"

"Yep."

Mike grimaced as Tuk pressed into the wound more. "I could have sworn I saw something at Jomsom."

Tuk smiled. "I'm afraid that was me." He leaned over Mike's thigh and stared at the wound.

"How is it?" Annja asked.

Tuk looked at her. "The bleeding is slowing, but I can't tell how bad the tear is. I think it's fairly certain that the femoral artery was not damaged, but he has lost a good amount of blood."

Annja looked around. "How long before they send a rescue team?"

Mike grunted. "I don't know. Depends if they got a fix on our location. There's a lot of real estate to cover up in these parts. All they knew was we were north of Jomsom. We could have gone down anywhere."

Annja sighed. Daylight was already starting to fade in the mountains and the chill that her adrenaline had kept at bay was finally working its way into her consciousness.

They needed shelter and fire. If they had to spend the night exposed to the elements like this, there would be no surviving it.

She looked at Tuk. "How well do you know the countryside around here?"

Tuk shook his head. "I don't know it at all. I'm an orphan and found my way into Katmandu when I was young. All the memories of my childhood have deserted me unfortunately."

Annja maneuvered around to where Tuk stood. She reached to take over the act of keeping pressure on Mike's wound. "Well, here's the reality check, Tuk. We need to find a place that is out of the wind. If we stay exposed like this on the mountain we're dead before anyone gets a chance to find us."

Tuk nodded. "I agree. What would you like me to do."

"Seeing that you're the most mobile out of all of us, you're going to need to find shelter of some sort. I know there are a lot of caves around these parts. What are the odds you can locate one for us to take shelter in?"

"I won't know until I get started," Tuk said.

Annja nodded. "All right, then. You go and see what you can locate. The bags in the back have some winter coats in them. You should take one along. And don't do anything silly. Mike's going to need help getting to wherever we hole up. Try to make it close. Otherwise, we'll risk worsening his wound."

"I understand."

Annja watched him get a coat out of one of the bags and zip it up. He brought them each a winter parka and then nodded to Annja. "I'll be back as soon as I can find someplace for us."

"Good luck," Annja said.

Tuk took a final glance at Mike and smiled. "Fast as I can."

He trudged off through the snow, but despite his small size, he seemed to make fast headway through the drifts. Mike's coughing brought Annja back to the moment.

"Is he gone?" Mike asked.

"Yeah."

Mike frowned. "Leg's killing me. Got any of that water from the cooler?"

Annja nodded and placed Mike's hand on the dressing. "Hold this here and press down on it. I'll get the water."

She scrambled back around to the cooler and winced as she did so. Her ribs were aching, but she fought off the desire to give in to the pain. Mike was the priority. He needed looking after and Annja's ribs were a secondary concern.

She dug a bottle of water out of the cooler and came back to Mike's side. "Here you go."

He tilted his head back and took several swigs. Annja eased the bottle back down. "Don't want you throwing up any of it. Just take it slow."

"What's the deal with our little friend there?"

Annja shrugged. "No idea. He was in the back of the plane. I passed out right after I found him. He could certainly have done me harm if he wished, but he was actually helping me when I regained consciousness."

"You trust him?"

Annja smiled. "I'm not exactly in a position where trust can be withheld, am I? We all need one another if we're going to survive this."

Mike nodded and took another sip of the water. "What if he works for Tsing?"

"What if he does?"

"He could have overheard our conversations. He might tell Tsing what we intend to do."

Annja frowned. "Mike, all we said was that we could handle Tsing later after all of this was over and done with. We didn't necessarily plan the guy's assassination or anything."

Mike grinned. "Good point."

"More to the point, Tuk needs us just as much as we need him. We're all in this together, and if one of us doesn't help, we'll all buy it. So you ask if I trust him? I trust him to do what's right for everyone involved. Beyond that, well, we'll take it as it comes. Once we get down off of this mountain."

"Always the pragmatic Annja," Mike said. "I've missed that over the years."

"I was busy being pragmatic elsewhere," Annja said.

"Apparently."

A strong breeze blew in from the mountain and Annja shivered in spite of the winter parka. The sun was starting to dip beneath the horizon, streaking the sky with purples and oranges.

"Some sunset," she said.

Mike stared out of the shattered windshield. "They're amazing up here. I just hope that our new friend finds us a place to spend the night."

"Me, too," Annja said. "Otherwise, that sunset could be our last."

11

Tuk forged through the waist-deep snow like an icebreaker and headed right for the side of the mountain, trying to get out of the open snowfield as quickly as possible. There could be a chasm hundreds of feet deep under any part of the snow. The closer he was to the actual mountain itself, the better he felt.

As soon as he was beyond range of being seen from the plane, he reached into his pocket and pulled out the cell phone he'd spent twenty minutes digging to find under all the snow in the plane. Luckily, it still worked. He opened it and prayed that he could actually get a signal.

He pressed the number two and waited. A series of clicks worried him at first but then miraculously he heard it ringing on the other end.

"Tuk?"

"Yes!"

Hearing the man's voice on the other end of the line reinvigorated him. Help would come for them!

"Did you all survive the crash?"

"Yes, but the man Mike is injured. He's got a bleeding wound in his thigh. We've stabilized him as much as possible, but we will need a medical team to come to us soon or he will not last the night."

There was a pause on the other end of the phone. "Tuk, I've got bad news. We can't get a rescue team out to you now."

"Why not?"

"There's a storm heading your way. A bad one."

Tuk looked at the sky. If he'd grown up with people who knew how to read the weather, he might have noticed the line of clouds forming and heading right for the peak he was on.

Already, he could feel the temperature falling.

"When?"

"Tomorrow if the storm breaks. But I'm not going to lie to you, Tuk. Not after everything you've done for me. The chances of a rescue early on are remote unless this storm breaks before dawn. The odds are long of that happening and you may be out there for a couple of days."

"We won't make it."

"Listen to me," the man said. "Remember how I told you to stay close to the plane?"

"Yes."

"Forget that advice. You need to find someplace else to take shelter while the storm rages. Get yourself into an overhang or some other piece of shelter close to the mountain itself, out of the wind. If you can do that, then you can survive this thing."

"The man may not survive."

"How is Annja?"

"She collapsed unconscious twice, but seems all right now. She apparently has two broken ribs but is mobile enough."

The man paused again. "I understand what you've told me,

Tuk. I wish I had better news. As long as Annja lives, that is the priority. Do you understand me?"

"Yes."

"Then you don't have any time to waste. Find a shelter and get as many of the supplies into it as you can. Wait this thing out. Keep the phone with you."

"I'm amazed I got any reception at all."

"It's not a cell phone, Tuk. Merely designed to look like one. You can reach me from anywhere on earth with that little thing. It's tremendously powerful despite its size. Just like you."

Tuk looked up into the sky. The wind was increasing. "I've got to go or I'll lose precious time."

"Understood. Call me tomorrow if you can."

"The woman doesn't know about you yet. I've kept it from them both. But I may not be able to much longer."

"Do your best, Tuk. That's all I can ever ask."

Tuk disconnected and frowned. The news that there would be no rescue irked him, but life had dealt him bad cards before and somehow he'd always managed to come out ahead.

The most important thing just then was finding them an adequate shelter. And fast. It would still take the time to reach it from the wreckage once Tuk found something.

The wind felt stronger on this side of the mountain. The storm appeared to be blowing in from the northeast so Tuk went around toward the other side. As soon as he cleared a large outcropping, the wind died down.

There'd be no guarantee that it would stay blowing in only one direction, but if they could minimize their exposure, then it would be better on this side of the mountain.

His legs kept churning beneath him and he glanced back at his own trail in the snow. If it started to snow, he would be in serious trouble. A rapid snowfall would erase his lifeline back to the plane. And then he would truly be alone.

He pushed ahead for another two hundred yards when he caught a glimpse of dark color in the field of grayish white twilight. He hurried over and felt a small depression in the side of a large rock face.

Tuk pushed his hand into the space and felt a rush of excitement as it seemed to open up into a larger area. The opening itself was barely twenty-four inches across and hardly a cave mouth.

But it would do. Tuk ducked inside and couldn't make out much in terms of detail. But it had a roof and it would offer them protection during the storm.

He had to get back to Annja and Mike.

Back outside, the first snowflakes swirled through the air. It would only be a matter of time before the storm would embrace the mountain in earnest. Tuk revved himself up and, with lungs already burning, trudged back hard through the snow toward the airplane.

As he came around the side of the mountain, the wind returned and slammed him so hard he fell on his back. He bent forward and made himself as low as possible, then kept fighting to make his way to the plane.

Finally, after another thirty minutes, he saw the tail of the plane ahead.

"Annja!" he called out.

His voice was barely audible over the encroaching storm, but after shouting two more times, the woman's head appeared and waved him on.

Back at the plane, she had a bottle of water ready for him. Tuk sucked it down, amazed at how hot and sweaty he was.

Annja eyed him. "Any luck?"

Tuk nodded and put the top back on the bottle. "It's a fair hike on the other side of the mountain, but there's a place we can use."

"Is it big enough for all of us?"

Tuk nodded. "I think so, but I couldn't be sure. I was just concerned with getting back. There's no time to waste. We've got to get going." He looked at Mike, who actually seemed better now. "Can you make it?"

Mike tried moving and gritted his teeth. "I'll make it."

Tuk glanced at Annja. "We don't have any time. We'll all die if we stay here. That storm is going to be massive."

Annja looked at Mike. "I'll carry you," she said.

Mike laughed. "Give me a break, Annja. I'll be fine. The bleeding's stopped and I'll make it on my own."

Tuk reached into the back of the plane and started gathering supplies. "I can carry two bags."

Annja took another and the first aid kit. "I arranged the contents so we've got blankets, food and the water," she said.

Tuk hefted the bags and found that, while they didn't weigh a whole lot, they made his walking cumbersome. "You'll need to help Mike. If the bleeding begins again, he might die," he said to Annja.

She nodded. "Start leading the way, Tuk. We're getting critical on time."

Tuk led them around the front of the plane and then started walking back through his own tracks. The snow increased and more flakes fell. Walking with the two bags strapped to his back made things even tougher, but he couldn't complain. The choice was clear—march or die.

They gradually managed to limp their way around the bend in the mountain and got out of the direct wind blasts that had assailed them since leaving the plane. Tuk called a halt and checked on Annja and Mike.

Annja looked cold and tired, but still in fairly decent shape. Mike looked pale and winded. He was limping along with Annja as a support for him.

Tuk cupped his hand over Annja's ear. "How is he?"

"He can make it. I think the bleeding started again, though. How much farther is it?"

"A few hundred yards," Tuk said. "You'll see the outcropping and that's it."

Snow continued to fall on them as they clawed their way those final few hundred yards. At last, Tuk spotted the outcropping, relieved that it hadn't been covered over with snow yet. His tracks made just thirty minutes earlier were already mere depressions in the snow.

He waved Annja and Mike over, helping them the last few feet. Annja handed Tuk the single flashlight that she'd retrieved from the plane. "Tell me what it's like inside."

Tuk ducked into the outcropping and switched the light on. His heart raced. He had found them a cave. A few yards in from the opening, the roof opened up to a height of seven feet or so and then seemed to go on right into the mountain.

There was always the danger that an animal lived inside, but Tuk was beyond caring. They had a place to wait out the storm.

He poked his head back outside. "Let's get Mike in here."

Annja eased him through the opening, which was barely big enough to accommodate his girth. Mike wasn't obese, but years of football had made him large. Getting him into the cave was a challenge.

Annja ducked through the opening a moment later, dragging the last of their gear with her.

She looked around and nodded. "Good work, Tuk."

"Thank you." He moved the flashlight around the walls and floor of the cave. It seemed remarkably dry. "We need a fire to get us warm," he said.

Annja grunted. "Wish we had some firewood."

Tuk looked at her. "You'll be okay with Mike here by the entrance for a little while?"

Annja nodded. "I need to change his bandage. He's bleeding again."

"All right. I'm going to see what there is to use in this cave."

Annja frowned. "You expect to find a tree?"

"You never know what might be around," Tuk said. "If animals have lived here, they might have bedding or even scat that we can use to burn. Anything to get our temperatures up would be good. Especially for Mike's sake."

"Well, you've already saved us by finding this place," Annja said. "Just don't be too long. I've barely got any light over here as it is and that flashlight is our only source right now."

"I'll be quick," Tuk said. He headed off toward the back of the cave and kept shining the flashlight around all the crevices. His feet brushed over bits of straw that he dutifully gathered up in his pockets. It would burn, but it wouldn't last long. They needed more substantial fuel if they were going to stay warm.

The cave seemed to descend toward a point where the walls converged. Tuk looked down at the ground and saw evidence of smaller animals living there, but again, nothing beyond that. As much of a blessing as the cave was, there seemed to be little of use inside its walls.

Tuk leaned back against the rock face of the wall and took a breath. He hadn't realized how utterly exhausted he was. Forging through the snow drifts had sapped all of his strength.

He decided to get back to Annja and Mike. They might not be able to have a roaring fire, but at least they were out of the storm.

"Any luck?" Annja asked as he came back around the bend.

"Unfortunately, I only managed to find a handful of straw. It is probably from an old bird's nest."

Annja had spread the coats around on the ground and layered them atop one another. "Well, so much for my picture perfect idea of a campfire and ghost stories tonight."

Tuk smiled. "How is he?"

Annja looked at Mike, who lay on the coats with his leg slightly elevated. "I've stopped the bleeding again, but he's lost a lot of blood. We're going to need medical help tomorrow or else…" Her voice trailed off.

"I understand," Tuk said. "We will get him the help he needs."

Annja waved him over. "I've got some survival rations here. It's not filet mignon but it will do. Eat with us. Then I think we're all going to have to cozy up to one another and share the warmth. That storm outside sounds pretty awful."

Tuk helped himself to some of the food and sat chewing for a while as the snow continued to fall outside of their cave.

He hoped the man on the phone would be able to find them.

Before it was too late.

12

Despite being out of the direct path of the wind, Annja could still hear it howling around the mountain outside of the cave. If we'd stayed with the plane, she thought, we'd already be dead.

Mike lay next to her. He was feverish and Annja was extremely worried about his injury. If the storm didn't break before morning, she doubted that any rescue party would ever find them. As it was, they were already quite a distance from the plane wreckage. And no one had any idea where they were.

But morning was still hours away. And they needed to get through the night first.

She felt Mike's head and checked his pulse. His heart rate seemed to have increased. At least he wasn't hypothermic. On the other side of Mike, Tuk lay on his back, perfectly still in the dark. His breathing seemed deep and level.

Annja thought about his sudden appearance earlier. Seeing him topple out of the back of the plane was a shock. She almost thought that Tsing might have stashed someone else aboard with a more evil agenda.

But Tuk had proven handy. He'd saved their lives by spotting this cave. Annja wasn't sure she would have been able to find the place on her own. And it was less likely she would have been able to get both the gear and Mike to the cave before the snow buried them.

The simple fact was that they owed their lives to the diminutive Nepali man.

The question that plagued Annja was very simple. What was he doing on their plane?

The excuse he'd given didn't hold up. Annja had a great nose for booze, and if Tuk had been drinking heavily the previous night she would have smelled it all over him, especially when he got back from his scouting mission. He was sweating so much that any booze in his system would have scented him like a perfume.

And yet, there was nothing about him that reeked of alcohol.

Which meant the little guy was lying.

But why?

Annja frowned. A stowaway on a plane that happens to crash who then saves their lives was a bit too much coincidence for her. And Annja wasn't big on believing in such things in the first place.

But Tuk seemed almost completely harmless. Almost. Annja knew better than to accept the notion that his small size meant he was a pushover. He'd already demonstrated his incredible drive to accomplish finding the cave. And he'd then come back, grabbed two bags and led them to the safety of this shelter.

Most people wouldn't be able to do that, she thought. But Tuk had accomplished it easily enough. It was almost as if his determination carried him along when physical strength did not.

And that made the little man dangerous. Or, at least, potentially so.

Annja took a breath and exhaled. She could just make out a bit of the breath as it frosted the air in front of her face. Her muscles slowly loosened from the earlier push to reach the cave. And the stress over Mike's injury had subsided somewhat, as well. He was resting comfortably and there was nothing more to be done for him at the moment. Mike wasn't out of the woods yet, but Annja needed sleep. Her body craved it like a drug, and mercifully, Annja felt the cloak of slumber reach for her and pull her into its embrace.

ANNJA TRIED TO RESIST the urging of her body to come back to a more conscious state. She wanted to stay asleep. Things were warm and happy there.

But she could sense movement. Maybe it was Mike needing some help.

Annja allowed one eye to open and glance around.

The interior of the cave was absolutely dark. She could see nothing. But she could feel something.

Mike was moving.

She rolled over and felt for him in the darkness. Her hand found nothing.

Annja sat up.

"Mike?"

She sensed another source of movement. "Tuk?"

"Yes?"

Annja relaxed a little bit. "Is Mike with you?"

"No. He's lying next to— Wait." Annja heard Tuk rustling around and then the flashlight beam cut into the darkness, illuminating the surrounding cave.

Mike was gone.

Tuk scrambled to his feet and shone the flashlight all around the cave. Annja was on her feet, as well. "Where the hell did he go?"

Tuk looked down at their improvised bedding and shook his head. "I don't see any fresh bloodstains. That's at least a good sign."

"Yes, but he's gone," Annja said. "And that's not a good thing."

Tuk looked around. "He was right next to me." He looked at Annja. "Forgive me. Ordinarily, I would have remained alert. But I'm afraid the exertion from my trek earlier quite exhausted my ability to stay awake."

"You deserved the sleep," Annja said. "I should have been on watch. I didn't think we'd have anything to worry about with such a crazy storm outside."

Tuk shook his head. "This doesn't make any sense. If Mike is gone and we cannot find him—"

Annja frowned. "How far back did you search the cave earlier when we got here?"

"Almost as far as I could go. The roof converges and the walls actually get much closer. I don't think there's any way that Mike could have gotten out back there."

Annja grabbed the flashlight and headed toward the back of the cave. Tuk followed along behind her. "Annja? I don't think he went this way."

"Then where did he go? Outside? That would be suicidal. And Mike's not the type to do that."

Tuk cleared his throat. "I don't mean to sound cold, but perhaps he was worried that he was weighing us down. That if we were concerned about him, then we might all die. Perhaps he thought—"

Annja flashed the light back on to Tuk. "Stop it. I don't believe that for a second."

"It was just a thought." Tuk clamped his mouth shut.

Annja shook her head. "Sorry, it's just that I know Mike and he wouldn't think of doing that. There would be another way to solve the problem. Besides, Mike was too fixated on the purpose of our mission."

"And what was that?"

Annja smiled. "We're searching for Shangri-La."

Tuk nodded. "Really?"

"You don't seem surprised."

Tuk shrugged. "You're not the first foreigners to come looking for it. The lure of an idyllic world isolated from the rest of the earth is a powerful one. Many people have come to Nepal looking for it."

"Do you believe it exists?" Annja asked.

Tuk shrugged. "I believe in only what I can control—my own future, until recently."

Annja reached the back part of the cave and frowned. Just as Tuk had said, the cave roof and walls all converged at a point that made any more progression in that direction impossible. Unless you had a drill or the means to pass through solid rock.

Annja had neither.

She supposed that the sword might be able to penetrate the rock at least for a few inches. But what was the point of that? she wondered. Unless there was a hidden route through the rock, it would be a useless gesture.

She glanced toward the front of the cave. As much as she hated the idea that Tuk might actually have a point with his suggestion that Mike had gone out into the storm, she had to at least satisfy herself that he hadn't.

She looked at Tuk. "Come on."

"Where are we going?"

"Outside."

Annja scooped up the jackets and tossed one to Tuk. "Put it on. I'm almost one hundred percent certain that he wouldn't do this, but in his feverish state, who knows how his mind might operate."

She zipped up the parka and watched as Tuk did the same. "You ready?"

He nodded. Annja held up her hand. "I'll keep the flashlight, if you don't mind."

Tuk nodded and watched as Annja swept the heavy beam over to the opening of the cave. "Here we go."

Tuk watched her scoot down through the thin opening. He followed her out into the storm.

Annja gasped as the first punch of cold wind knocked her sideways. The air outside the cave couldn't have been ten degrees. And the snow slapped her exposed skin like sharpened lead bullets.

She flashed the light along the ground and saw nothing. No footprints led away from the cave. And there was no way Mike could have left the cave without leaving some sort of sign.

Unless he happened to fly away.

Annja shook her head and turned to Tuk, shouting to be heard over the storm. "He's not out here."

Tuk nodded and gestured for them to return to the safety of the cave. He ducked back inside.

Annja took another second to look around, shining the flashlight in all directions. But the snow and wind combined to make the beam of the flashlight ineffective even out to twenty yards.

He's not here, Annja thought. He's got to be inside the cave.

Somewhere.

She ducked back through the opening and took a breath as she got herself out of the storm. Tuk had already ditched his coat and was jumping up and down to get his blood circulating.

"No one would last in that weather for more than ten minutes," he said a moment later.

Annja clapped her hands to herself, trying to warm up. "Agreed. But that still leaves us with the question of where Mike could have gone. If he's not outside, then logic demands that he's somewhere inside."

Tuk frowned. "We've seen all of the cave, at least as far as I can tell. And from what we know, it is also impossible that Mike is in here with us."

Annja shook her head. "I don't think he would have gone outside. But he's somewhere. People don't just disappear."

"I'm open to hearing your theories," Tuk said. "I must admit I have none at the moment that could explain this."

"Neither do I," Annja said.

Tuk sat down on the blankets. "What if there is another way out of here that we don't know about?"

"That's the only thing that makes any possible sense," Annja said. "But where? We're in the main cavern and then there's that back portion. Beyond that, I don't see any other spaces."

Tuk frowned. "Then there must be something that we have not noticed. Our perspective does not permit us to see what may be directly in front of our faces. Yet it would still exist."

"We have to search for it," Annja said. "Mike's life might well depend on it."

"Where do we start?" Tuk asked.

Annja pointed to the back wall of the cavern. "At what looks to be the dead end. If there's nothing there, then we'll work back toward the cave opening. But somewhere, there's got to be something. There has to be."

Tuk got to his feet. "And what happens if we search every bit of the cave and still don't know where he is?"

Annja bit her lip. "Then I'll have to accept the possibility that Mike has vanished off the face of the earth."

Tuk took the flashlight from her and aimed it toward the back of the cave. "Well, we're not there just yet. Let's see if we can maybe find a logical explanation for his disappearance before we write him off entirely."

13

Tuk set to check the back of the cave with Annja working over to his right side. He started pressing his hands into every inch of the rock, trying desperately to find some type of hidden spot that they couldn't see with their naked eyes.

He watched as Annja worked on her own section of the cave. She ran her hands up and along every bit of rock she could find. The worry on her face was apparent and Tuk frowned. He had to keep her focused but less frightened.

"How long have you known Mike?"

"Huh? Mike? I've known him for years. We did some graduate school work together. I always thought he wasn't serious enough. You know, because he played football and always seemed to be much more interested in sports than in anything to do with science and history."

"You were mistaken?"

"It's like what you were saying about perspectives just now. Sometimes what's right in front of our eyes can't be seen simply because we look at it from only one perspective. Mike was like that. And when I stopped seeing him as a football player, and instead looked at him as someone interested in many of the same things that grabbed my attention, then all of a sudden he became a great friend."

"How many times have you worked together?"

"On again and off again. It's how it happens in archaeology. You get together with some people for one thing and others for something else. Mike's teaching now and then takes long sabbaticals to go off and pursue those things he's really interested in."

"Shangri-La being one of them," Tuk said. He'd had no luck with any part of the cave so far. He ran his hands along the cave wall.

"Shangri-La is really the thing that drives him hardest," Annja said. "As long as I've known him he's always had a thing for lost lands and places that seem to defy convention."

"I guess Shangri-La is all of that. How long has he been searching for it?" Tuk asked.

"When we were in school, he wrote a thesis on its existence, which promptly got him laughed out of the first board. It taught him a valuable lesson about his passion."

"And what was that?"

"That sometimes people don't care how much you love something. If it doesn't look right or sound like something they want to hear, you may as well be the village idiot. There tends to be an acute lack of respect for passion in our society these days." Annja paused. "Well, unless it makes money."

Tuk nodded. "I think people fear their passion."

Annja looked at him. "Do you?"

He nodded. "Certainly. Passion for something means you don't care what anyone else thinks about it. You know in your heart that it's right and that's all that really matters. You're unstoppable in your love for something. Not a lot of people are confident or comfortable enough in their own skin to even acknowledge that emotion."

Annja smiled. "You're an interesting guy, Tuk."

"Thank you."

"And I never thanked you properly for saving our lives earlier," she said.

Tuk held up his hand. "Don't mention it. If I hadn't found this place, we'd all be in the same situation."

Annja turned back to the cave wall and kept pressing at the rock. Tuk watched her for another moment before doing the same. As the edges ran under his skin, he wondered what they could possibly be looking for. A hidden doorway? A trap floor compartment? There had to be something. As Annja said, Mike couldn't just simply disappear.

Tuk thought about the phone in his pocket and had the sudden desire to call the man who had hired him. He could let him know about their situation. Perhaps he had some ideas of his own about where Mike might have gone.

He frowned. That was foolish. How in the world would the man know anything about Mike's condition aside from what Tuk had told him earlier.

No, the time to talk to him would be in the morning. Hopefully when he was confirming that he was arranging the rescue for them.

"Annja?" Tuk asked.

"Yeah?"

"Am I right in saying that a missile brought the plane down this afternoon?"

Annja nodded. "Sure seems to have been a missile. Yeah."

"But who would have fired it? I mean, why bother with us at all? It doesn't make sense."

Annja shook her head. "I don't know what to tell you, Tuk.

All I know is the first missile barely missed us and then the second one took off our wing and we crashed as a result."

"But there's something else I don't understand."

"What's that?"

"Whoever shot us down doesn't seem to be around here."

Annja stopped and looked at Tuk. "What are you getting at?"

"Don't you see? We were shot down. Presumably because someone wanted us dead. Well, you and Mike, anyway. But then as soon as we went down, there was no follow-up."

Annja frowned. "You mean no one came to see that the job was done?"

Tuk nodded. "It's not like they didn't have time to do it. The weather hadn't gotten that bad yet. And unless we went down far away from where the missile was fired, they should have been able to get to us easily."

"And they would have killed us," Annja said.

"Exactly my point. Why didn't they follow up?"

"Maybe they didn't know where we went down." Annja shook her head. "I don't know that I have an answer for that one, Tuk. Except to say that we're obviously several times lucky today."

"Just strange, is all," Tuk said. "Sort of a half-finished job. It doesn't make much sense to me, but then again, it's probably beyond me."

Annja laughed. "If it makes you feel any better, it's seeming a bit beyond me, as well."

"You find anything?" Tuk asked.

"Not a damned thing."

Tuk looked back at the cave wall. He'd worked his way around to the left and was now about ten feet from where he'd started. He ran his hands from the floor to the ceiling and back again. But he found nothing of interest. And there seemed absolutely no way for someone to have passed through the wall to whatever lay beyond.

Annja had also moved farther from her starting point, and she was roughly in line with Tuk as they worked their way toward the front of the cave.

Tuk could still hear the storm raging outside. He wondered how much snow would fall and a brief worry gripped him. "I hope all that snow doesn't bury us in here."

Annja stopped working again. "You mean by covering the entrance?"

"Yes. If enough of it falls, we could get sealed up in here. It would become our tomb."

"Now you're making me worried. Please stop."

"Sorry."

Tuk went back to examining the wall. Where could Mike have wandered off to?

He had a sudden alarming thought. What if Mike hadn't wandered off at all?

What if someone or something had grabbed Mike?

Tuk glanced at Annja. She didn't seem to be in the mood for theorizing anymore. She intently scanned the rock in front of her and kept pressing her hands into every crevice, searching for something that would give them some sort of clue as to Mike's whereabouts.

Tuk wasn't sure what to think anymore.

He felt a breeze on the back of his neck and shivered. Even though they were working fifty feet from the front of the cave, the wind could reach inside and touch them. It was a reminder of how utterly harsh and merciless nature could be. Tuk shook his head and gave a silent prayer of thanks for finding the cave.

He wondered what would make the Americans come over to Nepal, so intent on finding a place such as Shangri-La. Why would they leave the comfort of their lives in order to look for something that might not even exist in the first place? What was the point?

Were they that unhappy in their lives that they craved something exciting and mysterious like this? Tuk sniffed and remembered that his own life until recently had been pretty unhappy, as well.

Better not to make judgments on people who sought excitement, he thought. Just let them do what they feel they need to do in order to be happy.

He thought about his own life and the retirement he was looking forward to getting under way. With the promise of the man's money, Tuk would be able to relax and enjoy his own life.

He wondered what that would be like. He'd spent so many years scraping a living together, hoarding his money and never living beyond his means.

But what was happiness to him, anyway? Tuk frowned. He wasn't even sure he would recognize it if it happened upon him.

And that felt pretty sad, he decided.

If we get out of here, he thought, I'm going to change that. I'm going to make sure I appreciate everything and go after what I want.

"How are you doing?" Annja asked.

Tuk realized several minutes had passed without either of them saying anything to the other. He cleared his throat. "Pretty much the same as you, Annja. Nothing."

Annja stopped working and turned around. "What are we missing here?"

"What do you mean? We're trying to do everything we can to find Mike and make sure he's safe."

Annja pointed at the wall. "We're missing it, I just know it. I can feel it. There's something here and we aren't seeing it. We could keep doing this all night and all day forever and we'd never find it, simply because we're not looking at it the right way."

Tuk frowned. "I'm not sure how else I can look at this. I'm trying to see it from every possible angle. It's not helping."

Annja nodded. "And yet…" Her voice trailed off and she suddenly frowned.

"What's wrong?"

"Do you smell that?"

Tuk started to speak but stopped. He caught a whiff of something on the breeze that seemed to circulate through the small cave.

Perfume? How could that be?

He shook his head and looked at Annja. The flashlight battery seemed to be waning and he could scarcely make her out, standing across the cave from him. "What is that?"

"It smells like perfume," Annja said. "Floral." She paused. "Gardenias?"

Tuk shook his head. "I'm afraid I don't know my flowers so I can't say."

He heard something.

Annja heard it, too.

And then Tuk saw something he didn't expect to see. There appeared in Annja's hands a sword that glowed and cast off a dull glow in the cave's interior. Tuk gasped. It was the same sword that cleanly sliced through the fuselage of the airplane earlier when Tuk tumbled out of the back compartment.

"What in the world is that?" he asked.

Annja held up her hand. "Stand behind me, Tuk."

"What for?"

"Because that smell doesn't belong here. We would have noticed it earlier. That means there's something else in the cave with us."

Tuk moved behind Annja and lowered his voice to a whisper. "Can you see it?"

Annja shook her head. "No. Not yet. But I can feel something. Something is in the cave with us."

"Right now?"

"Yes."

"Could it be Mike?"

Annja shook her head. "I don't think so. Mike doesn't wear perfume."

Tuk felt her suddenly move forward to the front of the cave. She was headed toward the opening.

"Are you sure this is a good idea?" he whispered.

"I'm not sure of anything anymore, Tuk."

Tuk felt himself drawn along. At least Annja had the sword. But how well would it work in the close confines of the cave? Tuk had to ask himself another question. If they really were in danger and couldn't fight, where could they run?

They were trapped.

14

With the sword held aloft in front of her, Annja could see several shapes now in the cave itself. That was the good news. The bad news was they were large. Very large. In fact, to Annja's perception, they could have barely fit inside the cave at all, let alone come through the narrow opening. This puzzled her. If they hadn't entered that way, then where had they come from?

She and Tuk had been working at the only part of the cave that might conceal something. But now it looked like they had missed entirely another possibility up near the cave's entrance.

Something had been, in effect, hidden in plain sight.

Annja flexed her muscles as the energy from the sword ran throughout her body. It felt good to have it back in her hands again. It warmed her and energized her at the same time.

She could sense Tuk behind her and he didn't seem overly panicked. She marveled at the little man and what he'd been able to accomplish. If he hadn't been afraid then, she doubted he would fear much now.

But the question still remained. Who or what were these things in the cave with them? And where did that floral smell come from?

She drew closer to the shapes in front of her. They appeared to be large shambling figures that vaguely resembled human beings. But large humans. A thought poked into her mind and Annja frowned.

They were, after all, in the land of the yeti. Could there be a pair of abominable snowmen in the cave with them right now?

If that was the case, would they be friendly or hostile? Annja didn't relish the idea of having to cut them down in order to protect herself and Tuk. But if she had to, she would. She still had to find Mike. His injury needed some serious help if he wasn't already dead by now.

She moved ever closer to the cave's entrance. The smell of the perfume, wherever it was coming from, was intoxicating. It seemed heavier toward the front of the cave.

Annja pressed on. It was now possible to see a lot better as she approached the cave entrance where the snow made everything brighter.

There was no mistaking the appearance of the two creatures. They were large and covered from head to foot in a coarse brown fur that hung long and matted about their bodies.

Yeti.

Annja racked her brain trying to remember everything she could about these things, but the one thing that stood out were reports by witnesses usually complaining of an awful smell in the presence of them.

Yet, Annja and Tuk were now extremely close to the yeti and Annja couldn't smell anything horrible at all. In fact, the heavy scent of perfumed flowers had exactly the opposite effect. She found herself almost smiling as warm thoughts of open fields and childhood joys of a type she'd never experienced in her own life ran through her mind.

"Is that what I think it is?"

Tuk's voice from behind her snapped her back to the moment. "I believe so," she said.

"I've lived in Nepal my entire life and the one thing I never expected to see was what now stands before us." Tuk's voice became a whisper. "They haven't moved. Do you think they mean us harm?"

"Your guess is as good as mine, Tuk," Annja said. But she didn't sense that they were waiting to attack. They could have already done that by sneaking up on them in the back of the cave.

They seemed to be watching Annja and Tuk.

Almost as if they were waiting for something.

Tuk sneezed.

Annja inhaled another breath of the perfume and found her concentration wavering. Her grip on the sword seemed to be ebbing.

The perfume—

"Tuk, try not to breathe," she said.

"Excuse me?"

"The perfume we smell is a gas. They're waiting for us to be knocked out by it before they do anything."

Tuk had no response. Annja kept her eyes on the yeti in front of her. "Tuk?"

She glanced back and saw that Tuk had simply slipped down to the ground and he appeared to be having a pleasant dream on the stone floor of the cave. Annja whipped her head back around.

The yeti were closer.

When had they moved? Annja brandished the sword. "Stay back!" But even as she did so, she felt her head start to swim again. Breathing was difficult now as she tried to force back the effects of the perfumed gas.

It was virtually impossible to do so. The sword, which had energized her before, now seemed to be waning in power itself. Annja's limbs felt heavy and droopy. The sword was growing heavier by the second. She wanted to drop the blade or at least return it to the otherwhere.

And Tuk looked so comfortable sleeping there on the floor. Why couldn't she take a few minutes to do the same?

Annja felt powerless. She looked at the yeti.

They'd advanced again without making a sound.

How was that possible?

Annja's vision swam and the walls of the cave seemed to turn into liquid. Tears ran from her eyes and then she had the distinct sensation of slipping and falling over a tall cliff toward a pillowy soft ground somewhere far below.

She heard a distant noise, like metal clanging on a rock. Her hands felt light. She drifted, floating, falling, spinning toward the darkness.

And she welcomed it.

ANNJA DRIFTED THROUGH a maze of dreams. Faces she hadn't seen in years swept past her. Some of these she spoke to and had strange conversations with. Then they, too, would pass on and Annja would see another face.

She flew over lands she'd visited before on other adventures. From the vast expanses of deserts to the freezing landscapes of both the far north and Antarctica, it seemed almost that Annja was playing out her entire life in one big flashback.

Throughout the entire experience, she could still smell that perfume. But it didn't annoy her any longer. Now she just accepted it, and when she did, she felt no more pain in her body. Her ribs didn't ache. Her head seemed clear.

She slept.

THE FIRST THING Annja noticed was the lack of the perfume smell. It had somehow vanished and she'd been far too exhausted to notice. But as her body returned from whatever dreamworld she'd lived in for several hours, it was now her main focus.

Her consciousness hauled her back up to a waking state, despite Annja's wish to remain asleep.

Reluctantly, Annja opened her eyes.

She was not in the cave.

A pair of eyes stared at her.

She rolled over, coming awake very fast. "Tuk?"

He smiled at her. "Good morning." He frowned. "Well, perhaps not. I'm not sure what time it is. I can only estimate that it might be morning. But who knows?"

Annja wiped the sleep from her eyes. "You seem to be in a good mood." Annja sat up and looked around. They were on large pillows embroidered with strange designs.

"Where are we?"

Tuk shook his head. "Of that, I have no idea. I only know that we are no longer where we were when we saw the yeti."

"The cave."

"Yes."

Annja felt the pillows. The fabric they were covered in felt smooth and silky to the touch. She looked around the room and saw that the same type of material covered the walls.

Light came from somewhere, but it was subdued and reflected inward from an outside source. The room seemed designed to transition people from wherever they'd been into this place. Waking up to a harsh lightbulb probably wasn't the best way to do that, so the lighting was dim, but Annja could still see everything.

"How long have you been awake?" she asked.

"A few minutes, no more," Tuk said. He smiled. "I'm afraid that when you told me to stop breathing, I did exactly the opposite and took a huge breath, which no doubt hastened my own demise, as it were."

Annja grinned. "You can't be faulted for that."

Tuk leaned closer. "You know, that is the second time I have seen that sword of yours. How is it possible for that to somehow conceal itself on your body and not be noticeable?"

Annja laughed. "If I tried to explain it to you, Tuk, you'd only have more questions. And they'd probably be questions I couldn't answer. Not because I don't want to. But because I don't know the answers myself."

Tuk leaned back. "I see. But you have it here still?"

Annja closed her eyes and saw the sword in its usual position. She looked at Tuk. "It's here."

"That's a relief," he said. "We don't yet know where we are. And while this room is lovely, we have no idea what may lie beyond its peaceful borders."

Annja nodded. "Something tells me that if they'd wanted to harm us, they would have done so by now."

"Perhaps," Tuk said. "But sometimes it is difficult to divine the intentions of others. I would prefer to not assume anything at this moment."

"Agreed," Annja said. "Have you seen or heard anything since you woke up?"

"Nothing. As I said, it has only been a few moments." Tuk glanced around the room. "Wherever we are, it is almost certainly not within the confines of the mountain, wouldn't you agree?"

"Unless the walls are rock and covered with that fabric." She leaned over to the closest wall and tried to see what was behind it. It felt solid enough, but didn't seem like a cave wall.

"I don't know. It could be anything. Metal, concrete, stonework. It's smooth, though."

Tuk looked around. Annja could see that he was mentally trying to process everything that had happened. She wondered if this was the first time he'd had his life thrown upside down.

Annja smirked. Hang out with me, she thought, and it won't be your last.

She wondered if Mike had come through this same experience. That would certainly explain his disappearance. And hopefully, if he had, then whoever had brought them here—the yeti, she supposed—would help Mike with his injuries.

She had the sudden urge to get out of the room and see if Mike was indeed here. But how? There was no door anywhere in the room. She and Tuk seemed to be in yet another space that had no exit. And, this time, it had no entrance, either.

At least the cave had had a way to get in and get out, small though it was, she thought. This place seems like a perfectly solid box.

Tuk pointed at the walls. "Where is the door?"

Annja nodded. "I was just noticing that myself."

He looked at her. "How is a thing like this even possible, Annja? I've seen a few strange things in my time, and this defies explanation."

Annja smiled. "I've seen plenty of strange things in my day, Tuk. And this still defies explanation." She fell silent and then heard something. A sound seemed to be coming from somewhere outside the box they were in.

"Do you hear that?"

Tuk glanced around and Annja saw him close his eyes to listen. He nodded. "Yes, what is it?"

"It almost sounds like music," Annja said.

"That is what I thought also," Tuk replied. "And it sounds as if it is coming closer to us."

"Maybe this means we're about to find out where we are," Annja said. "And, if so, maybe we can find Mike."

15

Tuk listened as the music grew louder. It sounded unlike anything he'd ever heard before. What is this place? he wondered.
And how does it exist?

The music stopped. There was a series of sounds that reminded Tuk of a bunch of locks being undone and then he
heard something that reminded him of the hydraulic hisses
he'd heard in Katmandu.

The walls of the room slowly pulled away.

Brilliant sunlight spilled into the room from all sides,
blinding Tuk. He turned to Annja but she had her eyes firmly
clamped shut, trying to ward off the intensity of the sun.

Warm air hit them, a lush tropical balminess that wrapped
them in its embrace. Tuk heard Annja sigh contentedly as the
last vestiges of the cold they'd borne with them seemed to
evaporate in the sunshine.

Tuk allowed his eyes to open again and what he saw
shocked him.

A long line of people stood looking at him. They wore a

brilliant array of clothing woven with golden thread and bright colors. It had all the appearance of a parade that seemed to stretch as far as Tuk could see.

He knew it had to end somewhere, but the length of the parade wasn't what shocked him the most. It was the people themselves. Each of them was exactly the same size as him.

He scooted off of the pillows and came down the set of steps that appeared before him. Tuk stood in front of the first person in the parade, a man of his height and width whose eyes crinkled as a big wide smile broke out on his face.

"Welcome."

Tuk's heart raced. What was this magical place? And how was it that everyone here was the same height as him? He shook his head. "I am still dreaming."

The man's smile never wavered. "No. You are not dreaming."

"Then where am I?"

"Don't you know? You're home."

Tuk looked at the other members of the parade. All along the line, the faces shone with bright smiles of happiness. The music began again, but softly. From the depth of his soul, Tuk remembered the tune. He began humming along with it and tears welled up in his eyes, streaming down his face.

Annja came down the steps and stood next to him. "What's the matter? Are you all right?"

Tuk nodded through blurry vision. "I think I am now. Yes, I think so."

The man turned to Annja. "We welcome you to our kingdom, Annja Creed."

Tuk fought back a grin as he saw Annja's eyes widen. "How do you know my name?" she asked.

"We were told your name by your friend, who is here with us, as well," the man said. "Would you like to see him?"

"Mike is here?" Annja asked.

"Indeed. And it is a good thing he is," the man said. "Otherwise, we fear he would have expired a few hours ago. That would have caused you a great deal of distress, would it not?"

"Definitely," Annja said.

Tuk looked around the land they were in. A flight of birds soared aloft under a blazing sun and brilliant blue sky. Fruit trees of every type swayed in the balmy breeze. And he saw a stone path leading toward a series of structures farther away from where they stood. "This is Shangri-La?" he asked.

The man at the head of the parade smiled. "This is your home. You may call it whatever you wish. Names as such do not concern us as much as making sure all who enter our kingdom are treated with dignity and respect."

"Thank you," Tuk said. "But I have many questions."

"Which will all be answered in time," the man said. "But for now, you must accompany me to the royal court. There are others who would like to see you…again."

"Again?"

"Please," the man said. "It is better if you come with me. I assure you that all of your questions will soon be answered." The man gestured to Annja. "And she is anxious to be reunited with her friend, the one who calls himself Mike."

"You can take me to him now?" Annja asked.

"Indeed."

"Thank you!"

Tuk watched as the man made a simple gesture with his hand and the entire parade abruptly turned in the opposite direction. Tuk held up his hand. "Wait, what do I call you?"

The man smiled again. "My name is Prava. And I am honored to meet you at last, Tuk."

"You know my name, too?"

Prava nodded. "Come, let us proceed to the court where all will be revealed to you and your friends."

Tuk gestured for Annja to follow the parade and the two of them walked behind Prava and the others.

Tuk glanced at Annja, but she seemed just as mystified as he was. And what was it that Prava had said? "Home?" Did he mean that Tuk had once lived here? The tune they had played brought back a cloudy thought in Tuk's mind, but he couldn't clarify it. It seemed so utterly alien to him.

And yet…familiar.

"Do you know this place, Tuk?" Annja's eyes bore into him. "I heard what Prava said to you back there. About this being home. Well, is it?"

Tuk shook his head. "I do not know. I don't remember it, and yet the music they played…it was strangely known to me."

"You said you were an orphan."

"I am," Tuk said. "I mean, I thought my family was killed or they'd abandoned me, but I guess I don't really know."

Annja smiled. "If you're from this incredible place, then that's not the worst news you could have gotten, huh?"

Tuk laughed. "No, I guess not. And Mike is here. That's more good news."

"Sounds like they've saved his life," Annja said. "We'll be indebted to them for that."

"I don't think they would view it like that. I get the distinct impression they are motivated to help simply because it's the right thing to do."

Annja nodded. "I kind of got that impression, too."

Tuk turned back to the path they walked along. On either side of them, gleaming golden statues rose out of the lush grass. Strange faces and animals contorted and twisted together in a variety of poses and postures that reminded Tuk of some of the Tibetan Buddhist paintings he'd seen displayed in Katmandu.

The sunlight reflected off of the statues and dazzled his

eyes. The music that swept them along sounded like a celebration tune and swept Tuk's soul into its joyful refrain.

He heard squeals from somewhere farther ahead and then saw a series of fountains spraying jets of crystal-clear water high in the air. Under the arcs of water, children splashed and played as the parade marched by. They waved to Tuk and he smiled in spite of himself, waving back.

"Seems like you're a popular guy here," Annja said.

Tuk shrugged. "I have no idea what's happening to me, but I am struck by an almost overpowering sensation that I have been here before."

"Is it possible this is your home?"

Tuk looked at her. "I suppose it is, but the question then becomes, when did it stop being my home? And for what reason?"

Annja shrugged. "Prava said we would find out when we got to the court. I take it there is someone we're having an audience with."

"I gathered the same," Tuk said. "To say I am beyond anxious would be a terrible understatement."

Annja nodded. "I know how you feel."

"Do you?"

"I'm an orphan, too, Tuk."

Tuk smiled. There was much about Annja he didn't understand. But what he did understand, he liked. She seemed to be a complicated woman with a fierce and passionate heart. And he respected her loyalty toward her friend Mike. That was to be admired, especially when the rest of modern society seemed to care little for helping others unless they gained something from it.

"If this is indeed my home," Tuk said, "then you are forever welcome to call it your home, as well."

Annja smiled. "Thank you, Tuk. That's a very kind thing to say."

Tuk watched as they approached the structure ahead of them. He might have called it a temple or a castle, but it looked more like a combination of both. He could see a grand entrance capping off an approach of hundreds of steps that led skyward. Behind the structure, it looked like a mountain went clear up to the heavens.

Was that the mountain they'd been inside earlier?

Was the building they were entering a part of the mountain or was it the mountain itself?

Prava's voice was low. "Tuk, we must hurry now. The king awaits."

"King?"

Prava smiled. "Yes. I believe he's very anxious to meet with you and hear of your travels."

"My travels…" Tuk's voice trailed off. "This is all quite a marvel to me. I'm sorry if it seems like I'm a bit slow."

Prava shook his head. "You are responding exactly as we knew you would when you returned."

"I've been here before?"

Prava pointed. "Your answers are in the royal court. They are not for me to reveal to you. I do not have that right."

The parade drew to a halt in front of the grand staircase and parted into two columns. Prava nodded at Tuk and Annja to proceed. "You must ascend the stairs and take your place in the royal court now."

Tuk glanced at Annja. "I guess we go on without them."

Annja nodded. "Seems that way. You nervous?"

"I don't know what I am, honestly. I seem to be caught in the sway of a number of emotions right now. I suppose the best way to resolve this is to proceed and see where the answers lie."

"I agree," Annja said. "And maybe Mike is up there waiting for us, too."

Tuk started up the steps and found them perfectly suited for his small size. He chuckled.

"What is it?" Annja asked.

Tuk pointed at the stairs. "My entire life I have been forced to deal with stairs that are made for larger people than myself. I've had to adjust my stride accordingly. And yet here…"

"They are made for people of your size," Annja said. She seemed to be having trouble walking up them. "I can see that."

"It is another indication, I suppose, that this may be my home."

Annja took the steps two at a time. "I'm understanding the trouble you might have had back in the world I'm used to."

Tuk shook his head. "It wasn't trouble. Just one of those things. When you don't feel normal, it seems the rest of the world doesn't quite fit you all that well."

"And here, everything seems to fit."

"Perfectly," Tuk said. He paused and looked back at the parade of people who remained motionless as they watched him.

He couldn't see a single face that did not bear a wide smile. "They seem so happy," he said.

Annja nodded. "I think they are happy because you have come back."

Tuk frowned. "Really?"

Annja nodded and continued up the steps. "We've got a few more steps to climb. Let's get moving."

At the top of the staircase, Tuk again paused and looked back. Prava nodded his head slowly, still smiling.

Tuk turned back and saw the brilliant red tapestries swaying in the breeze. And beyond them, he could see an open pavilion. In the middle of the pavilion sat three stone thrones.

Two people sat on either side of an empty one.

And Tuk stepped forward to receive his answers.

16

Annja crested the steps and took a breath. She hadn't realized quite how troubling they would be, and even after resorting to taking them two at a time, she still found herself struggling to keep up with Tuk. The smaller man seemed to simply float up the stairs with no problem. Not for the first time, Annja had a pretty good indication of how it felt to be different from the world around you.

As they came off the steps at the top, she marveled at the brilliance of the red tapestries fluttering in the tropical winds. Their finery could not be underestimated, she decided. They looked nothing like any of the fabrics she had seen during her many travels. But she did have the feeling that they were all handmade. There didn't seem to be any type of machinery present in this place so far.

Stone thrones in an open pavilion in front of her beckoned them. Tuk walked ahead and Annja rushed to stay beside him. As they got closer, Annja could see that two of the thrones were occupied. An old man sat on the one to her right and the throne on the far left had an old woman seated there.

The throne in the middle was empty.

The smiles the old man and woman wore were indescribable in that they seemed to contain more joy than Annja thought possible. Tears rolled down their faces as they watched Tuk approach them.

They exchanged a glance and their smiles grew even broader. The old man lifted his hand and urged Tuk forward to a spot on the pavilion ten feet from the thrones.

The old woman gestured for Annja to stand back a little bit. Annja stopped on the spot the old woman indicated and contented herself with observing everything that seemed to be unfolding in front of her.

Tuk stopped at the prescribed spot and the old man and woman took an entire minute to examine him up and down. Finally, with a great deal of clearing of his throat, the old man spoke.

"Tuk, you are returned to us by the will of the harmonious universe seeking to restore that which was, for so long, the cause of unbalance within our hearts and within our kingdom."

Tuk said nothing, but Annja noticed that there was a smile building on his face that seemed to be spreading with every second.

The old woman spoke, as well. "I have dreamed for so long of this day—the day of your homecoming—that I often feared it would never come. But my faith in the universal scheme of totality has been rewarded and you have found your way back to your rightful home."

"My rightful home?" Tuk's voice sounded small.

The old man nodded. "You are not just Tuk. You are the one who was stolen from our kingdom."

"Stolen?"

The old woman smiled. "Long ago we helped a traveler who had fallen ill in the snows outside of our walls. We brought him here and nursed him back to health. He was beyond words with gratitude, but when he looked around at what we had here, he wished to tell the world of us. We begged him not to, but he seemed determined to persevere."

The old man cleared his throat again. "This man stole you from the royal nursery when you were but a single year of life." He glanced at the old woman. "Your mother and I despaired beyond whatever may be deemed reasonable. We searched for you for many years, never knowing if you had survived your ordeal and lived somewhere out in the other world."

"I did," Tuk said. "I did survive. But I must admit I have no recollection of this man of whom you speak."

"That is because he did not survive the journey back to the other side. When he stole away from us in the middle of the night, he took you wrapped up under his arms. But as soon as he got back to the other side, he was struck by what must have been a terrible storm. He lasted long enough to get you to safety—and for that we must be eternally grateful and forgiving of his transgression—before he himself succumbed to the elements and perished in the snows of the mountains."

"You know this for certain?" Tuk asked.

"We found his body within a week after you were taken," said the old woman. "But you were nowhere to be seen."

"We searched everywhere for you," the old man said. "And when it became apparent that you could not be found, we had to face the possibility that something terrible had befallen you. Our hearts grieved, but perhaps something within us would not let us completely believe that you were dead."

"I could not feel your death," the old woman said. "And you were bonded to me like nothing else in this world. I felt certain that I would know if you had perished on the other side. And yet, I never once did."

"She knew you were alive. Somewhere," the old man said.

"And it appears that she was right. You were alive. But you were also alone."

Tuk smiled. "I am alone no longer."

The old woman started weeping with joy and Tuk rushed to her side, hugging her tightly. She clutched at him and kissed his cheeks. Annja found it difficult to watch the scene through her misted eyes.

Tuk rushed and hugged his father and the old man's voice cracked with joy at his touch. "Long have I waited for the second coming of my only son," he said. "My heart has always been heavy with grief and guilt over something I should have been able to prevent."

"I do not blame you, Father," Tuk said.

The old man nodded and then gestured to the empty throne next to him. "Then take your rightful place beside your father, my son. And rejoice, for you have found your home once more after many years away."

Annja felt tears flowing down her face as she watched Tuk seat himself on the throne that looked like it fit him perfectly. He smiled at his mother and father and then at Annja.

Annja waved and felt silly at the same time. She'd known Tuk for barely a day and yet she was moved to tears watching the reunion between a child and his parents.

"Annja."

She looked up and saw that Tuk's mother was now gesturing for her to come forward. Annja walked closer and then stopped just short of the throne.

"You have played a part in bringing Tuk back to us. For that, we are beyond grateful."

Annja shook her head. "It wouldn't be right for me to take any credit for what has happened. Any part of mine in this has been purely coincidental."

Tuk's mother smiled. "I know that one such as your-self doesn't truly believe in coincidence. You have seen things—done things—that defy such an explanation as simple chance."

Annja said nothing. Tuk's mother was right. Annja didn't believe in coincidence, but that didn't mean she'd helped bring Tuk back, did it?

"If anyone deserves your gratitude, it is Tuk himself," Annja said. "Although I've only known him for a day he has impressed me in ways I could never imagine. Your son is a force unto himself. He saved my life and the life of a dear friend of mine. Were it not for Tuk's help, we would have certainly perished."

Tuk's mother smiled. "And yet you were the catalyst for bringing him home to us, so please do accept my gratitude."

Annja bowed her head. "Thank you."

"You mentioned your friend. This is the one called Mike?"

Annja looked up. "Yes. He was badly injured out on the mountains." Did it make sense to mention the airplane crash? Did they know what airplanes were here? Annja decided to keep things as simple as possible.

"He is no longer injured," Tuk's mother said. "He is resting now comfortably. I believe he will awake within the hour if you can wait."

"His rest is more important than me seeing him," Annja said. She smiled. "So, it was your people who took him from the cave while we slept?"

Tuk's mother nodded. "When we learned that someone had found the portal, we sent people to investigate. As you can imagine, we are much more guarded about our existence as a result of what happened to our son so many years ago."

"Understandably so," Annja said.

"While you slept we were able to observe and see that

Mike was badly injured. We brought him through first since he would have died had we not."

"I am indebted to you for that act," Annja said. "And I'm sure I speak for Mike when I say thank you."

"We have spoken to Mike. It was he who told us about both you and our son. It's how we knew that there was a chance our boy had returned to us."

Tuk's father coughed once. "As you can imagine, we were beside ourselves with hope. And I apologize for the manner in which you were transported. But we've found it's best if no one knows quite how they get here."

"The perfume," Annja said.

Tuk's father nodded. "A slight sleeping gas derived from some of the flora that grow here. It's quite harmless except that it does produce a nearly complete state of slumber. It wears off with no adverse effects after a time."

"It was a beautiful scent," Annja said. "But I suppose that's the point, isn't it?"

"Indeed."

"How should I address you both?" Annja asked. "I'm assuming that you are both rulers of this incredible place. Are you the king and queen?"

Tuk's father nodded. "Officially, we have those titles, but we are known by much simpler names. I am Guge and my wife is known as Vanya."

"Guge?" Annja frowned. "There was a monarchy of kings in Tibet known as the Guge. Are you related to them?"

Guge nodded. "I am a descendant of that dynasty. I am Guge XXV. Tuk is actually Guge XXVI."

Tuk blinked. "I rather prefer my own name, actually."

Vanya laughed and Annja was surprised at how musical she sounded. "We will call you whatever you wish to be called, my son. It does not matter so long as you are here with us."

Guge nodded. "It is as your mother says, Tuk. However

you wish to be known is acceptable. You were named Guge at birth, but if Tuk suits you better, then we will make the alteration accordingly."

"Thank you."

From the left side of the pavilion an attendant swept up toward Vanya's throne. She hurriedly whispered something in the queen's ear. Vanya turned and looked at Annja.

"Your friend Mike, is he rather a stubborn sort?"

"Mike?" Annja frowned. "Well, I guess you could describe him that way. When he gets his head wrapped around something, he does tend to be a little tenacious."

"It appears he is a bit headstrong about his condition and is refusing treatment because he—"

A sudden noise to her left made Annja turn. Hobbling in on a crutch was Mike, brushing aside his medical staff with a flick of his hands. "Leave me alone, dammit. I'm fine—" He stopped short.

"Annja?"

Annja broke into a wide grin. "Hey, Mike."

The effect on Mike was instantaneous. He broke into a hobbled run that carried him across the pavilion toward Annja. He dropped the crutch and swept her up in a bear hug.

"Jesus, I thought I'd never see you again!"

"Put me down, you big lug." But she hugged him back and felt an immense joy over his apparent healthiness.

Mike put Annja down and reached for his crutch. Annja looked at his thigh and saw it was bandaged in some of the same gossamer material that comprised the tapestries and clothes of everyone present.

"Your leg—how is it?" she asked.

Mike shrugged. "It feels marvelous, actually. I was in a bad way when they brought me here. I was in and out of consciousness. Fever. The works. I don't think I would have lasted another hour to be honest."

"That doesn't seem to be a problem now," Annja said.

"Good to go in a short time, I think," he replied. He turned and bowed to the queen and king. "I can't thank you enough for taking care of me."

Guge smiled. "We help others where we are able to do so. It was our pleasure to aid you. Although I am told you must still be careful and not exert yourself until your leg has enough time to heal."

"I won't run any marathons, that's for sure," Mike said.

He looked at Annja. "So, what do you think about this place, huh? Pretty amazing, isn't it?"

Annja nodded. "You've made a believer out of me, Mike. I doubted you before, but there doesn't seem to be any getting around the fact that you've found Shangri-La."

Mike smiled. "Guess it was worth the effort, huh?"

"The plane crash?" Annja asked.

"Tsing, the money, all of it," Mike said. "But I just wish I knew how we actually got here. Because when we were in that cave, I didn't think there was any other way out."

"There wasn't that we could find," Annja said. "And Tuk and I searched the entire place." She frowned. "Well, at least we did until the yeti showed up."

Mike looked at her. "What did you say?"

"The yeti."

Mike smiled. "You mean abominable snowmen? You saw some?"

"In the cave with us," Annja said. "Right about when we smelled the perfume that knocked us out."

"Are you sure you weren't just hallucinating?"

Annja frowned. "We most definitely were not hallucinating, Mike."

"They did indeed see the yeti," Guge said. "And if you would like, we will show them to you again."

17

Tuk watched the tearful reunion between Annja and Mike and was happy. He looked around the pavilion and at his parents and felt a kind of peace the likes of which he'd never known before. This was his home and he felt incredible being back among his people.

But who exactly were they? And why were they smaller than other races of humans?

He turned to Guge and asked him that very question. Guge coughed twice and then began telling his long-lost son the tale of his people.

"More than a thousand years ago, the Guge was a kingdom in western Tibet, established by a wise and benevolent ruler who split his kingdom into two, allowing each of his sons equal sway.

"They built their capital cities at two locations—Tholing and Tsaparang. For many years our people lived in brilliant harmony. Several of our rulers embraced an esoteric version of Buddhism, which further brought us into harmony with the universe. Together, we lived rich lives of enlightenment and prosperity.

"The first time any people from outside of our kingdoms actually found us was almost four hundred years ago. Jesuit missionaries came and marveled at what we had accomplished."

"What we'd accomplished?"

Guge nodded. "You know of the land that surrounds this region. High snowy mountains and arid deserts. Farther south there is a much more temperate climate, but here and in parts farther north, there exists no such lushness. And yet, through our enlightenment and harmony with all things of nature, we were able to produce a wonderful habitat for ourselves. Using advanced techniques of irrigation, we created a paradise where our people frolicked and sought to better themselves and their fellow people."

Tuk noticed that both Annja and Mike were now paying attention to every word coming out of Guge's mouth.

"Opening ourselves up to the people of the West proved to be a tragic mistake. The Jesuit missionaries insisted on building a chapel in Tsaparang, saying that the teachings of Christianity were even more profound than those of the Buddhist traditions we all followed.

"The ruler of the time allowed the construction to begin. Thereafter, the missionaries began teaching the people of Guge about Christianity. This did not sit well with some of the other rulers in the area who were devoutly Buddhist. To their way of thinking, all was well and harmonious with Buddhism and these new teachings contrasted with what they believed. Worse from their perspective was that the missionaries succeeded in converting the king and his wife to Christianity. This led to an open battle between the opposing factions."

Guge coughed again and then cleared his throat. "Regrettably, this led to an almost complete slaughter of the Guge people. Only a few hundred survived and fled from Tsaparang, which was later razed."

"Where did they go?" Tuk asked.

"They fled to Qulong, a city closer to the border with Nepal. There, they rested and spoke openly of the need to once again find their way back to their Buddhist teachings. But with so few survivors, it seemed unlikely that they would be allowed to live in peace in order to repopulate themselves."

"What did they do, Father?"

"They took all that they knew about living in harmony with nature and the universe and found a secret valley—this valley—hidden between two massive mountains. One that is always visible to the outside world and one that remains hidden from view. They retreated into this valley and set about turning it into the lush paradise of their past greatness."

Vanya smiled. "And they succeeded. Within a generation, they had created a marvelous kingdom, shielded from the outside world and prying eyes. No one knew that our people existed here. The way the two mountains come together forms an almost impenetrable descent that would be too risky for anyone to attempt, if they even knew where to look."

Tuk could see that Annja was dying to say something. "What is it, Annja?" he asked.

"I'm just wondering how that is even possible? I mean, we've got satellites in space that can peer anywhere on the planet. Wouldn't they be able to discern the presence of two mountains and a secret valley?"

Vanya smiled. "While I do not know what these things called satellites are, I can tell you that the universe acts in ways that have thus far enabled us to live without molestation from the outside world. Once we retreated into this valley, our lives became a constant wonder."

"It's just incredible," Annja said. "And it honestly strikes me as impossible. But I can't argue with the fact that we're standing here."

Tuk looked at Mike, but found him still paying attention to everything being said by his mother and father.

Vanya kept smiling. "Every once in a while someone finds their way here, through the portal or just outside of it. We take care to extend to them the utmost courtesy and respect, but for some reason, none of them ever sees fit to tell of the place they've seen. We remain safe and secure."

"Except for that one time," Guge said to his son. "When you were taken from us and brought to the outside world, that man was punished by the universe for his transgression. Otherwise, we have never had any problems."

"But what about the reason we seem to be so much smaller than other races?" Tuk asked. "Is it because of our isolation?"

Vanya nodded. "Apparently, yes. In some ways, we believe that evolution has altered us in this fashion. This valley might not support our population if we were all normal-size humans. But small as we are, our people are perfectly sustained within this environment. We don't use what the earth cannot replenish when we need it. And as such, we make it a point to never overindulge or otherwise create something that would destroy this place and all its beauty."

"What about the tropical environment?" Annja asked. "How is it that immediately outside this place it is freezing cold and yet, in here, there are plants and birds that would usually grow in a much more equatorial climate?"

"We are positioned directly over a series of hot springs and vents that feed a luxurious warm air current up through the soil," Guge said. "The air here is what nourishes this place and the hot springs help us irrigate the entire valley, keeping it in optimal growing conditions."

Tuk looked at Mike again, but still the big man didn't

speak. He seemed utterly enraptured with everything that was being said.

Annja, for her part, still seemed mystified. Tuk supposed that was because she was a scientist and naturally cynical about stuff like this. Of course, there was a difference between being skeptical of a legend and actually witnessing the legend itself.

"I can't explain it all away so easily," Annja said after another minute. "But the fact remains, we're here and this place is absolutely amazing."

"And most importantly," Vanya said, "our son has returned. Now he can assume his rightful place as heir to the throne of Guge."

Tuk looked at his mother. "I'm to be the king of this land?"

"That is how it is written, my son, yes."

Tuk looked at his father and saw now that time had aged the old man terribly. Tuk couldn't even begin to calculate how old his father was.

Guge smiled at him. "We have been waiting a very long time for your return, my son. I am a tired old man. And your mother is tired, as well."

Vanya laughed. "Not nearly so now that my son has returned. But we are weary of ruling. It is time for a new generation to take over and guide our people onward through time and history."

Tuk couldn't believe it. Yesterday, he'd been a small man of no consequence who worked as a tracker for criminals and spies. Today, he was to be the king of a legendary kingdom.

Annja bowed her head. "Congratulations, Tuk."

"Thank you." Tuk frowned. Life certainly was a strange thing. "I still have a lot of questions about all of this," he said to his parents.

Guge held up his hand. "In time, my son. In time. For now,

the people of your kingdom are excited to see you again. And they have prepared an elaborate feast in your honor."

"Already?"

Mike smiled. "I kind of mentioned you to them when they brought me here. Once I saw how small they were, I couldn't help but let them know about you."

Vanya nodded. "And I believe they have been working steadily ever since it became apparent that you might finally be coming back after all these years. It wouldn't do to disappoint them now."

"I wouldn't dream of it," Tuk said. But he felt bad that the people of this place worked so hard for the likes of him. It didn't seem right somehow.

Guge patted Tuk's thigh. "I can see the trouble in your face, my son. You haven't put anyone out, if that's what you're thinking. This is a time of celebration and as such, the work that goes on is not considered toil as much as a chance to revel in the fact that you have returned to the kingdom."

"I guess so."

Vanya nodded. "A feast is being laid out down below." She turned to Annja and Mike. "You are, of course, more than welcome to join us."

Annja bowed her head again. "Thank you very much."

Mike nodded. "I could eat a horse."

Vanya looked horrified. "Why would you do a thing like that?"

Annja elbowed Mike. "It's merely an expression meant to convey extreme hunger, Your Highness," he said.

Vanya laughed again. "Oh, I see. Very well." She looked at Guge. "Shall we descend and join our people?"

Guge held up his hand and pointed at Annja. "You had a question a few minutes ago. About the yeti."

She nodded. "Yeah, I'd like to see them again if that's possible."

"Of course it is possible," Guge said. "They are here with us now."

Tuk turned on his throne and Annja and Mike followed his gaze. Guge clapped his hands twice, and from the back of the pavilion, two shambling furry creatures wandered over.

In the sunlight, the yeti didn't look nearly as horribly matted. Their fur shone like a luxurious coat. They didn't smell, either. Tuk marveled at them standing as tall as they did, which was nearly two feet taller than Mike.

Mike whistled. "That is amazing."

Guge smiled. "They help us keep track of the outside world. And in some cases, they are used to ensure our survival here."

Annja seemed disappointed by that statement. "You keep them here as slaves to do your bidding?"

Guge recoiled. "Certainly not. The yeti are not slaves. They are part of our kingdom and our people."

Annja's eyes narrowed. "What do you mean by that?"

"Just what I said," Guge replied. "The yeti are part of us and we would never do anything to harm or otherwise subjugate them."

"I don't see how you can say that about them and then ask them to serve you."

Vanya smiled. "No, it's apparent that you do not see. But, of course, that is because of your perspective. And from where you stand, you see only one aspect of the situation instead of the other."

Annja's frown stayed locked in place and Tuk worried for a moment that she might draw her sword and try to do something rash. But instead, she shook her head. "I am trying to understand."

"Then look," Guge said. "And understand." He turned to the yeti and nodded once.

Instantly, the yeti moved and each creature reached up,

and then they heard a series of clicks. In a second, the yeti separated and became two parts, an upper torso and a lower torso.

And concealed inside was one of the Guge people.

"A costume," Mike said. "Incredible!"

Guge smiled at Annja. "You see now?"

Annja smiled. "I do."

Vanya continued. "The yeti were once real creatures that walked these lands. Their legends have come down to us for thousands of years, but human encroachment eventually led to their extinction. We have found them to be useful in helping us preserve the sanctity of our kingdom. So we use their legend to keep us safe. We don't think they would mind if they knew."

"I don't think they'd mind, either," Annja said.

"Now that that's settled," Guge said, "perhaps we can go attend the feast. I, for one," he said winking at Mike, "could eat a horse."

18

Annja watched as the Guge people entered the long field carrying huge elaborate trays of fruits and vegetables that had been prepared in every conceivable manner. Big bowls of steaming white rice adorned the simple tables that had seats for hundreds of people. Annja realized with a start that she was desperately hungry. Her mouth watered and she fought to restrain herself.

Vanya and Guge seated themselves at the head table. Tuk, Annja noticed, chose to remain close to her and Mike. She smiled. It was a touching gesture of friendship. They were all placed at the head table.

A plate was put in front of her and platters of food were passed around. Annja helped herself to the meal and ate and drank her fill of peppers, carrots, rice and strange and wonderful-tasting plants and fruits she'd never seen before. She drank out of a cup filled with a fruity wine that quickly relaxed her and allowed her mind to open to the wonder of the scene before her.

The Guge people seemed genuinely ecstatic that Tuk had returned to his homeland. They kept approaching him and talking to him about his adventures in the outside world. Annja noticed that there were several women who made it apparent they thought he was quite handsome.

Mike sat next to her, eating his way through plate after plate of food. Annja looked at him. "Aren't you full yet?"

"Not even close. I'm famished."

"You're healing. Your body knows it needs fuel for the repair process." She glanced down at his torn pants. "How's the leg?"

"Feels great. After they stitched me up, they put some type of balm on it that I think acts as a pain reliever." He reached for another helping of food and looked at Annja. "Everything okay?"

"Everything's great," she said. "I guess I'm just a little bit in awe of this place. It seems almost too amazing to be true."

"I know what you mean. I've been here longer than you two and I'm still in shock."

"Not that it's affected your appetite," Annja said with a laugh. "Apparently."

Mike held up his hands. "I'm a growing boy. I need to have my strength, you know."

"Yeah, I got that." She looked at Tuk, who was talking with his parents again. "He looks so happy."

Mike nodded. "Orphan suddenly finding out that his parents are still alive and that he's going to be the king of some long-forgotten land? Yeah, I'd bet that would put a smile on my face, too."

Annja nodded and reached for her glass of wine. Mike nudged her.

"Hey."

"What?"

"You sure you're okay?"

Annja sipped the wine. "Yeah. I don't know. I've never known my own past. And I guess it's kind of being brought up again seeing Tuk find his way back to his family. But I'm still searching for the answers I need." She sighed. "Maybe I'm just jealous."

"Anyone would be," Mike said. "This is a pretty damned amazing thing to have happen. But I guess we're lucky to be here, right?"

"And what about Tsing?"

"What about him?"

Annja looked at Mike. "Well, what happens after we leave this place? Tsing is going to want to know how we found our way here."

"Who says he has to know?"

Annja frowned. "When we come walking back from that plane wreck with little to show for it, I don't think he's going to be the understanding type."

Mike bit into a peach. "Maybe we don't go back."

Annja shook her head. "We can't stay here, Mike. We don't belong here. This isn't our home."

"Home is where the heart is," Mike said.

"Thank you, Mr. Cliché." Annja sighed. "Look, Mike, this was never my obsession. I signed on to help you find this place. But I never said I wanted to run away from the real world when we found it."

"Run away? Is that what you think I'm doing?"

"If you want to stay here, then that's exactly what it looks like."

Mike frowned. "Annja, you don't know everything that's happened in my life since the last time we got together. A lot of crap came down on me. Not the least of which is my failing health."

"Your cholesterol? That's easily taken care of if you simply change your eating habits."

Mike smiled but there seemed little mirth in it. "It's not just my cholesterol, Annja."

"Something else?"

Mike nodded. "I'm dying."

"What?"

He put a hand on her arm. "This isn't the time to bring it up. But the fact is, I have a very short time to live. I have an inoperable brain tumor. If they try to crack my skull and get it out, it will just kill me."

Annja felt her throat swelling shut. "How long?"

Mike grinned. "I didn't ask. I didn't want to know. It always seems to me like that's just a death sentence right then and there. Doctors tell you that you've only got six months and, whammo, you drop dead at exactly six months. All I know is the tumor is there and it's a ticking time bomb. And, eventually, I will die."

"Eventually, we all die," Annja said.

Mike nodded. "Granted. I would have liked a little more time, though. Say thirty years or so. Get married, have a few kids of my own. Would have been nice to have those experiences."

"You could still have that."

Mike shook his head. "I'm not that selfish. What would I do, go out and find someone to fall in love with me, have children and then crush their hearts when I kicked off? That would really make me something of a jerk."

"It's not selfish to want to be loved, Mike."

Mike took a drink of wine. "However, my time is extremely limited. And personally, I can't think of a place I'd rather be than here with these people. I mean, if you could choose how you wanted to go out, wouldn't it be in a place like this? Surrounded by beauty and peace. Everything here is so utterly perfect."

"I guess it is," Annja said. "But I don't want you to stay. I want you to come back with me."

Mike grinned. "Now you're being selfish."

"Yes. I am."

Mike hoisted his glass and they clinked them together. "At least I'm not the only one."

Annja took a drink and then looked around the table. The party had lost all of the joy for her. She watched, as if peering in through a window, how Tuk and his people bonded.

Music started as the meal finished. More wine flowed and the people took to dancing all over the grass. Even Guge and Vanya enjoyed a few dances before sitting down again. At one point, Vanya looked over at Annja and smiled. Annja smiled back but she felt no happiness.

The idea that Mike would be dying soon felt like a hole had been torn in her heart. She'd lost close friends before, but this felt different. Mike was a different kind of man. He never expected anyone to understand what it was that drove him. He made no apologies for being who he was, and he was utterly comfortable in his own skin.

Annja respected that. And she respected what he had accomplished in his life. Barring the incident with Tsing, Mike had nothing to be embarrassed about. He pursued what he loved and did so with all the joy of a child.

Annja wished she had some more of that mirth in her own life. But that seemed to be a precious commodity. And somehow, the music that played around her tugged harder at her heartstrings than she cared for.

"Annja?"

She looked up and saw Guge standing there. She tried to smile but felt it die on her lips. "Hi."

Guge's eyes peered deep into hers. "Perhaps we could walk awhile?"

"Sure." She rose and followed the king away from the party and back toward the grand staircase.

Guge smiled at her. "I'm afraid I'm not as young as I used to be. These celebrations tend to wear me out."

"I see."

"But what's your excuse?"

"Sorry?"

He turned to her. "You wear the look of someone who has lost a friend."

Annja sighed. "I guess in a way I just did."

"Who? Surely not Tuk. He seems to have a genuine fondness for both you and your friend Mike."

"It's not Tuk," Annja said. "It's Mike."

"Oh?"

"Apparently, he's dying."

Guge said nothing for a moment and then looked at her. "Surely it is not the injury to his leg?"

"No. He has a brain tumor. It's a disease where something grows inside his head until it kills him."

Guge nodded gravely. "I see. And there is nothing that the doctors in the outside world can do for him?"

"According to him, no. They've told him that it is inoperable. They can't take it out for fear of killing him."

"That is unfortunate," Guge said.

"I don't mean to be down during such a time of celebration," Annja said. "He only just told me, though. It's weird. I was so overjoyed to see him earlier and everything seemed so great. And now I feel like he's already dead."

Guge laid a hand on her arm. "He is most certainly not dead yet, Annja. And you should remember that."

Annja nodded. "I know. I just can't stop thinking about it. We've always been friends and now I'm not sure what to do."

"That is the thing about the universe, my dear. It doesn't

succumb to the desires of the likes of us. It simply is. And the things we wish to change are the very things that often must happen. We simply don't have the power to make the universe obey our whims."

"Yes," Annja said. "I know from experience it doesn't listen to the likes of my desires, but that doesn't stop me from trying again and again."

"That's because you are a human being," Guge said. "And ours is always of the mind that we can control our destiny."

"He's just such a good person. I hear about the evil men that walk among us and wonder why the universe doesn't take them?"

"The universe doesn't distinguish between good and evil, per se. Only in certain incarnations will it see things in such a light. To the universe, evil and good simply exist. Neither is better than the other. They simply are."

Annja sighed. "I wish it was easier than it is."

"If it was easier, then we would have no chance to learn and evolve ourselves to a higher level of existence."

Annja sat on the stairs and hugged her knees. "I don't know how long he has. And he's thinking that he doesn't want to leave here to go back to his home. He's entranced with this place."

"We have noticed. You, however, don't seem so."

Annja smirked. "I've been told my destiny lies elsewhere."

Guge nodded. "So it would seem. You carry a burden unlike any other outsider we have ever seen."

"You have no idea," Annja said.

Guge cleared his throat. "We will talk more of this in the coming days. But we must return to the party now."

"Why?"

Guge's brow furrowed. "Because I think Tuk has just received what the outside world calls a phone call."

19

Tuk nearly jumped out of his seat when the tiny phone began vibrating in his pocket. He'd forgotten all about it in the rush to celebrate his homecoming. It was something he'd longed for for so long that this sudden reminder of the world he used to know at once shocked him and made him melancholy.

He excused himself from the table amid many startled glances, and walked away from the party, pulling the cell phone out of his pocket.

"Hello?"

"Tuk, where are you?"

Tuk glanced around at the lush valley. "I'm not exactly sure where I am, to be honest with you."

"You're not still by the plane, are you?"

"No, no. I found a cave for the three of us to take shelter in. We spent the night in it." He paused. How was he going to put this in such a way that the man on the phone didn't think he was completely insane. "But then something…happened."

"What happened?"

"Mike was near death, but holding on. Annja and I slept, and in the middle of the night Mike disappeared."

There was a pause on the phone. "He disappeared? How is that? He couldn't have just gotten up and walked off. Not in his condition."

"Yes, I know," Tuk said. "We didn't at the time, of course, and we searched frantically for him. But we couldn't locate him."

"So, he's dead, then?"

"No. He's alive and well."

"You're not making much sense, Tuk. I'm at Jomsom now and will be coming for you shortly. But I need you to tell me where you are exactly."

Tuk sighed. "I understand, but it's not as easy as that because I'm not sure where we are. I mean, I know where we are—I'm just not sure how we got here. That's what I'm trying to say."

"All right, then. Where are you?"

"In a place called Shangri-La."

Tuk heard the sharp intake of breath on the other end of the phone. "I think you'd better explain yourself a bit more carefully, Tuk. And I sincerely hope you're not lying to me."

"Why would I do that?" Tuk asked. "After everything I've done already. I have no reason to lie."

"Fair enough. Tell me what happened."

"Annja and I searched the cave and came across two yeti."

"Abominable snowmen?"

"Yes. I realize it sounds ridiculous but please hear me out."

"I'm listening."

"They were standing in the cave and then we smelled something like flowers. It was some type of gas. When we awoke, we were here in this beautiful land. I have no idea how we came to be here. One moment we were in the cave and the next we were here."

"All right."

"The thing is," Tuk said, "this is apparently my home— where I'm from. I'm surrounded by people who look just like me."

"You mean they're small like you?"

"Yes, exactly that. And an outsider who broke the rules here apparently kidnapped me as a child. He took me out, which is how I came to be in Katmandu. He died, and I was left to my own devices. But I'm home now. It's absolutely incredible."

"I see."

Tuk frowned. For some reason, he'd expected a different reaction from the man than what he seemed to be having. Tuk sighed. "I'm sorry if that disappoints you, but I am truly amazed at this place."

"I have no doubt that you are, my friend."

Tuk paused. "What is it? I feel like there's something you're not telling me."

After yet another silence, the man cleared his throat. "Do you remember what you told me about the woman in Tsing's apartment? The one who rattled your nerves a good bit?"

Tuk shivered at the sudden recollection of her and her fingernails. "Yes. I remember."

"I did some checking on her."

"And?"

"It took me a considerable amount of time, but I managed to dig up a few things. I don't think you're going to like hearing any of them."

Tuk looked across the way at the party still raging in full force. Katmandu and the penthouse infiltration seemed years ago and a world away from where he stood just then.

"Tell me."

"The woman's real name is Hsu Xiao. She is what is known as a Black Pole."

"I'm not familiar with that term."

"Most people aren't. The term itself derives from Red Pole, which in Chinese Tongs is an enforcer. The leg breakers. If you owe them money and don't pay, the Red Pole pays you a visit."

"I see."

"Hsu Xiao doesn't break legs. She kills. She is—according to my sources, anyway—one of the most highly adept assassins in this part of the world. Her skills are highly prized."

Tuk was alarmed. "It didn't much appear that Tsing prized her lethal charms all that much."

"That's because Tsing doesn't know what her true nature is. She has concealed it from him."

"Why would she do that? Is she going to kill him?"

"No, I don't think she is. If she were going to kill him, she would have done so already. She's had plenty of opportunity to do so and hasn't yet acted. This leads me to believe her real target isn't Tsing at all.

"Then who? Which person would Chinese organized crime want to kill?"

"Well, that's the other thing I discovered. She's not working with any form of Chinese organized crime."

"Then who is she working for?"

"The Communist Chinese government in Beijing. Hsu Xiao is a high-level operative for the intelligence service. She works exclusively in covert operations, liquidating targets of opportunity that her government deems acceptable."

Tuk's stomach ached. "It still doesn't explain why she would be at Tsing's penthouse. Who would she be after and why would she be there?"

"I'm not quite sure yet." The man paused. "I have another question to ask you."

"Go ahead."

"How are the people there?"

Tuk smiled. "They're absolutely marvelous. It's like one big family here. My parents rule this kingdom and I am apparently the heir to the throne."

"Is that so?"

"Yes. Needless to say, I'm a bit overwhelmed by the entire affair, as you can imagine."

The man laughed a little. "Yes, yes, I can see how you would be. I would urge you to be careful, however."

"Why is that?"

"Because Hsu Xiao is no longer in Katmandu."

Tuk frowned. "Then where in the world is she?"

"That, my friend, is the problem. No one seems to know where she is. She has quietly and subtly gone to ground and vanished. I don't know if she was recalled to Beijing or if she is somewhere close by."

Tuk shook his head. "Well, why would she be interested in me, anyway? I've had no interaction with her or her superiors. I shouldn't even be on their radar. I'm insignificant to them."

"Are you really?"

"Of course."

"Perhaps Hsu Xiao was positioned near Tsing for the purpose of discovering the location of Shangri-La. It's no surprise that the Chinese government has long sought to strengthen its grip on this region. When it took over Tibet in the fifties, it made no pretext about its ambitions to squash the spiritual kingdoms in this area of the world since it saw them as an affront to Communism."

Tuk gulped. "You think Shangri-La might come under attack?"

"I'm not saying it could, but I'm also not going to lie to you and say it won't happen."

"This is all so bizarre," Tuk said. "I felt positive the outside world could be kept at bay."

"I doubt that very much, Tuk. It would only be a matter of time before your kingdom is discovered. And you wouldn't be able to count on anyone for assistance. Especially if the Chinese enter with a big enough force to seize control and eradicate anyone they don't approve of."

"Eradicate?"

"Your people might become extinct, Tuk."

"My God."

"Are you aware of what side of the border you're on right now?"

"You mean the Nepali or Tibetan?"

"Yes, exactly."

"I don't know."

"Here's the deal. You're in an area of Nepal that juts into Tibetan territory. It's like a middle finger in the face of the Chinese. They would like nothing better than to simply take that finger and break it in half by annexing the entirety of Mustang. And they would certainly have no problem doing so. They have a sizable force in Lhasa that they could mobilize and get into the region within forty-eight hours at the maximum. That's not nearly enough time to evacuate your people, is it?"

"I don't know," Tuk said. "I wouldn't think it would be."

"So your position is extremely delicate. If I know the Chinese, they are going to doggedly pursue the idea of locating your kingdom, if that is indeed what Hsu Xiao is after. And when they find it, they will simply crush the entire valley."

"What can we do to stop it?"

"I don't know if we can do anything, my friend. The odds are that the Chinese already have people in that region searching."

"How do you know this?"

"You said a missile brought your plane down, right?"

"Yes."

"No doubt it was fired from a soldier on the ground. And if Hsu Xiao radioed them to let them know the tail numbers on your plane—Tsing's plane—then they would have been able to positively identify you and take you out as they attempted to do."

"But no one followed up and made sure we were dead."

"Well, perhaps you crash-landed away from them and they couldn't reach you. Look, Tuk, I'm not saying this is exactly what happened. But I'm saying there exists a real danger here. And I hate having to be the one who tells you, but I owe you the truth."

"Are you coming here?"

"As soon as I can. But you need to find out how I can actually get there. I can't do much from this side."

Tuk caught sight of movement out of the corner of his eye and saw Annja striding down the steps and headed in his direction.

"Annja sees me on the phone."

"Does she really?"

"And she doesn't look pleased."

"No doubt she thinks you were holding out on her and Mike. Don't worry about it. She'll get her cool back soon enough."

But Annja looked hot enough to fry an egg on, Tuk thought. And she was going to grab the phone from him. He could just tell from the way she stalked across the grass.

"I think she wants a word with you," he said into the phone.

"Oh, dear," the man said. "Well, better hand her the phone, then. Put it on speaker first, though."

"Tuk!"

Tuk turned and smiled at Annja. "Hi, I was just—"

Annja grabbed the phone. "You had a phone this entire time and you never said anything? How dare you hold that back from us."

Tuk shook his head. "I wanted to tell you, really, I did."

Annja held up her hand. "We'll discuss it later." She looked at the phone. "Now, who is this exactly?"

Tuk looked at the phone. For a moment, no sound emerged and he wondered if he had hit the speaker button. Then, at last, he heard the man's voice.

"Hello, Annja. It's been a while."

20

Annja grimaced. She knew the voice on the phone. And it always had a way of popping up when she least wanted it to. "Garin."

"The same."

"What in the world are you doing calling Tuk?" she asked.

"Tuk is working for me. He has been for some time now."

Annja laughed. "Please. What would Tuk ever do for someone like you?"

"You say that like I'm the worst person on the planet, Annja. I might take offense."

"I can think of a few who might be worse," Annja said. "But it's a close race if it makes you feel any better."

"The only reason you don't love me to death is because you've just never understood my agenda." Garin chuckled into the phone. "If you did, there might be hope for us yet."

"Doubtful," Annja said. "We've come out of things at

different extremes far too often for me to think there'd ever be a peaceful alliance there. I can't tell you how many times you've made me want to scream."

"I make lots of women scream. Usually they don't complain about it afterwards," he said.

"Don't you wish that was the reason."

"I'd never deny that bedding you would be one of the best experiences in my life. It would be for you, as well, if you'd only give in to what you feel and admit that you love me."

"I most certainly do not." Annja felt her face redden. Despite the fact that she definitely did not love Garin, she was physically attracted to him. She'd never admit it, though. Garin's ego was massive already.

"If you insist." Garin paused. "Don't be upset with Tuk. He was only following my orders. And it's not like he betrayed you or anything."

Annja glanced at Tuk. He looked positively embarrassed. Annja sighed and waved it off with her hand. "All right, fine. Whatever. What's he been doing for you, anyway?"

"Keeping track of you."

Annja's eyes flashed back at Tuk with murderous intent. "He's been following *me?* So that's why he was in the airplane. He told me he was a drunk and fell asleep trying to get over a hangover."

"You were too smart to fall for that, Annja. You never believed it from the moment he told you so stop pretending to be angry now that I've confirmed it. It's unbecoming."

Annja felt her blood pressure rising. She glanced around and then decided that Shangri-La likely didn't have any heavy bags hanging off of trees that she could pummel for a solid hour. "Why has he been following me? What's the big deal?"

"I asked him to look after you so I could make certain you were safe."

"I'm in danger?"

Garin laughed. "Annja, you are very rarely not in danger in that so-called life of yours. Most of the time, I believe you're miraculously lucky to walk down the street without someone dropping a piano on you." He paused. "It amazes me you even manage any type of social life at all."

Annja smirked. "Who said I have one of those?"

"I'm being kind, my dear."

Annja nodded. "You'd better explain yourself, Garin. I'm not liking the way this conversation is headed."

"Tuk's been with you since you landed the other day. I set it up well ahead of time, but it was necessary for me to keep tabs on you. I believe you've stumbled into something that you don't fully understand. And for purposes best known to myself, I find it necessary to make sure you stay safe."

"I thought it was because of my sparkling personality."

"More likely your spectacular ass."

Annja blushed again. "Garin, is there a point to this conversation or is all this just making you feel good about yourself?"

"I just informed Tuk that the woman you saw in Tsing's apartment the other night works for Chinese intelligence."

"Taipei or Beijing? There's a difference."

"Beijing."

"Oh."

"And she is an expert assassin. If she's been let loose from her cage, you can bet that it is because there's a major target in play. I have no idea right now who that might be. It could be you. It could be Tuk. It might be someone I don't even know about yet. But considering that she was positioned near Tsing, it's more than likely it's someone involved in your little jaunt to discover Shangri-La."

Annja frowned. She never truly trusted Garin because of all the times he'd conned her in the past. And yet, when he told her certain facts, there did seem to be an element of truth to them. The key with Garin was figuring out which nuggets were true and which ones were bogus.

"All right, so where do we go from here?" she asked.

"I need to see you."

Annja smirked. "Here? You want to come here?"

"That would be optimal, yes."

Annja shook her head. "I can't tell you the first thing about getting here. As far as I know, we could have been taken here in a time machine."

"You weren't," Garin said. "If there was a time machine on this planet, I would know about it."

Annja raised an eyebrow. Was that just one of those things he said in passing or was there some truth to that statement? She shook her head. "What I mean to say is, I don't know how we came to be here. I'm sure Tuk will verify this for you."

"He did. Regardless, I need to get there. So I've instructed Tuk to figure it out and then call me back."

"Where are you now?"

"Jomsom. I'm close. But for all I know, the assassin could be closer."

"Great."

Garin paused. "Listen to me, Annja. I know that we haven't always seen eye to eye in the past. I understand that my motivations may not coincide with your own. Despite that fact, I am being very serious when I tell you that there is something going on here that I don't fully understand."

"All right."

"Tuk tells me you were shot down by a missile. Is that right?"

Annja nodded. "I'm no expert but we definitely took rocket fire yesterday."

"Any idea what kind?"

"None. First we knew about it we were flying over a

snowfield near Dhaulagiri. Mike threw the plane into all sorts of maneuvers and it missed us. We swept back to land at Jomsom to try to figure out who might be shooting at us and then got nailed by the second missile."

"You shouldn't have turned back."

"We were on a direct course to cross the Tibetan border. The alternative didn't look so good, y'know?"

"You think it was shoulder-fired?"

Annja frowned. "Again, I don't know. We didn't see a thing down there except a snow-white blanket. It could have been an emplacement. It might have been fired from someone's shoulder if they were well camouflaged. I just can't say."

"Very well." Garin paused. "Take care of yourself, Annja. Just because you're in a supposed utopian world, don't forget that there's a very real world back out here. And sometimes those two worlds can get crossed. When they do, bad things can happen."

"I'll see you if Tuk manages to figure out a way to get you here," she said.

"Keep things to yourself, Annja. Don't be so trusting— even when you're there."

"I understand."

The phone went dead in her hand. Tuk bounded over.

"Annja, I'm sorry. I didn't mean to mislead you. But I didn't think I was doing anything bad. Garin, as you call him, seemed most concerned about your safety and welfare. I didn't think it was wrong what I was doing."

Annja looked at him. "I know. How did he manage to find you anyway?"

Tuk frowned. "In my old life I worked for intelligence services operating in Katmandu. I was a tracker. I freelanced for them all and did my job very well. But then things changed and the world of espionage was not what it used to be with all its modern technology. I was forced to seek employment with criminals and thugs, the likes of which I have hated from the start. When Garin found me, it made my heart leap at the chance to once again do some good work."

"And he paid well, didn't he?"

"Extremely so. All I wanted was enough to retire on. I wanted to buy a home in the countryside and leave my former existence behind."

Annja smiled. "I can't blame you for that, Tuk. I just wish you'd been honest with me from the get-go."

"I had my orders, Annja. I hope you can understand. Part of what made me such a great tracker was my obedience to mission parameters."

"Yeah, I understand. I don't like it, but I understand."

Tuk chewed his lip for a moment. "Did you listen to what Garin had to say?"

"I did."

"And what do you think about it?"

"I'm not sure yet. Garin sometimes says things that aren't wholly factual."

"He lies?"

Annja smiled. "Hate to burst your bubble about your employer, pal, but yeah, he's been known to lie before. He's lied a lot to me personally."

Tuk frowned. "That is unfortunate."

"But who knows," Annja said. "He could be completely honest right now about this thing. You just never really know with Garin until all the cards are on the table and you can see what he's got." She smirked. "Even then I wouldn't buy into everything. Garin's been known to have a few extra aces up his sleeve."

"He sounds like a most interesting man."

"Something like that." Annja glanced back at the party. "What do you think of this notion that the Chinese are involved here somehow?"

"I don't know what to think. But I saw that woman Garin mentioned. And she terrified me."

"So you think she's capable of being what Garin said she was?"

Tuk nodded fiercely. "I was in Tsing's penthouse the night you and Mike were there, as well."

"You were? How did you manage that feat?"

Tuk shrugged but Annja could see the little man was proud of what he'd accomplished. "I managed to infiltrate the apartment successfully in order to keep an eye on you."

"Oh, yeah? And what would you have done if Mike and I were in danger?"

Tuk frowned. "Honestly, I have no idea."

Annja laughed a little. "So you saw this woman?"

"She had stepped out of the apartment and that enabled my entrance. I was caught unaware when she returned. But whereas most people will walk right by my hiding spots and be none the wiser, she seemed to sense my presence there in the darkness. Her eyes pierced the night and seemed to stare right into my soul. And I shall never forget the image of her fingernails. They looked like claws or blades. She struck fear into my very soul."

Annja nodded. "Great. Sounds like just the kind of woman I could have a beer with."

"That," Tuk said, "is something I doubt very much."

"I'm being sarcastic."

Tuk grinned. "Sorry."

Annja looked at the party. Mike had noticed the two of them were missing out on the festivities and seemed intent to wander over. Annja glanced back at Tuk. "I don't think we should talk too much about this with anyone else."

"I agree."

"It's just that it might make people upset. If something happens, then we'll deal with it."

"With your sword?"

Annja smiled. "Maybe. And don't you dream of mentioning that to anyone, either."

"Especially, I'm assuming, Garin?"

Annja shrugged. "Nah, he already knows about it. Too late to keep that secret from him." She took a breath. "In the meantime, you have to figure out how to get Garin over here."

"I'll speak with my father," Tuk said. "I'm certain he will tell me what we need to know."

"He seemed to know all about your phone call," Annja said. "I'd be curious as to how he pulled off that trick."

"Maybe I'll ask him that, too."

"You do that."

"And if it's true what he says, that there is indeed an assassin headed here at the behest of the Communist Chinese? What then?"

Annja shrugged. "Then she and I will just have to have a serious talk."

21

"You guys okay?"

Tuk had wandered off to find his father and Mike had come across the field. In the background, the music continued to play and Annja wondered how long it would carry on for.

She nodded. "Just going over some things."

"Was that a cell phone I saw in Tuk's hand?"

Annja smiled. "Yes, it was. Apparently, the little guy had it with him the entire time."

Mike frowned. "You mean we could have been rescued before all of this?"

"I doubt it, actually. There would have been no way to get a team in for us with the storm coming down. And I believe that Tuk would have used it to do just that if he thought there was enough time."

"Who was he talking to?"

Annja smirked. "An old friend of mine. Of sorts. I guess he thought I was in some kind of danger and asked Tuk to keep an eye on me."

"Tuk was your guardian angel?"

"Seems to have been, yes." Annja shrugged. "Although, I'm still not quite sure what he might have been protecting me from. And that's the bone of contention right now."

"What is?"

"There is apparently something much bigger going on than any of us realized." Annja sighed. "And it shows signs of infecting this place if what I just heard is to be believed."

"Are you kidding me? How would it impact this place? It's like an unspoiled paradise here." The expression on Mike's face betrayed his sudden worry and apprehension.

Annja tried to calm him down. "Mike, I know that you're loving this place, but we aren't the only ones who have been looking for it."

"I know that," Mike said. "People have been searching for Shangri-La since it was written about all those years ago. It's a given that others would want to find it. And yet, somehow I don't think they'll be able to."

Annja shook her head. "I wish that was the case, but I think it's safe to say that right now there is a very concerted effort to discover exactly how to access this valley from the outside world. And the people involved in that hunt are anything but friendly."

"Are you talking about Tsing? I didn't get the idea that he wanted to destroy this place. I thought maybe he wanted to come and live here in seclusion. Maybe find a cure for that weird vampire condition of his."

"I'm not necessarily talking about Tsing," Annja said. "I'm thinking about the Communist Chinese. I just don't know all of the details yet and, until I do, I'm not quite sure what we're supposed to do. This doesn't look like the kind of place you could easily defend." Annja swept her hand up, pointing out that they were in a valley bordered on all sides by mountains.

If someone invaded they would immediately hold the high ground and therefore the strategic advantage.

"Maybe it doesn't need defending," Mike said. "It's been able to remain hidden here for years. Maybe that is its best defense."

"That was also before satellite technology," Annja said. "And despite what Guge might say, I'm not ready to believe that it's invisible to what we have flying around the earth. Someone knows about this place or they will soon enough. And when that happens, there's going to be a rush to get here and exploit whatever natural resources they have."

"Probably the geothermal ones," Mike said. "Hot springs and underground vents that could produce this type of environment would be badly sought by governments around the world."

Annja nodded. "And the Chinese have one of the fastest-growing populations in the world, coupled with a real energy crisis. Even being able to tap into this place to help them offset the energy requirements of Tibet would be a boon and a massive savings for them."

"You think that's it? That they want to channel the geothermal heat out of here to run power in Tibet?"

Annja shrugged. "Like I said, I don't know. I just got handed all of this information and I'm still processing it. If I had to guess, I'd say they're as likely to grab the entire Mustang province as they would be to just take over this valley. But we've also got a very real geographical dilemma here."

"Which is?"

Annja looked at him. "We don't know which side of the border we're on. We were straddling it when we were in the mountain. Presumably we're someplace else now, but where exactly? I don't think Guge and Vanya have the latest maps to show us. And if it turns out that we're on the Tibetan side, then we are, in effect, in Chinese territory. They could literally do anything to this place and suffer no repercussions."

"And we'd be screwed," Mike said.

"Definitely," Annja replied.

Mike looked around and let out a huge sigh. "Isn't it always like this? Doesn't it just suck that you think you finally find something amazing—something that has driven you your entire life. I read James Hilton's novel *Lost Horizon* when I was just eight years old and it captivated me so entirely that my life was devoted to this even before I knew it would be." He shook his head. "And now at last, when I'm on the threshold of my own lost horizon, I find the place of my dreams, only to have to come to grips with the idea that it may be taken away from me."

Annja put a hand on his arm. "Mike, I don't think we should jump to any drastic conclusions yet. Like I said, I'm still processing the information I was just given."

Mike sighed again. "What's the point anymore? Where is the harmony in the universe that would allow a place like this to blossom only to stub it out and wreck the happiness it provides to so many people?"

"I don't know that there is any universal justice," Annja said. "Despite what people think and believe. Sometimes it really does seem like the bad guys get to win and the good guys go home without the ball."

"It shouldn't be like that," Mike said. "And you can bet that when I get to whatever afterlife awaits me, I'm going to have some really hard questions for the people in charge."

Annja smiled. "I don't doubt it at all."

Mike pointed at the party, which was finally beginning to show signs of breaking up. Dozens of people were now clearing the tables and carting off chairs to some other locale. "These people seem to have lived in peace and prosperity for years, only rarely coming into contact with the outside world. How is that now they're in jeopardy?"

"I don't know," Annja said. "I just don't know."

Mike shook his head. "That's not a good enough explanation, Annja. And it's not one I can accept."

Annja watched him storm off. She took a deep breath. She couldn't blame Mike for feeling this way. With a brain tumor growing in his head and only a matter of time before his last days on the planet, all he wanted was to find a peaceful place to spend his final moments.

And now that seemed to have no chance of happening.

Annja wandered away from the party and back to the grand staircase. There she sat and looked up at the sky. She could see the stars twinkling above her head and had to wonder exactly where she was. And why was this place in danger, now of all times?

Her gut response didn't make her feel any better. What if Shangri-La was being threatened as a direct result of events set into motion by Mike? What if his lifelong obsession had enabled the possibility of Shangri-La's very extinction? By being so driven to find this place, Mike might have unleashed the very forces that will lead to its downfall.

Annja frowned. And she might be helping them, too. Just by agreeing to tag along on this adventure, Annja could be just as culpable in the demise as Mike.

Wonderful, she thought. Now I'm destroying whole worlds instead of just evil people. I'm really embracing my inner destructor.

"You look troubled."

Annja looked up and saw Vanya approaching her. For an older woman, she looked remarkably vibrant. Her skin seemed to glow almost translucently in the twilight. And her smile radiated a peace and warmth that Annja found comforting.

"I suppose I am," Annja said.

"Here? Of all places? You've managed to be troubled about something?"

Annja nodded. "Trust me, if anyone can find something to be troubled about, it's me."

"Surely not by desire, though."

Annja shook her head. "Nope. Trouble seems to find me wherever I am. I don't go looking for it, but it seems drawn to me."

"Very often trouble finds us not because we are bad people, but because we have the opportunity to help set things right. Perhaps instead of focusing on why trouble always finds you, you should focus on the good you've been able to do when put to the challenge."

Annja smiled. "I appreciate that, but I sometimes question whether I've been able to do any good at all. Or are my efforts merely wasted breaths in the universe. It's impossible for me to know for certain."

"Does it matter?"

Annja looked at her. "What do you mean? Of course it matters."

Vanya shook her head. "I don't think you believe that. You don't act as a force for good simply because you want to be recognized for it. That doesn't really even matter to you."

Annja shrugged. "Possibly…"

"Your actions in this world bear out a destiny you have been born to. You are where you are supposed to be for that very reason. Our personal agendas have little to do with the nature of our divine purpose."

Annja looked at her. "You truly believe that?"

"We all have a part to play, Annja. No one role is more important than any other. We are all interconnected and therefore reliant on one another. Even those who may never know us by name or by face will still find that our journey through this universe is not taken alone, but in the breadth of a complete human experience."

"We're all in this together, in other words."

Vanya nodded. "That is an easier way of putting it, yes."

"And if you knew that something bad was going to potentially happen, what would you do about it?"

Vanya smiled. "There exists in everything and every one of us the potential for anything to happen at any time. Potential is simply misguided energy careering around. It is only when that potential is harnessed and then focused into something that we can decide for certain if it is good or evil."

Annja sighed again. "I suppose I could stand to wait a little longer before I make certain decisions."

"It sounds," Vanya said, "as though you have already started making those decisions."

Maybe I have, Annja thought.

"The universe is a quirky thing," Vanya said. "It simply goes on oblivious to whatever our personal desires may be. The real way to impact the universe is not to wish and pray for good things to happen."

"A whole lot of people are going to be pretty disappointed in that statement," Annja said with a grin.

"If you want to change the universe, then you must set things in motion starting at the most basic level. Waiting and then trying to change what already began years or centuries before will not be enough to impact the course of the future. By that point, it is already too late."

"But how do you know when to start?"

Vanya smiled. "We are always at the starting point of something, somewhere. The real trick is knowing where you are at any given moment. Find out the answer to that, and then you will become truly unstoppable."

"Have you figured it out yet?"

"Me?" Vanya laughed. "Oh, no. I imagine that will take

me many more lifetimes to understand. Perhaps then I will escape the wheel. Until such time, I will be back to learn more and continue to evolve."

"You don't seem disappointed."

"Why be disappointed? Time is a function of humanity. The rest of the universe doesn't seem to care how long something takes or whether things are on schedule or not. It simply continues, regardless. So, too, will my personal evolution. When it is time for me to move on, I shall."

Annja smiled. "Thanks for your help."

"It is my pleasure. Thank you for bringing my son home."

"My pleasure."

Vanya drifted away, leaving Annja to ponder a lot more than what she'd started with.

22

Tuk walked with his father, Guge, toward the royal pavilion hours after the last of the partygoers had wandered off to sleep. He couldn't stop thinking about the phone call from Garin earlier and what ramifications it might have for his kingdom. But Garin had specifically asked Tuk to find out how to cross over to this land. And Tuk knew his only chance at getting that information was from his father.

"You're enjoying yourself, my son?"

Tuk smiled. "What's not to enjoy? For my entire life I've always wondered who I was and what I was supposed to do. I thought I'd found my life's work and then that vanished. I was despondent. Unsure of where I was supposed to go. And then this happened and everything seems so utterly perfect."

Guge smiled. "Your mother is beside herself with joy. She blamed herself for many years after your disappearance. She was inconsolable in some respects. Guilt is a terrible burden to handle, but especially so where it concerns a child."

"I would imagine," Tuk said. "But I don't hold either of you responsible. How could you have known that your kindness would be repaid with betrayal."

"That's the thing that one can almost never guard against," Guge said. "Betrayal."

"But surely you can look out for such things. If a person's actions are suspect, then you can remain on alert for their traitorous ways to emerge."

Guge nodded and then fell silent for a time. Finally, he looked at Tuk. "You wish to ask me a question."

"I do."

"Then why haven't you yet?"

Tuk smiled. "How is it that we came to be in this place? We examined the cave as much as we knew how. And yet, here we are."

Guge smiled. "You want to know how you crossed over."

"Yes."

"It's quite simple, actually. Would you like to see it?"

Tuk looked at him. "Right at this moment?"

"Certainly. Why not?"

Tuk shrugged. "I thought there might be something complicated about it, something that would require more preparation time."

"Not at all." Guge pointed toward the temple ahead of them that was connected to the royal quarters. Like the pavilion and court, it was constructed out of stone and seemed to be part of the mountain itself. Intricate carvings bordered every doorway and window.

Tuk was amazed at the workmanship. "How long has this been here?"

"Hundreds of years." Guge pointed inside a darkened corridor. "Come with me and you will learn the secrets of our kingdom."

Tuk fell into step behind his father. Guge traveled over the polished stone-floored corridors without a sound, seeming to almost levitate as he walked. Guge's cough had also ceased, which made Tuk feel better about his father's health. He'd secretly wondered if the coughing might be a sign that his father's life was nearing its end.

They walked past giant stone gods squatting in amazing detail with their hands knotted into intricate mudra for calling down favor from the universe. Spectacular colored wall reliefs showed ancient battles between the good and evil forces.

"I come here a lot to be alone with my thoughts," Guge said. "It is a place of contemplation for me as I imagine it will be for you also."

"I'd like that," Tuk said. "I have often thought my life could use a lot more meditation than action."

"Some people don't like to think," Guge said. "If they are not solely preoccupied with action, then they have time to realize the truly infantile aspects of their essence. A brain in constant need of action is no better than a fool's mind. Only the truly wise and intelligent may devote themselves to inaction from time to time without fear or prejudice."

Tuk saw that there were lit torches ahead, casting light into the darkened gloom of the temple. The flames danced and bit at the night air, throwing shadows across the walls and paintings with reckless abandon.

"How much farther is it?"

Guge shrugged. "Not very. Are you in a hurry, my son?"

"Not at all. I am tired, however. I fear that I might collapse from exhaustion soon from all the dancing earlier."

"Your people have missed you. And there was quite some concern as to who would assume the throne when your mother and I pass on. Some of our people suggested that it was time for a new ruler to assume command. But your mother insisted we wait a little longer before making a decision. She is very wise."

Tuk smiled. "Maybe she knew I was coming home."

"Perhaps she did."

Guge led them down yet another corridor and the air grew cooler. Tuk shivered slightly and Guge noticed. "Yes, this is much deeper into the mountain now. And you can feel the temperature shift, can't you?"

"Yes, it's much cooler."

Guge nodded. "So, you see that we are part of the same mountain. But our position makes all the difference."

"How is that possible?"

"It just is."

Tuk frowned. "Forgive me father, but that's not much of an explanation."

Guge turned around and, for a moment, Tuk thought his father was angered. But the expression faded then and Guge merely smiled. "Do not allow yourself to get caught up in the need to have everything explained to you so completely. Doing so robs the world of its magic."

"I understand, Father. I merely thought that there would be an explanation that made more sense. You know, from a scientific perspective."

"Science cannot explain everything, my son. And science should not try to explain everything. For then it becomes a crutch and imagination departs the soul." Guge shook his head. "It would be truly tragic for the human race if that were to happen."

"All right."

They walked down a flight of stairs and then entered a long hallway leading toward another portal. A lone torch flickered on the wall ahead, but Tuk could not see beyond into the absolute darkness of the portal.

Guge stopped. "This is the way you came across."

"Through there?"

Guge nodded. "It leads to a path that will take you back to the arctic side of the mountain." He glanced at Tuk's clothes.

"Perhaps now is not the time to try it out and see. You seem a bit underdressed."

Tuk smiled. "I'd just like to take a look."

Guge shook his head. "I don't recommend it, my son. There is little to see over there that you have not already seen. Why go through again? Are you merely attempting to satisfy your own curiosity?"

"I suppose I am."

Guge sighed. "I am old, my son. This is nothing of consequence. You should be content to know that it exists and that there is a way to get from our kingdom back to the real world. But I don't think you will be needing it. Unless you don't intend to stay?"

Tuk shook his head. "I'm not leaving."

Guge smiled. "Excellent. Then perhaps we can satisfy your curiosity another time? I am getting tired myself."

Tuk smiled. "Perhaps I could take one quick little peek across? That wouldn't be so bad, would it?"

"You won't stop badgering an old man unless he lets you go, will you?"

Tuk smiled. "Probably not."

Guge sighed again. "Very well. Go ahead. But I am not coming with you. That cold air makes my old bones hurt. And there's nothing there that I haven't seen before now. If you want to go, you go by yourself."

"Are you sure you won't come along?"

"Completely."

Tuk paused and looked down the hallway at the portal. The torch fire danced from the slight breeze that seemed to snake through the hallway. Tuk caught a touch of the chill across his neck and shivered involuntarily.

For a moment, he seriously considered going off to bed and doing this later. But then he shook his head and started forward toward the doorway.

He paused and looked back. "Can I bring the torch?"

"Are you afraid of the dark?"

"Not at all," Tuk said. "I'm afraid of what I can't see. I don't want to step over the edge of something that would send me hurtling toward my death."

"I don't believe you will."

"And yet…?"

Guge took a deep breath and blew it out slowly. "Oh, very well, take the torch along. But be ready for it to go out the moment you cross over. The winds are strong. And there may be a lot of snow."

"I'll be ready."

"And make sure you pay very close attention to where you are," Guge said. "If you don't, you will never find the way back to us and you will perish in the cold over there. Your mother would never let me hear the end of it."

Tuk paused and a slight frown crossed his face. That almost seemed an odd thing for his father to say. But Tuk shook his head and then grabbed the torch from the wall bracket.

He looked back toward his father. "All right. I'm going to go through the doorway now."

"Good luck."

"Thank you.

Tuk turned back to the blackened doorway and held the torch aloft. But for some strange reason, the torchlight could not penetrate the interior of the doorway.

Tuk held the torch up and ran it all along the perimeter of the door, but there was nothing that he could see inside.

"You will not be able to see until you actually cross the threshold," Guge said from behind him.

Tuk looked back. "Why is that?"

"It is that way simply because it is that way."

Tuk nodded. Another strange answer from his father. Very well, he thought. If there's only one way to do this, then he would simply do it. Perhaps then he would know what to tell Garin when he called again.

Guge's voice was behind him then. Very close. "I nearly forgot to ask you something."

Tuk turned around. "What is it?"

"You received a phone call earlier this evening. Didn't you?"

Tuk felt his face redden. "I did. I forgot that I had the telephone with me."

Guge pointed at the doorway. "You cannot go through with the telephone from this side."

"Why not?"

"As far as I understand it," Guge said. "The technology is too advanced to be transported back."

Tuk frowned. "But I came through with it from the other side and it seems to work just fine."

Guge shrugged. "I will hold on to the phone for you while you go through. That way, you can be sure it will work."

Tuk took the phone out and hefted it in his hand. "All right. I'll just take a quick peek and then come back."

Guge nodded. "Good. I hope you will satisfy your curiosity once and for all. Then we can move on to other things."

Tuk smiled. "We have a lot to talk about, I assume."

"A great deal indeed."

Tuk turned back to the doorway. "All right, I'm going through." He held the torch high above his head and then stepped closer to the doorway. He still felt Guge behind him, though, and turned back around. "Aren't you too close?"

Guge smiled. "I just wanted to make sure you are certain of this."

"I am, Father."

Tuk turned around. Before him, the gaping maw of the darkened doorway stood.

Tuk took a deep breath and then started to step through the doorway.

The phone rang.

He stopped.

Then felt a heavy push from behind, and before he knew what was happening, Tuk went sprawling through the doorway and into the darkness beyond.

23

Annja tossed and turned on the bed of silky soft pillows and tried to get comfortable. From her quarters, an open window looked down upon the pavilion. Tropical breezes swept through the curtains and across her skin. The temperature was absolutely perfect for sleeping.

And yet, she couldn't.

The idea that Garin was somehow involved in this whole mess had her confused. Why exactly had he hired Tuk to watch over her? Since when did Annja need a guardian angel, anyway? She had her sword. And the sword could handle anything that she'd ever come up against.

Although, she thought, she hadn't had much occasion to use the blade on this outing. Something told her that if Hsu Xiao was really coming here, then that would soon be rectified.

Annja wondered how Mike was doing. After he'd stormed off, she'd tried to find him but he seemed intent on avoiding any contact. Annja decided that he needed some alone time and had gone to bed to try to get some rest. She would have thought that would be an easy task given how much the strain of the past day had worn on her. But after nearly an hour of tossing and turning, even she had to admit that something wasn't letting her sleep.

She sat on the stone window ledge and peered out across the land. The winds swept through the trees, rustling leaves. She could see the tall grasses sway. And all about this place, everything seemed perfectly still. Perfectly...perfect.

Annja frowned. It wasn't that she didn't believe in an absolute peace. It was just that she had never seen anything that even approached the tranquility of this land. It was an oddity to her.

How is this even possible? she wondered. Where are we... exactly?

The idea that Shangri-La existed on the other side of Dhaulagiri Mountain didn't sit right with Annja's analytical mind. Some part of her rejected that outright, saying that it would be impossible for such a place to exist and stay hidden from the technological eye of modern man.

Despite what Vanya and Guge might want her to believe, Annja couldn't buy into it.

Still, if they were in some sort of magical location, then what was it? How did it operate? Annja wasn't naive enough to think that just because something may or may not be magical, there weren't rules that it would have to abide by, as well. She'd seen enough crazy stuff in her life to know that all things in the universe—even those that were presently unexplainable—still had a rule book they had to follow.

So how did Shangri-La function?

She dressed quickly and walked down the stairs back toward the pavilion. The amazing thing about this place was there seemed to be very few individual homes anywhere. And everyone seemed to disappear to sleep at the same time. Earlier this evening, right after the party had disbanded, people simply vanished. Annja wrote it off as everyone going off to bed, but now it triggered an alarm bell inside her gut.

Her footfalls were silent on the courtyard stonework. Annja moved across the open pavilion and stole back down the grand staircase toward the fields below. As she walked, she kept her senses alert for any movement that might alert her she was not alone.

But as far as she could tell, she was just that. Alone.

This is weird, she thought. Where is everyone?

Even Tuk seemed to have vanished earlier. Annja had last seen him walking with Guge. Presumably, Tuk was going to get his father to tell him how to cross over so that Garin could find them.

Annja frowned. She wasn't sure that was such a good idea. The times she'd been around Garin in the past had usually amounted to a lot of tension between them and then a differing agenda that left Annja on the losing end of things.

But then again, Garin had seemed sincere about wanting to keep Annja safe. But from what? The Chinese assassin? Was Annja truly in the crosshairs? And, if so, how did the Chinese know she would be coming over here? Couldn't they have taken her out when she was back in Brooklyn?

Too many things just didn't make sense. Her mind and spirit were at odds and the resulting battle had one casualty—Annja's sleep.

She crossed into the open fields and started walking toward the groves of fruit trees farther ahead. She could smell their scent as she approached. Their branches looked strong and supple. Annja reached up and twisted a peach from one of the branches and held on to it as she continued toward the edge of the field.

Overhead, the stars winked at her and, somewhere far above, clouds wove strange patterns across the night sky. The effect was incredibly peaceful.

Annja bit into the peach, aware of how incredibly juicy it was. She ate it quickly and then tossed the pit onto the ground.

Annja looked around in every direction and saw nothing that would lead her to believe this place was inhabited. No lights, no noise, no nothing.

Everyone seemed to have disappeared.

Except for her.

Annja started walking back to the grand staircase. Surely there would be attendants awake in the temple corridors. Perhaps she could ask them a few questions and try to put her mind at rest.

But as Annja ascended the stairs, she heard nothing.

Back at the top, as she traveled down corridor after corridor and checked out room after room, she found nothing. There were no people anywhere. And worse, there were no personal belongings to speak of.

It was as if she was on some sort of weird soundstage in a movie production lot. But the land was real and surely the peach she'd eaten was real.

So where the hell was everyone else?

She ducked back upstairs to her room and tried again to sleep. Perhaps, she thought, if I go to sleep, tomorrow will sort things through.

But her mind raced as soon as she lay down.

Annja sat up and frowned.

Shangri-La was turning out to be anything but paradise.

She yawned and realized how utterly fatigued she was. Even if she couldn't sleep, maybe just closing her eyes would make everything feel better. She leaned back and felt her head sink into one of the pillows.

A delicate scent of honeysuckle tickled her nostrils and Annja smiled. She loved that scent. Always had.

She thought about the golden sunshine and how warm it

had been earlier today. It reminded her of sitting on a tropical beach somewhere watching the blue-green waves crash in against the sandy shore, frothing white before retreating once more to the water.

Annja stretched her limbs and tried to release all of her nervous energy. Wherever she was, she decided, it was better than being back in that cold, snowy cave.

In the next instant, driven purely by instinct, she leaped from the bed into a standing position. In her hands, the sword had already materialized.

Several images registered at once as she came fully awake.

A dark shadow behind her bed.

Hands extended over the pillow where she'd been lying.

Claws.

Annja flicked the sword up in front of her and, from behind her bed, tracked the shadow. It was bathed in black cloth, invisible in the dim twilight of the room. There was no moon, making the landscape even darker.

But the shadow that stalked Annja seemed to simply bleed across the floor toward her, its hands upraised in a fighting stance vaguely reminiscent to Annja. She'd seen it somewhere before, but where?

The figure in black didn't scream or jerk its body in any fashion. One second it was coolly regarding Annja as a cat might look at a mouse.

The next instant, it attacked.

Annja was almost stunned by the sudden ferocity of the attack. The figure slashed at Annja's face with its claws.

Annja deftly flicked her sword up, intending to cut the attacker's hands, but she heard something she didn't expect. It was the clang of metal against metal.

Annja moved back for more room. Swinging a sword in a confined space wasn't the best use of it as a weapon. The shadow had the advantage of a smaller tool used in a close environment.

But Annja didn't intend to go down without a fight.

As the shadow advanced again, Annja could see that the skin around the eyes had been darkened, as well, rendering the figure nearly invisible save for the whites of the eyeballs themselves.

Again and again it came at Annja. Annja used the sword to ward off the attacks, but her own offensive struggled to get off the ground. Annja stabbed and took short cuts at the shadow, but the figure merely moved out of the way and out of range.

Annja shook her head. She needed open space to use her sword to its fullest advantage. But how would she convince the shadow to pursue her? She had to assume the shadow knew how to fight and do so extremely well. There was no way it would simply follow Annja if it meant giving up its advantage in the room.

Annja attacked savagely and thought she felt her blade slide into a piece of flesh. But the shadow never once uttered a sound.

Instead, it came back at Annja, swinging its claws with full force. Annja was driven back to the doorway and then beyond into the corridor.

Instead of continuing the fight, though, Annja ran.

She dashed down the steps back into the open pavilion. She had no idea if the shadow had followed her or not. She couldn't hear anything. Even her own footsteps had been virtually silent thanks to the thick stone steps.

Annja whirled in time to see the shadow floating down from the second floor bedroom window of Annja's quarters.

It flies, Annja thought. How is that possible?

But she had no time to think it through. The shadow attacked again, this time kicking Annja in the stomach.

Annja flew back, feeling her wind rush out of her body.

The shadow followed up with a resounding punch to Annja's chin. Annja saw stars and tried to blink away the tears that welled up in her eyes.

Annja crouched, pivoting on her knee, trying to cut the shadow open at the midsection.

But the shadow backflipped away, tumbling across the pavilion and disappearing into the corridors beyond.

Annja stood there with her sword gleaming in the night.

Stay or follow?

She'd tricked the shadow into coming down here where she could better use the blade. Now the shadow probably wanted to return the favor.

Annja shook her head. No way was she following.

From the darkness across the courtyard, Annja heard a soft whisper cut through the night air. She jerked her sword up and cut it across her face, severing the arrow that had been fired at her from somewhere beyond the range of her sight.

The two pieces fell and skittered across the stone floor.

Annja heard another series of whispers and twisted to avoid the bolts that flew at her.

Again and again, arrows flew at her body and Annja found her lungs heaving as she struggled to avoid them. I'm silhouetted out here in the dim light, she thought. I need to be invisible, too.

Annja ran toward the darkness where the shadow had fled. Rushing through the doorway, she cut right and left and above and below, trying to score a direct hit with her offense.

But she cut nothing.

She heard a soft peal of laughter ring out, carried to her ears on the breeze that brushed past her face.

Annja pivoted and sliced nothing but air.

But she'd sensed movement.

Something had rushed past her back into the open court-yard of the pavilion.

Annja raced back out, still keeping the sword in front of her to protect her if need be.

Perched atop one of the stone walls leading up toward Annja's quarters, the shadow was hunched. Against the night sky, it looked like a feral cat.

And it cast one final look at Annja before leaping off into the night.

24

The ringing of the phone echoed in Tuk's ears as he pitched and fell headlong through the doorway into the blackness beyond. His hands instinctively shot out, reaching, grabbing for anything to help break his fall. He felt a weird fabric brush against his hands and he clutched at the material before it gave way under his body weight. It enshrouded him as he continued to fall forward until he hit his face against something hard.

For a moment, he lay there unsure of what had just happened. His phone had rung and then he'd been shoved from behind. But had his own father pushed him through the doorway? That didn't make any sense.

Tuk heard a heavy rumbling sound and yanked off the black material in time to see a giant slab of stone slam shut, enclosing him in a small ten-by-ten-foot room.

"Hey!"

Tuk's voice echoed back at him. He could tell the walls must have been exceedingly thick. He didn't think any bit of sound would escape this room no matter how hard he tried to shout.

He looked around at the sparse room. It resembled a prison cell. Overhead, a single light illuminated the room behind what looked to be a Plexiglas housing. This suddenly didn't look very much like Shangri-La.

Had he come across some kind of gap in time and space and he was back on the other side in some strange location? This certainly wasn't the mountain cave they'd come through.

So where was he?

He paced off the room, confirming in his own mind the measurements. Other than the light fixture, there was nothing else in the room with him. Tuk was, for all intents and purposes, in a perfectly square stone box.

His mind raced. Surely his own father hadn't done this to him, had he? He felt like a prisoner and he was rapidly suspecting that he'd somehow been betrayed. Was everything a hoax here? Was this place just a fraud? And if it was, then that meant that Annja and Mike were in serious trouble.

He pounded on one of the walls but found it as solid as he thought it might be. His hand came away badly scraped. Tuk sucked it for a moment and then sat down on the floor, trying to make sense of things.

Garin was obviously attempting to get in touch with him again. But why? Had he learned something that would help? Or was he calling to see if Tuk had managed to find a way for Garin to cross over?

Either way, things didn't look good.

Tuk leaned against the wall and folded his arms. Nothing made sense except for the fact that he'd passed through a doorway and into some type of prison cell, cut off from his friends, and seemingly at the mercy of his so-called father.

Perhaps his father didn't really want him back, after all. Maybe Tuk was a threat to his rule.

No.

Tuk shook his head. His father was old. Guge himself had said how happy they were about his return.

But why?

If that was how they showed their happiness, then things were truly askew.

Tuk examined his hand again and made sure that the bleeding was minimal. It wouldn't need any medical attention, but it hurt for the time being.

"You shouldn't have punched the wall like that."

Tuk looked up and saw that a section of the stone wall had slid back, revealing a piece of Plexiglas. It looked to be some type of observation window. And Tuk couldn't see beyond the one-way glass into the other room.

"Father?"

He heard laughter. "He still thinks you're his father."

"Who is that?" Tuk got to his feet, feeling his heart thunder in his chest. Now they were mocking him. He felt his face redden at the thought of it.

"Sit down, little man. Sit down and listen."

Tuk sat, still feeling furious.

"It's a shame you had to be so curious about things. We were hoping you would hold out long enough for us to complete what we're working on here."

"I only asked a question," Tuk said.

"Yes, but you asked the question we didn't want you to ask. Don't you see? And now you're paying the price for that curiosity."

"Where is my father?"

More laughter sounded. Tuk got back to his feet. "Stop laughing at me!"

He heard a voice that sounded vaguely familiar. Guge. "I'm here, Tuk. What can I do for you?"

"You can explain yourself. All of this. Tell me what is going on here. I want to know."

"Yes, I know you want to know. The thing is, I can't tell you just yet. I'm afraid you're going to have to be a little more patient. When everything is done, you will be allowed to see it."

Tuk stopped. "I will?"

"Certainly."

Tuk didn't like the tone of his voice. "What's the catch?"

"There's no catch…son."

Tuk frowned. "You're not my father."

"Oh, now don't take it so personally. It was important for us to make you feel welcome when you first arrived. After all, it wouldn't do to have you come here and not roll out the welcome mat."

"Why, though? You could have just left us alone in the cave on the mountain."

"No. Unfortunately, as much as we would have liked doing just that, we couldn't leave you there."

"Why?"

"Because the woman you are with is far more adept at ferreting out things than we would like. And inevitably you would have located the passageway that bridges us with the mountain entrance."

"So you took us over with the intention of doing what?"

"Sending your friends back on their way when the one called Mike was healed. And keeping you here."

"Why keep me?"

"We have our reasons."

Tuk sighed. "Well, now you've got me. Are you going to let Annja and Mike go?"

"I'm afraid things have progressed beyond us being able to do that now."

"Why?"

"Your cell phone for one. Who is the man you are speaking with on the other end of the line?"

"None of your business."

"Tsk, tsk, Tuk, that's no way to treat your friends."

Tuk sniffed. "Friends…right."

"We need to know. We must ensure the secret is still safe. Does he know where you are?"

Tuk frowned. "I don't even know where I am. How would I be able to communicate anything to him?"

"All right."

Tuk rubbed his hand. "So how long are you going to keep me here?"

"Just a little while more."

"My friends aren't going to stand for this. Once they see that I've gone, they're going to start asking questions."

"Yes, Annja is already being somewhat troublesome."

Tuk smiled. You have no idea what she's capable of, he thought. "Oh, really?"

"Indeed. And we have another problem."

"Good."

"Don't be like that, Tuk. This can all go so much smoother if you simply cooperate and answer our questions. If you do that for us, we'll make sure your time with us is relatively comfortable. And painless."

"You're going to torture me if I don't talk? How refreshingly original."

"Torture tends not to work that well. The results are usually mixed. Unpredictable, even. But there are other alternatives."

Tuk frowned. "I'm not answering any more of your questions."

"Where is Mike?"

Tuk looked back at the one-way Plexiglas. "You lost him?" He couldn't help it and a smile broke out across his face. "That's fantastic. You guys must be so proud of yourselves."

"Tuk, this isn't helping us."

"You are absolutely correct. It's not helping you. And you can bet there's more where that came from."

Another voice spoke now but it wasn't directed at Tuk. "This is getting us nowhere. I told you he wouldn't cooperate."

Guge's voice broke into a different language. Tuk frowned. Mandarin Chinese. He heard the tones and had spent enough time around some of the Chinese transplants in Katmandu that he knew how the language sounded even if he didn't understand a word.

The conversation continued for several minutes and sounded quite heated. Tuk leaned back against the wall with a smug look on his face. Good, he thought, let them get annoyed with me.

"Tuk."

"What?"

"My comrade here thinks we would be better served if we simply started making you as uncomfortable as possible right now. He thinks I am wasting my time trying to talk to you like a civilized human being."

"Maybe you are."

"Don't say that, Tuk. Things can grow truly unpleasant here. You have no idea how enterprising some of my colleagues can be. And I mean that in the worst possible way."

Tuk sighed. "I'm done helping you. Until I get some answers, I'm not saying a thing."

"Where is Mike, Tuk?"

"I don't know. And that's an honest answer. Seriously. I will give that one to you for no charge."

"Where is he?"

Tuk patted the stone walls of his cell. "You guys are about as thick as this wall, aren't you? I just told you the truth. I don't know where he is. The last I saw of him was right after Annja spoke to him and he went off in a huff about something. I don't know anything else."

Guge and his colleague exchanged another battery of Chinese conversation. Back and forth for a minute this time and then, finally, Guge's voice came back on.

"All right, Tuk. That's fine for now. We will see if your story checks out. If I were you, I'd spend my time praying that it does."

"Really?"

"Oh, most definitely. Because if we find out you've been lying to us, there's going to be little I can do to stop my colleagues from exerting themselves upon you in a most terrible fashion."

Tuk bunched his knees up and leaned his head back against the wall. "I have nothing to hide. I've told you the truth."

"Let us hope so."

"How soon can I get out of here?"

"I told you. When we are finished. Not a moment before that time."

"And then you'll let me go?"

There was a pause. "We never said anything about letting you go, Tuk."

"I'm no use to you here. Let me go back to Katmandu. Or better yet, let me leave the country. I've got a little money. I can go anywhere. Trust me, I'm no bother to you here."

"You won't be a bother."

"Absolutely not."

"Well, there's one thing we agree on, Tuk."

Tuk nodded. "Good."

"Unfortunately, we don't agree on how to make sure that you do disappear."

"I just told you that I can vanish."

"It's too risky, my little friend."

Tuk swallowed. "I don't think I like where this is going."

"Then perhaps you should stop talking. Before your worst fears are confirmed. Good night, Tuk."

And the room plunged into darkness again, leaving Tuk very much alone in the cold stone cell.

25

Annja ran through the deserted corridors of the temple searching for her adversary everywhere, but to no avail. She paused, the sword still gleaming in the night air. There was no way she was going to release her blade until she knew exactly what the hell was going on around here.

But after a full minute with no action, Annja calmed her heartbeat down and retraced her steps to the courtyard. The night seemed even more still than it had before.

Something was definitely not right.

And where was Mike?

Annja wanted him around now especially so since there was apparently some kind of assassin in the grounds. Was it the Hsu Xiao character that Garin and Tuk had mentioned? Or was it someone else eager to dispatch the outsiders who had come into their land?

Annja headed left of the courtyard, following her gut instinct. Ahead of her, she could see flickering torches in the distance, illuminating aspects of the stone corridors. She passed the giant carved Buddhist sculptures and bizarrely colored tapestries and paintings all showing universal conflicts.

Where the hell was everyone?

She walked faster and then heard something in the distance.

Voices.

She slowed to a stop and strained her ears to pick up anything of importance. She frowned. They weren't speaking English.

She listened closely.

Annja frowned. Someone was speaking Chinese. Did that mean they were on the wrong side of the border? And if that was the case, then Annja was in serious trouble.

She stalked farther ahead, keeping the sword tucked behind her back to avoid its gleam giving her away. She stayed in the recesses of the shadows and hugged the wall farthest away from the torch brackets.

Annja could hear them more clearly now. They seemed to be arguing. And one of the voices sounded familiar.

Guge?

She waited and then almost gasped when she saw Guge stalking away from someone dressed in combat fatigues. A lone red star appeared on his shoulder epaulets.

Chinese military.

Here?

But this was supposed to be a sacred land far removed from the outside world. How was it possible that the Chinese were here? And if they were, why so? What was their purpose?

What did the people of Shangri-La have that would interest the Chinese military so much? She sighed. Maybe the geothermal theory was right. Maybe the Chinese wanted free energy to run part of their country. Already the global economy had hit China hard. Thousands of laborers had been laid off from shuttered factories reliant on American consumerism.

And with so many people to take care of, energy costs might push the government to the brink of almost anything. If they couldn't keep their people happy, they'd have a serious revolt on their hands. And China couldn't afford bad will. Another Tiananmen Square incident would turn the world against them. And that would cost them billions upon billions of dollars.

So what was the alternative? Find Shangri-La and plunder its geothermal supply for Chinese use only?

Annja frowned. She really needed Mike.

And it wouldn't hurt to have Garin along, too.

She knew how much he would have loved to hear Annja say that to his face.

Fat chance of that happening.

Annja snuck down the corridor closer to where she'd heard the men speaking. She could feel the cold air now. How deep was she into the mountain? It almost felt as cold as it had back in the cave they'd been taken from.

Guge strode away from the Chinese soldier, leaving him behind. He seemed to be intently watching something through a pane of glass. But what? And where had Guge gone?

Annja decided she couldn't worry about him right now. She needed to see what the soldier was looking at. Perhaps it would clear up this mess.

But how was she going to get close enough to do it?

She could just run him through with the sword, of course. But, despite her apprehension at the appearance of the Chinese military here, so far they hadn't done anything to warrant murder.

Annja might even be the one breaking the law if she was on sovereign Chinese territory. She could just imagine the scope of the international incident if she attacked the solider for doing nothing other than peering through some glass.

Still, she needed—wanted—to look and see what he was

watching. She regarded the soldier. He was armed with a pistol on his right side, but otherwise, there didn't seem to be another weapon about. Annja figured him for an officer. They were the ones who normally wore sidearms.

Annja returned her sword to the otherwhere and then flexed her muscles. She would sneak up and take him down with a choke hold. She'd been practicing some of them at the traditional jujitsu school that had recently opened in Manhattan. But this form of jujitsu wasn't like the mixed martial arts silliness. This was authentic jujitsu from Japan, with holds and chokes designed to immediately incapacitate or kill an opponent.

Annja stole down the corridor toward the solider. She prayed he wouldn't turn around and see her.

She drew closer.

And then she immediately leaped up and onto his back, wrapping her left arm around his windpipe and using her right arm to tighten the hold. She positioned her head down at the base of his skull.

The soldier's instant reaction was to snap his head back, trying to head butt Annja in the face to make her release him. When that didn't work, his right hand scrambled for his pistol.

But Annja twisted him off his feet and brought him down to the ground. She could feel his strength waning already as he convulsed once, twice and then went still.

Annja kept the hold on for a few seconds longer and then released him. She checked his pulse and breathing. Both of them seemed fine. The soldier would recover in a few minutes.

But it didn't give Annja much time.

She rose and looked through the glass.

"Tuk?"

He sat there on the stone floor in almost complete darkness. What the hell was Tuk doing in there?

Annja searched, trying to see if there was a button she could punch so she could speak to Tuk. She found one and keyed it. "Tuk? Can you hear me?"

She saw him scramble to his feet. "Annja? Is that you?"

"Yeah, what the hell is going on around here? Why are you in this…whatever it is?"

"I asked Guge how to cross over and then he pointed me to this doorway. My phone started to ring and then he pushed me through here. I don't know what's going on!"

Annja looked around but saw no way to free him. "I can't see how this cell works. Is there a door in there?"

"None that I can see. Annja, what is this all about?"

"I'm not sure. But I'll get some answers. Do you know this place is deserted out here? I saw your father speaking Chinese to a soldier."

"They want to know where Mike is. And who Garin is. I didn't tell them anything."

"Not much to tell," Annja said with a grunt. "I don't know where Mike is and trying to explain who Garin is would take a very long time."

She kept looking for a release button or panel or something that would free Tuk but she saw nothing. What kind of place was this?

She looked back inside. Tuk was right up against the Plexiglas and he looked scared. "Annja, I don't think that's my real father."

"I'm starting to think that, too."

"I can't see you, by the way. This glass is one-way."

"All right. I'm trying to get you out, but there doesn't seem to be any way to trip the door release."

"If there even is a door," Tuk said. "I can't see anything

in here to tell you where it might be. The four walls appear completely solid."

Annja frowned. "Well, there's got to be a release somewhere. Just hang on."

"Garin was trying to reach me when I was put inside. Find my phone and maybe you can guide him here."

Annja shook her head. "I have no idea how I'd even do that, Tuk. I'm not sure where we are anymore. If I even knew at all."

"We've got to be somewhere close to the mountain we stayed in. They couldn't take us too far, could they?"

"There's no telling how strong that gas was they used on us. We could be in Brazil now and not know it."

Tuk sighed. "You're right."

"I'm going to keep searching, but you just—"

Annja felt her legs kicked out from under her. She crashed to the ground and nearly snapped her head against the stone floor.

"Annja?"

She rolled, ignoring Tuk's voice, and concentrating on the Chinese soldier who had a quicker recovery time than she'd given him credit for.

As she rolled she saw the pistol in his hand and immediately lashed out her leg, knocking the firearm out of his grasp. It skittered away across the stones. He watched it for a second, determined it was too far away to go after and then glanced back at Annja with a grin on his face.

"So, the mighty Annja Creed makes her appearance at last."

Annja groaned. "I've been here all day. It's not my fault you're late to the game."

He whipped out a knife and the blade caught the flickering torchlight. "It will be my pleasure to kill you," he said.

Annja blinked and had her sword out in the next instant.

The soldier's eyes went wide with awe. "So, it is true."

"What is?"

"The sword. The mystical sword we've heard rumors of."

Annja slashed at him. How had they heard of the sword? As far as Annja knew she'd managed to keep its existence secret from all but a few individuals over the years. And now this Chinese soldier was telling her that he knew of it?

"What have you heard?"

The soldier ducked and came back at Annja with a stabbing shot aimed at her heart. Annja deflected the blow and the soldier caught her with another quick kick that scraped Annja's shin and sent pain echoing through her body.

"You've been in too many battles for your enemies not to notice the sword's existence, Annja. And not all of your enemies died as you thought. It's funny what people tell you when you help them live for vengeance."

"Vengeance?"

The soldier cut back at her. "How do you control the sword? Where does it come from?"

"If you don't know, why should I tell you?"

He smiled. "Because I'm not going to kill you, Annja. I'm going to disable you and then torture you until you tell me every last secret of that blade."

"You think so?" Annja cut down at him again but he managed to vault out of the way. Whoever the solider was, he'd been extremely well trained in hand-to-hand combat.

"I know so. You can hold out for a little while, but eventually you will cry and weep with joy when you tell me what I want to know. When I'm done with you, you will give me the sword."

Annja smiled. "I'll give you the sword right now."

The soldier stopped. "You will?"

Annja plunged the blade directly at him so fast, the soldier had no time to react and the blade stabbed through his fatigues and directly into his heart. Blood spurted out, coating the floor. The air was thick with the smell of copper and death.

Annja yanked her blade back out and let the soldier slide down to the floor, his eyes already wide-open and unfocused as he died.

"You should be careful what you wish for," she said.

26

Annja turned back to the window. "Sorry about that, Tuk."

"What happened? I can't see a thing in this place but I heard you fighting."

"We were momentarily interrupted." Annja cast a quick glance at the dead solider and the rapidly expanding pool of blood spreading out from his corpse. "I don't think it will happen again."

"You killed him?"

"I had no choice."

Tuk stayed silent for a moment. "Well, now you most certainly have to figure out how to free me. If you've killed one of their people—whoever they are—then they will hold me responsible for his death."

Annja shook her head. "How could you kill him if you were inside this cell? They can't blame you for it."

"All the same, I'd rather take my chances with you."

Annja searched the dead soldier's pockets and found nothing to indicate how the cell operated. She patted him down and didn't even find an identification card. Annja frowned. There were no tags of any type except for one red star on his epaulets.

She stood and walked over to the other wall, but again, could find nothing to indicate how the stone walls operated. As far as Annja could see, they were set perfectly flush with the other part of the corridor.

Tuk was trapped.

"I can't find anything," she said to Tuk.

"There's got to be a way. Some kind of trip switch. When I was pushed inside, the wall slammed shut quickly. There's got to be an activation button," he said.

Annja turned her attention away from the walls of the cell to the area behind her. She had to take care not to slip in the soldier's blood. But her heart thundered and she knew that if she didn't find the trip switch soon, she'd have a lot of company to worry about.

Finally, on the third time around the walls, she found a shallow depression painted exactly to match the color of the stone walls. She pressed into the depression and heard the rumbling sound of walls sliding away.

Turning, she saw Tuk standing there looking relived. He rushed over to her and smiled. "Thank you!"

Annja nodded. "We don't have any time. We've got to get out of here and figure out what happened to Mike."

"We need to get my phone back, too," Tuk said. "It's critical that we find a way to get Garin here. He can help us."

Annja nodded. "Much as I hate to admit it, I'm sure he can. But how are we going to do that. Didn't you say that Guge took it?"

"Yes. He told me that for me to cross back over, I couldn't have any technology with me."

"Probably just a con to get you to give up the phone."

"I know that now."

Annja indicated the corridor running off to their right side. "He went that way after he and the soldier had a few choice words."

Tuk looked down the darkened hallway. "I suppose we should go that way, too, huh?"

"As much as I'd rather get the hell out of here, yes, we need to go in that direction," she said.

"What about Mike?"

Annja shook her head. "I don't know what to do about Mike. As far as I know he's on his own somewhere. Right now our priority is to get the phone, get Mike and then figure out a way to get some help to get out. This place is no longer a paradise. And I have serious doubt as to whether it ever was."

"Meaning what?"

"Meaning this whole thing feels staged."

"For whose benefit?"

Annja frowned. "Mine, yours, who knows? Whatever it's for, it's not anything good."

Tuk nodded. "All right, Annja. I'm with you. Let's go."

Annja summoned her sword from the otherwhere and they stole down the hallway. Annja would have liked to dispose of the soldier's body properly but there was no time. And they would have had to clean the blood off the floor, anyway—a nearly impossible task given the little time they had. They would have to take a chance that there were too few people around to notice the body for a while.

Something told Annja it wouldn't happen that way but there were no other options.

Ahead of them, the corridor forked and Annja frowned. She wanted to cover both hallways at once, but she'd only just reunited with Tuk. And splitting their forces didn't seem prudent at this point.

"Which way?" she muttered.

Tuk sighed. "Left?"

Annja nodded. "Left, it is."

The hallway descended and the air grew starkly colder. Annja's breath appeared in front of her face. Just where were they? Annja wondered. Behind her, she heard Tuk's teeth chattering. She glanced back and put a finger to her lips. "Keep the noise down, Tuk. You'd be surprised what people can hear in the darkness," she whispered.

Tuk clamped a hand over his mouth and they traveled on. Annja's sword lit the hallway for a small area around them, reflecting the flickering torches up ahead.

The floor started to slope back up and then Annja stopped.

She could hear voices.

Tuk had stopped immediately, keenly aware of Annja's movements, as she suspected he would be given his past as a tracker. Annja crept up inch by inch and heard more voices.

"Mandarin," Tuk whispered.

Is this entire thing some type of Chinese operation? she wondered. And, if so, how high up did it go? All the way to Beijing?

She took a calming breath and moved forward a few more feet. The torches ahead seemed to bracket a doorway carved out of the tunnel. Annja wanted to see what was beyond that doorway.

More soldiers?

The shadowy figure she'd fought before?

Guge?

She frowned. She couldn't just burst into the room, although it was tempting. Not being able to see what lay beyond was a problem. She didn't know if she could get that close without alerting them to her presence.

She felt Tuk nudge her from behind. She turned and saw

him gesturing to himself. Annja frowned and then understood. Tuk wanted to do the recon.

She raised her eyebrows. Are you sure?

He nodded. He could do it.

Annja moved out of his way and watched as the little man crept soundlessly up the corridor toward the twin torches. Fortunately, because the torches were in front of him, they cast Tuk's shadow behind.

The little spy moved easily and quickly and Annja almost thought at one point that he had become part of the wall. It was easy to see why Tuk's skills had been so highly valued by the intelligence services of so many countries.

He must have some stories, Annja thought.

She looked back down the corridor and then up at Tuk. At any second, they might be discovered. Annja kept a firm hand on her sword and then watched as Tuk reached the periphery of the doorway, sank down on his knees and, ever so slowly, peered around the corner.

Don't stay too long, Annja thought. Just get a glimpse of the room and then come on back.

The little man seemed to know exactly how much time he had and retreated back down the corridor toward Annja quickly and silently. He motioned for her to follow him back into the darkness and there he squatted. Annja crouched next to him and whispered, "What did you see?"

Tuk cupped his hand to Annja's ear and replied. "Guge is in there. He's not dressed like my father anymore."

"How is he dressed?"

"Military fatigues."

"Chinese?"

"I don't think so."

"What else?"

"There are several soldiers in there. They're all armed with automatic weapons. And there's one other person in there, as well."

"Who?"

Tuk frowned. "Hsu Xiao."

Annja sighed. So the assassin was involved in this somehow. But what did Guge have to do with this and why were they connected?

"How should we play this?" Tuk asked.

"We need your phone, right?"

"Yes."

"And Guge has it, so we need to get it back from him. The sooner we can call in the cavalry, the better."

"You mean Garin."

Annja nodded. "I'd settle for a Boy Scout troop if I thought it would help. But yes, Garin should be brought in here if possible."

Tuk nodded. "All right, then. Let's go get the phone."

Annja stopped him. "How many soldiers?"

"Four."

Annja frowned. Six to two. Not good odds. Especially since Tuk was unarmed and they were facing automatic weapons and a top-drawer assassin. Taking the room down would be a challenge even if Tuk had a weapon. But going in there without one was virtually suicidal.

"Stay here," she said.

Tuk frowned. "I'm going with you."

Annja shook her head. "I understand that you want to come with me, but you can't. You don't have a weapon, and the instant the bullets start flying I won't be able to protect you. Those soldiers will turn you into Swiss cheese if they get even half a chance."

"Don't I have any say in this?"

"No. I rescued you back there, so you owe me, right?"

"I suppose."

"Then do as I say."

Tuk held her arm. "Annja, that assassin—Hsu Xiao—she's not going to be easy to kill."

Annja shrugged. "They never are."

Tuk released her arm. "Just be careful."

"As much as I can."

Annja crept back up the corridor. She could sense Tuk watching her from behind and hoped he would be all right. She didn't like the idea of leaving him alone in the corridor, but it was better than if he came with her.

She paused outside of the room and checked her position. Inside an animated conversation continued.

Wish I knew what they were saying, Annja thought.

She gripped her sword and looked into the blade. Her own reflection stared back at her and she smiled in spite of herself. Here we go again, she thought.

She took several deep breaths, flushing her system with an abundance of oxygen. Adrenaline dripped into her veins and Annja's heart thundered again, ticking into overdrive in preparation for battle.

There was movement in the room. Some part of Annja's gut told her that, in a few short seconds, the hallway was going to become very crowded.

It was time.

She gripped the sword.

Took a final breath.

She burst into the room, her blade already starting to spin and cut and slash as if under its own control.

Annja was merely along for the ride.

27

As Annja entered the room, she took in everything at once.

One soldier on the right, hands off his weapon.

Two soldiers at ten o'clock chatting with each other in low voices.

Guge talking with a woman draped in black who must be Hsu Xiao.

One other soldier sitting at a computer terminal.

A door on the far side of the room, closest to Hsu Xiao.

At Annja's sudden appearance, the room stopped moving. The soldier on her right managed to react first. He gripped his AK-47 and started to thumb the safety off.

Annja's sword cleaved the barrel of the assault rifle and she backhanded the blade up and into the soldier himself. He screeched as the blade tore into his upper torso, slicing deep into his thorax, dumping blood on the room's stone floor. The soldier twisted in agony and then dropped.

Annja kept moving, making a beeline for the pair of soldiers. The one farthest away brought his gun up and then

Annja heard the terrible sound of fully automatic gunfire. The AK-47 selector switch went from safety to full auto and the soldier seemed content to spray the room full of lead.

Annja twisted and leaped through the air, arcing high and then coming straight down at the soldier who was attempting to jerk the barrel of the gun around toward her even as he still unleashed the hail of lead.

Annja sliced down, landed and then cut back up under the gun, driving the sword into the young soldier's lower torso, severing entrails and disemboweling him. Blood sprayed everywhere and the soldier died on his feet.

A bullet ricocheted off the wall nearby as the second soldier abandoned his rifle and went for his pistol instead. Annja flicked her hands up, catching the soldier's gripping hand just beneath the wrist. The soldier screamed as he looked down at the bloody stump of where his hand had been seconds before.

Annja spun and cut the man across the throat. He dropped to the floor and lay still.

She caught movement out of the corner of her eye and saw the door open and close quickly. Her consciousness registered that Hsu Xiao had fled the room.

Annja wondered why, but she couldn't afford to get distracted.

As Guge backed up against the wall and attempted to get out of the door, only to find it locked from the other side, the soldier seated behind the computer terminal stood and rushed Annja headlong.

He caught her around the waist and they went down in a tangled heap. Annja lost the sword and then felt the impact of a punch in her face that seemed like it had jarred a few teeth loose. The soldier brought his head down hard against the cheekbone and Annja grunted from the impact.

She pushed him off and tried to get the better position, but his legs came up instinctively, using them against her hips so she couldn't get any purchase.

Another punch caught her in the chest and she gasped as the wind burst out of her lungs. Annja heaved and dropped an elbow onto the soldier's sternum again and again. She drove the elbow hard against the xyphoid process and heard the small bone break. She let her full weight come down and then she felt the soldier stiffen before going slack as Annja drove the fragmented bone into his heart.

She rolled off the soldier just in time to see Guge going for her sword. Annja concentrated and the sword vanished. Guge stood there mouth agape.

"It was just there!"

Annja rolled off the dead soldier and then grabbed Guge by his lapels and tossed him against the stone wall. "It's time you and I had a talk," she said.

Guge shook his head. "Where did the sword go?"

Annja paused and suddenly the sword was back in her hands. She held the gleaming edge of the blade under Guge's chin, pressed it ever so slightly against the skin on his neck and allowed it to bite just enough to score a thin line of blood.

Guge gasped at the pain. Annja pressed her point once more and then removed the sword.

"There. Now that I've got your attention…" Her voice trailed off.

Guge felt his neck and saw that his hand came away bloody. "You wouldn't kill me, Annja."

Annja smiled. "What makes you think that?"

"Because we saved you. We rescued you. If it hadn't been for us, you would have died in that cave."

Annja shook her head. "We were fine."

"Mike would have died."

Annja paused. "Perhaps you're right. But don't assume that

means I won't kill you. Especially since it looks like you've been lying this entire time."

"It couldn't be helped."

"The lying?"

"Of course! How else could we accomplish this?"

Annja shook her head. "All right, Guge, or whatever the hell your name is. You and I are going to have a nice long talk. And you're going to sit down and explain every last bit of what's happening to me."

She shoved Guge into the chair behind the keyboard. Annja studied the screen but it was filled with complex Chinese characters that she couldn't understand. She pointed at the screen. "Does that have something to do with what's going on here?"

Guge glanced at it. "Of course."

"And you understand what that says?"

Guge smiled.

Annja frowned. "Don't even think about lying to me again. I heard you speaking Chinese right before I freed Tuk."

Guge looked shocked. "You freed Tuk?"

"Of course I freed him."

"How did you figure out how to do that?"

Annja sighed. "I'm not a moron, Guge. I discovered the depression in the wall. The button disguised as a part of the rock. It took a little time, but I found it."

"You must be proud of yourself."

"I'm not proud of anything. What I am is beside myself with wanting to know what exactly is happening in this place. And you're going to tell me."

"Hello, Father."

Annja looked up as Tuk entered the room. "Tuk, maybe you should stay outside."

He shook his head and looked at Annja's handiwork. "It smells a lot worse than I thought it would."

"Stick around a while and it gets much, much worse."

Tuk knelt and removed a pistol from one of the dead soldiers. He slid the magazine out and made sure there were still bullets inside. Then he slapped it home again and racked the slide.

"Tuk, tell Annja to let me go."

Tuk looked up and almost laughed. "I'll do no such thing. I'm as anxious to hear your answers to her questions as she is."

"But I'm your father, Tuk. You can't do this."

Tuk rushed over before Annja could stop him and placed the barrel of the pistol on Guge's left knee. In an instant, there was a muffled pop and Guge screamed as if he'd been set on fire.

"Tuk!" Annja said.

But Tuk had already placed the gun barrel next to Guge's other knee. "Are you my father? Tell me!"

"No! No! I'm not your father!" Guge's face was pale and sweat boiled off his head, running down into his neckline. He clutched at his wounded knee and Annja could see that the bullet had effectively hobbled him.

"Tuk, let me do this, will you?" she said.

Tuk stepped clear of Guge. "Well, at least we've established that he is not my father."

Annja glanced at him. "What if he had been?"

"Then I would apologize for crippling him. But that's a moot point now, don't you think?"

"Apparently."

Annja looked at Guge, who was moaning and clutching his injured leg. "As you can see, Tuk is pretty upset with you for lying to him."

Guge rocked back and forth, cradling his leg. "My God, it hurts."

"It's going to hurt even worse if you don't start telling us the things we want to know."

Guge looked up at Annja. "You don't understand what's happening here. You don't get it."

"That's our point. You're going to tell us now."

Guge shook his head. "She'll kill me if I tell you."

Annja leaned in closer to his face. "And I will kill you right now if you don't tell me exactly what I want to know."

Guge looked at her and then nodded. "Very well."

Annja leaned back. "First, where is Tuk's cell phone?"

Guge gestured at his right leg. "In my pocket. The cargo pocket halfway down my leg."

Annja felt around for the phone and found it. She handed it to Tuk. "Call Garin. Find out where he is and if he's any closer to finding a way to get through to this place."

Guge laughed. "He'll never find it. It's too well hidden."

"You thought I wouldn't be able to find the cell release for Tuk and I found that easily enough. Garin's a pretty sharp guy. Something tells me he might just figure it out even without our help."

Guge looked up at her with hatred in his eyes. "You'll never leave here alive, Annja Creed."

"Why not?"

"Because this is all about you. From the top down, this is all about you. Don't you get it yet?"

Tuk looked up from the phone. "I'm not getting a signal."

Annja frowned. "I thought that thing could get reception anywhere?"

"I thought so, too. But the walls of this place must be extra thick or something."

Guge laughed. "They are thick. You're inside a mountain. You won't be able to reach anyone by phone while you're in here."

"We need to get outside," Annja said. "You'll get a signal out there."

Guge moaned. "Good luck. The alarm will have already gone out and you'll get a very different reception than the one we staged for you this evening."

"What do you mean this is all about me?" Annja asked.

Guge shrugged. "Well, in truth, it's not *all* about you. You are just one person, after all. But combined with everything else, we thought this would be a very nice way to take care of some loose ends all at once."

Annja regarded him for a moment. She needed Garin here. But Tuk couldn't reach Garin unless they went outside. But outside meant more troops presumably. At the very least, Hsu Xiao would be waiting for them.

Annja made a decision and dragged Guge to his feet. Instantly, as weight came down on his hobbled knee, he shrieked. "I can't walk on that leg."

Tuk looked up. "What are you doing?"

"We need him to keep us alive. If we go outside without him, they'll shoot us. At least with Guge, we can keep them from unleashing a lead shower on us."

"You think that will work?"

Annja shrugged. "I really don't know. But I'm running out of ideas."

Guge leaned against the computer desk and gritted his teeth. "They won't hesitate to kill me to get to you, Annja. You've got too high a bounty on your head for them to even blink at taking me out."

Annja shoved him toward the doorway. "Well, maybe we'll just go outside and test that theory of yours, shall we?"

"It will be the last thing you do."

"I can't tell you how many times I've heard that before," Annja said. She looked at Tuk. "Better grab some firepower.

Bring both rifles and the magazines. This thing could get really hot."

Tuk bent and scooped up the guns and ammunition. When he was ready he nodded at Annja.

Annja shoved Guge forward. "All right, old man, let's get going. Something tells me things are about to get interesting. And you can spill all your secrets on the way out."

28

Annja led Guge into the corridor and back down the slope toward the opening near the prison cell. As they walked, Tuk brought up the rear, with the two AKs dangling from his shoulders.

"Tell me what this is about," Annja demanded.

"It's about you dying, Annja Creed," Guge said. "We've known about you for a while now."

"Who has known about me?"

"Various members of the Chinese intelligence service."

"You mean the whole of the Beijing political apparatus?"

Guge laughed. "Of course not. Only a few select members. Can you imagine how crazy it would look if we went with this before the premier and his people? They would have had us all shot for suggesting that there is a woman with a magical sword roaming the planet who should be assassinated."

Annja felt a small measure of relief. "But why target me? I wasn't harming anyone."

"It's not necessary that you were harming anyone," Guge said, still gritting his teeth to ward off the pain he must have been feeling from the bullet hole in his leg. "It's that you have access to that sword."

"So the sword signed my death warrant?"

"Something like that. It was felt that it would be good to try to acquire the sword for our own usage."

"Whose usage?"

"Our leader."

Annja stopped and shoved Guge against the wall. "Who is it? Is it Hsu Xiao or whatever her name is—the woman in the room with you?"

Guge laughed. "Hsu Xiao is nothing but a tool of our leader. She does what she's told to do, which just so happens to be dealing death. But she is nothing close to the brains of this operation."

Annja then shoved him forward again. "Keep moving."

Guge stumbled along. "It's quite funny, actually. Seeing you so concerned about this. I mean, we heard that you didn't even like having the sword. That you'd rather go back to the normal life that you had before the sword came into your possession."

"Whoever you guys are, you've certainly had some highly placed sources near my life for some time."

Guge smiled. "Our leader doesn't do anything halfway. She's special that way."

"She?"

"Does that surprise you? That a woman would be in charge?"

"No. I'm all for equal rights. Madmen, madwomen, what's the difference?" Annja shrugged. "It always come down to the same thing. How soon can I get rid of them?"

Guge shook his head. "You won't be getting rid of her so easily. She knows all about you. She's taken the time to study you intimately, in fact. She's watched you over the years and has learned how to play you. This setup alone should prove that as fact to you."

"What setup?"

Guge laughed. "Our little fantasy world here. It's something, isn't it? This make-believe Shangri-La? That's the irony. We're making believe that it's a make-believe place. The irony is so thick you could cut it."

They'd reached the prison cell and Guge blanched when he saw the dead Chinese soldier on the floor. "You certainly don't seem to mind all the killing you unleash, do you?"

"I do what's necessary. I choked him out first but then he came to and attacked me. I had no choice but to kill him," Annja said.

"Is that what you tell yourself before the demons come at night?"

"Shut up."

Guge shrugged. "You're more like her than you know. I think that's why she went through all this trouble just to catch you and get the sword."

Annja pulled him to a stop again and got up close to his face. "Listen to me, pal. Even if I wanted to hand over the sword, it wouldn't leave. It's not something I can give away. And if I could, I sure as hell wouldn't pass it to some nutball organization that wants to use it for evil purposes."

"Actually, it's our theory that you *can* give it away."

Annja stopped. "What?"

Guge nodded. "We think you can give it away. Of course, there happens to be a downside."

"Yeah, and what's that?"

"You have to do it as you're dying. Sort of like a final wish or command, if you will. If you manifest the sword as you are dying, then we believe you can hand it over to whomever you want."

"That's some theory."

Guge giggled. "Well, you know what they say about theories—all it takes is one damned fool to try it out to see if it works."

Tuk swept past Annja. "Can we shut him up now? I'm getting tired of listening to him babble on and on."

Annja ignored Tuk. "And just how are they going to test that theory?"

"I already told you, Annja. You'll have to die."

Annja backhanded him across the face and shoved him forward down the corridor again. She could still see the flickering torches stuck in their brackets down the hall where the giant Buddhist sculptures sat.

"So all of this is nothing but a joke, huh? This must have cost millions to create. Millions of dollars just to get to me?"

Guge shook his head. "Don't be so egotistical. She's not a fool. Diverting that kind of money would have raised alarm bells and gotten us all killed. No, we needed a place that already existed. So we found it."

"This already existed?"

"Sure."

"Why is this the first anyone has known about it?"

Guge shrugged. "Isn't it obvious? You found this place because we wanted you to find it. It's all part of the plan, sweetheart."

Annja kneed him in the back. "I'm not your sweetheart. Now keep moving before I do get tired of you and let you rot here."

Guge stopped. "Wait—before we go any farther, I've got to tell you something."

"Yeah? What's that?"

"When you meet our leader—because you will soon—you should know one thing about her."

Annja sighed. "What?"

Guge licked his lips. "She—"

The sharp retort of gunfire exploded down the hallway and three rounds tore a line across Guge's chest, stitching him from one side to the other. His body spasmed and jerked from the impact.

Annja spun even as Tuk started shouting for her to take cover. Automatic gunfire sounded and Annja bent forward, looking for any type of protection.

"Annja! You okay?"

Annja crawled and found a shallow depression by one of the torch brackets. She reached up and pulled the torch out of the bracket and then smashed it to the ground. Darkness enveloped the hallway.

"I'm all right. You got some cover?" she called to Tuk.

"By the nearest statue."

Sporadic gunfire broke out and bullets zipped past in the air. Annja kept her head down.

She heard closer gunfire and saw that Tuk was firing back at the end of the hallway.

"Are they down there?"

"I think so. I caught a glimpse of movement right before the whole place exploded."

"I need a gun. Slide one over to me," she said.

Annja heard the skid of metal on stone and reached out as the assault rifle slid into her grasp. She picked it up and ratcheted the slide. Annja set the selector switch down past full auto to semi and brought the butt to her shoulder.

Along the hallway, she caught a muzzle flash and ducked back as a bullet plowed through the air near her head.

Tuk was firing back in two-round bursts. Annja caught a glimpse of him in the muzzle flash and then fired off a few rounds herself. She had to let them at least know they were armed.

She wasn't going down without a fight.

Thoughts swam through her head as she looked for any target of opportunity. Just how much of what Guge had just told her was truth? He'd already admitted to lying. Would he still be lying to her up until the moment he died?

And if he wasn't lying, then could this whole thing really be just one big plot to get Annja's sword?

Who would go to those lengths?

"Reloading!" Tuk called out.

Annja brought her weapon up and squeezed off several rounds. She realized they would have to conserve ammunition. Once they ran out, that was it. They'd be defenseless.

"Tuk! We can't stay here!" she shouted.

"I know. What do you want to do?"

Annja squeezed off two more rounds. "I'm coming to you. Cover me."

"Go!" he said.

Tuk started firing and Annja crept out of her space, then ran toward the shadowy figure of the little man. Annja slid in next to him and felt the reassuring presence of the giant statue. It was more than enough to provide them with exceptional cover from the bullets coming at them.

Tuk paused. "You all right?"

Annja nodded. "Who taught you how to shoot?"

Tuk grinned. "Reruns of *The A-Team*. For a while that was the only American programming we got over here."

Annja wanted to laugh. But they had problems to face. "We can't stay here. They'll wait us out and then come and kill us."

"Agreed, but what do we do? If we try to go at them, they'll simply mow us down."

Annja chewed her lip. "I'm open to ideas."

"I'm not sure I have any." Tuk frowned. "Hold that thought." He ducked back around the edge of the statue and let out a burst of gunfire. From somewhere down the hallway, Annja heard a scream and then silence. Tuk must have tagged one of them trying to sneak up.

"It got too quiet out there," he said a moment later.

"Do you think Guge was telling the truth? That this is a plot to get my sword?"

"I don't understand your sword, Annja," Tuk said. "But it certainly seems a bit too massive an operation to go through just for a sword. But then again, I'm not some insane despot. So who knows?"

Annja nodded. "We'll have to make a run for it. Somehow we have to get out of here. You've got to call Garin and we need an escape plan."

"I'm with you. I'm just not crazy about the whole running right at the gunfire thing."

"We may not have a choice."

"Annja Creed!" The loud voice echoed down the hallway. The gunfire had ceased. Annja was puzzled. "Who the hell is that?"

Tuk frowned. "It sounds like my so-called mother," he said.

"Annja Creed!"

"Vanya?" Annja looked at Tuk. "I think you're right."

"What does she want?" he asked.

Annja shrugged. "One way to find out." She crawled around Tuk but stayed behind cover. "I'm here!" she shouted.

"I'm giving you exactly two minutes to come out of there with your hands raised and no firearms in your possession."

"Why on earth would I agree to something like that?" Annja called out. "You'll just kill us."

"You don't have any choice. You're trapped. Sooner or later we will simply come down there and kill you. I'm offering you an alternative to that."

"Doesn't sound like it. You'll just kill us one way or the other."

"You, perhaps. But if you come out right now, I'll spare the little man."

Tuk frowned. "Who's she calling 'little'?"

"No way," Annja said. "We might die but at least we'll take a lot of your men with us when we go. Maybe even you."

Vanya's laughter echoed through the hallway. "No, I don't think you'll take any more of my people. In fact, I'm sure of it. You come out in two minutes or you will die there, trapped beneath tons of rubble."

"What do you mean by that?"

"The entire room is wired with explosives," Vanya said. "And I'm holding the detonator in my hand right now."

29

Annja looked at Tuk. "You think that's true?"

"Stay here." Tuk crawled away into the darkness and Annja sat very still for a lonely minute until Tuk's face reappeared next to her. "She's not lying. This place has more high explosives than a military facility. If she triggers that detonator, then the whole room will cave in. And I don't know if she has the corridor behind us wired, as well."

"Can we snip the wires?" Annja asked.

Tuk shrugged. "Maybe, but I wouldn't know the first thing about how to do it. The other thing is the number of boxes with blinking lights leads me to believe that she's got them remotely keyed to explode rather than a hardwire landline kind of thing."

"Great." Annja slumped back against the wall. "This is not the news I was hoping to hear."

Tuk nodded. "Sorry."

"It's not your fault." She glanced back around the statue

and saw a single figure illuminated down at the far end of the hallway. "I wonder if I could hit her from this distance?"

"Probably not. And if you grazed her, she'd just blow the whole room up. I think it's likely that the only thing they're interested in right now is getting you out into the open."

"Presumably to kill me."

"Presumably," Tuk said. "But who knows, they may have something else in store for you, as well."

Annja smiled. "Like what? Long bouts of extreme torture? Sounds like a great time."

"I'm not sure what our alternatives are right now," Tuk said. "And we're out of time."

On cue, Vanya's voice found them again. "Time's up, Annja. I am going to turn that room into a pile of smoldering rubble. Come out now."

Annja shook her head. There had to be something she could do. But what? There was no way she'd be able to disarm all the explosives, and if Vanya saw them retreating back the way they'd come, she'd just detonate the bombs. Annja and Tuk were about to be buried alive under a mountain.

"This sucks," Annja said. "I don't suppose your phone is getting any reception now that we're closer to the outside?"

Tuk's face lit up. "Let me try." He yanked the cell phone out of his pocket and examined the screen. "I see one bar on the reception. I suppose it's worth a shot."

"Anything is," Annja said.

Tuk pressed the number two and waited. Finally, Annja saw him sit up. "It's ringing."

"Give it to me," she said. She grabbed the phone as Garin's voice could be heard.

"Tuk!"

"It's Annja, Garin."

"Where the hell are you?"

"I don't have any time so shut up and listen. This place,

wherever we are, is a staged thing. Some rogue Chinese military woman who calls herself Vanya is running the show here and the aim seems to be to get me to give them the sword."

"Annja, that's impossible, isn't it? You can't give anyone the sword. The sword chose you. And when you're gone, presumably the sword will choose someone else."

"Well, I'm having a hard time selling them on that notion. Apparently, they think that as I'm dying I can command the sword to pass to the person of my choosing."

"Rubbish!" Garin said, although he didn't sound entirely convinced.

"I don't have any time. Tuk and I are in a room that is wired with explosives. This Vanya woman is telling me that unless I come out and give myself up, she's going to blow it up."

"You go out there and they'll kill you."

"I know."

"I need more time, Annja. I can't find you guys. I've been searching everywhere and there's no trace."

"All I've got is that this place—wherever we are—was previously constructed. It's got to be something big. And somehow it's tropical here, and that means it would take a lot of heat coming from something. I don't have any idea what, but it's a sure bet it would have taken millions to make this place."

"That's it?"

"I'm not exactly having a great day, Garin."

"I'll do what I can and get there as fast as possible."

"I hope so."

Annja closed the phone and handed it back to Tuk. "So much for that."

"Did he say they were close?"

"He's got no idea where we are."

"This is your last warning, Annja!"

Annja frowned. "I'm getting tired of hearing her voice. She sounds incredibly egotistical."

"She's probably quite happy about the situation she's got you in," Tuk said.

"No doubt."

Tuk laid a hand on her arm. "I don't mind dying, Annja Creed. I've had a good life. I've done a lot given the paltry amount I started with. So if you say we're going to rush them, then that is exactly what I will do."

Annja smiled. "I don't doubt it, my friend. But I don't think that's the best way to play this."

"Then how."

Annja took a deep breath and told Tuk what she wanted him to do. When she was finished, Tuk looked up at her. "Are you sure?"

"Yes. It's the best option we have right now."

"It's not really much of an option, if you ask me."

"I'm all out of ideas," Annja said.

"As am I."

Annja nodded. "All right, then. Are you ready for this?"

Tuk took a deep breath and closed his eyes. "I think I am."

A second later a single shot rang out. Then Annja got to her feet very calmly and shouted down the hallway.

"I'm coming out!"

"What was that gunshot we heard?"

Annja was fifty yards from the entrance. But she could see Vanya standing there surrounded by a squad of Chinese soldiers all aiming their weapons at Annja.

"You left me no choice."

"What are you talking about?"

"You said you wouldn't kill Tuk, but neither of us believed you. And he preferred to die by my hand than by yours. So I did him the favor."

Vanya regarded Annja as she approached. "But you didn't choose suicide? How interesting."

"I don't think I'd be able to do it," Annja said. "I guess I just know my limitations."

Vanya nodded. "Come out here into the light so I can see you properly. And if you try any tricks, my men are under orders to fill your body full of bullets. You'll die standing up."

"That wouldn't really help your end game, would it?"

"To get your sword?" Vanya grinned. "I suppose it wouldn't, but I'm not a fool, either. I'd rather you were dead than give you even half a second to unleash that blade against us."

Annja cleared the remaining distance and came out into the light, blinking her way back to full vision. As she did so, she caught a glimpse of movement and suddenly Hsu Xiao had her claws positioned around Annja's throat.

"Move and you will die," she whispered.

"Nice welcoming committee you have here," Annja said.

Vanya nodded at her men. "Go and check on the little man. I want his body dragged out here so I can make sure there's nothing going on."

Annja shrugged. "I told you he's dead."

Vanya smiled. "And if he's not, he soon will be."

"And to think I almost believed your promise that he would be set free. I'm glad we chose the route we did."

"You're a fool, Annja. And you had no options left. In fact, from the moment you set off on this particular adventure, your destiny has been predetermined. At every step of the way, you were channeled exactly in the direction I wished you to go."

"I'm so glad I've lived up to your expectations," Annja said. "So, assuming you're able to get my sword, who does it go to? You?"

Vanya smiled. "Oh, that I were young enough to wield it with the elegance such a blade deserves. But no, regrettably my advanced age makes that a little foolish for me to attempt."

"So, who, then? Crazy Nails here? She'll bust them gripping the hilt."

"Hsu Xiao will inherit the blade. Yes."

Annja shook her head. "I don't know if that's such a great idea. You see, the sword doesn't like being told what to do. Trust me. I've tried several times."

"Quiet," Hsu Xiao said.

Vanya laughed. "I marvel at your humor. I really do. You know, when the rumors reached us about an American woman who had this mystical sword, at first we suspected it was some type of American intelligence operation. That maybe they had created a super soldier that they could unleash at will."

"Nope. Just little old me."

"Imagine my delight when I learned everything I could about you. Your past is one shrouded in secrecy for some reason and yet I was able to trace your lineage back hundreds of years."

Annja frowned. "You're lying."

"Oh, no, I'm not. I wanted to know everything about you. It was my way of trying to decipher why the sword chose you as its wielder. I thought that if I could uncover what made you so special, then the questions about the sword would reveal themselves to me."

"Interesting theory. Too bad you don't know squat. No one does. I'm an orphan and I've got no family."

Vanya shook her head. "You disappoint me, Annja. I really expected that you would have taken the time to search deeper and go back further than a mere generation. The answers to your past lie in full view, provided you know where to look."

"And why do I find this so difficult to believe? I don't know, could it be because you're a liar?"

Vanya frowned. "I'm not lying. You must think me a fool if you believe I would undertake something of this magnitude and not do my homework. Whatever you may think about me, Annja, know this. I am not lying when I tell you that I have learned every aspect of your past. Every family member who has passed his or her genetic material down through your bloodlines to make you what you are today. You are not a mere orphan. You are something wholly incredible. And yet, you fail to realize that, save for the sword being in your possession."

Annja felt her heart beating faster. Was Vanya telling the truth? If so, what answers did she have?

"So tell me something," she said, fighting to remain calm.

"About your past?" Vanya smiled. "Perhaps I will. Right before I kill you and Hsu Xiao takes the sword. At least then you will die with some measure of peace."

Vanya glanced down the corridor. "What is the holdup down there? Bring the body out!" she shouted.

Annja saw the two soldiers approaching. They were dragging a limp body behind them.

"What took you so long?" Vanya said.

"We couldn't find him at first. She must have shot him behind the statue on the far side of the room."

"You saw the bullet hole?"

"We couldn't see anything in the room. It's too dark," the first soldier said.

"There's a blood trail," the second soldier said. "And it's a lot of blood."

Vanya nodded and cleared her throat. "All right then. You've done well. Turn the body over so I can see him."

The soldiers turned the body over. Vanya looked and then

frowned. "He still looks alive to me. Put another bullet in his head to be sure."

Vanya looked at Annja. "After all, if he's truly dead, one more bullet won't make a difference now, will it?"

Annja shrugged. "I guess not. Shame he'll have to have a closed casket, though."

"I don't think anyone will really care about that. And why should they when we dump his body into the nearest gorge and be done with it?"

"Disrespecting the dead will come back to bite you," Annja said. "Trust me on that one."

"Trust you?" Vanya asked. "Why would I ever do a thing like that." She turned to the soldiers. "Shoot him again. Shoot him now."

30

One of the soldiers chambered a round in his weapon and, as he did so, Tuk came alive, suddenly kicking at the exposed knee of the soldier with the gun aimed at him. The gun went off and the round fired wild.

Annja jerked her shoulders up, knocking away Hsu Xiao's hands. Then she pivoted and drove two punches into the assassin's exposed sternum. Hsu Xiao recoiled and thrust her hands forward, but as she did so, Annja leaned back, just barely out of range of the slicing claws that would have surely severed her carotid artery.

Annja kicked up at the same time Hsu Xiao backflipped away and Annja's kick hit nothing. She summoned the sword in time to cut down the other solider who was aiming his gun at Tuk.

Annja's blade cut him through the shoulder and ripped a chunk of flesh out of his neck. He went down screaming.

Tuk grabbed the closest gun and aimed a volley of bullets

at Hsu Xiao, but the assassin twisted away. Annja saw her flick her wrist ever so gently.

"Tuk!"

The throwing spikes embedded themselves in Tuk's shoulder and upper chest. He went down clutching at the exposed pieces of steel.

Vanya grabbed a knife from a hidden sheath in her dress and came up behind Tuk, placing the point of the knife under his right ear. "Drop the sword, Annja. Drop it or he dies."

"You'll kill him, anyway," Annja said.

"I won't. I only want the sword. This man is inconsequential to me."

Tuk grimaced. "Don't listen to her, Annja! She won't stay true to her word. You know this."

Annja held the sword up in front of her. Hsu Xiao came back to stand beside Vanya. The look on her face made Annja's skin crawl.

"Let him go first," she said.

Vanya sniffed. "I'm not a fool, Annja."

"Neither am I. And you don't exactly have a good record of keeping your word. So we do this my way or no way. You let Tuk go. Once he's clear, then I'll surrender the sword. You tell him how to get out of here and he's gone. It's that simple."

"I can't tell him how to leave. He'll bring back help."

Annja shook her head. "We're out in the middle of nowhere. What help is going to come for us?"

Vanya's eyes narrowed and she had a whispered conversation with Hsu Xiao. Vanya nodded. "All right. I will tell him how to get out of here. Once he's gone, you turn yourself over to us."

Annja pointed at Hsu Xiao. "Crazy Nails stays here with us the entire time. Once Tuk has enough time to get away, then I'm yours. Not a moment before. You try anything at all, any kind of ambush, any funny business, and Tuk's death will be the least of your worries."

Vanya sighed. "Fine. You have my word." She pushed Tuk away from her. "But make it quick. I have a schedule to keep and, right now, I'm behind."

Annja leaned over Tuk and tugged the three spikes out of him while he gritted his teeth. "You going to be okay?" she asked.

He nodded. "Yes. I think so. None of them went too deep. Hurts like hell but I can endure it."

"Get clear of this place. You hear me? Get clear and don't stop to look back. You can bet as soon as they're done with me Hsu Xiao will be on your trail. She's going to want to make sure there are no witnesses. You understand?"

"I understand." He looked into Annja's eyes. "Thank you for doing this for me. I don't think I've ever had a friend like you."

Annja smiled. "Hey, you watched over me. This is the least I can do."

Tuk looked at her and nodded once. "All right, then."

Annja smiled. "All right."

Tuk turned to Vanya. "I'm ready to leave now."

Vanya sighed. "Fine, fine. Go back to the statue room and continue to where your cell was. Beyond the doorway is a false wall. Press it and a door will open to a small staircase. Travel up the staircase and you'll come to a trapdoor in the floor of the cave you and Annja were in when the yeti found you. That's your way home."

"A trapdoor in the floor of the cave? That was the big secret?" Annja said.

Vanya smiled. "No one ever checks the floor. All anyone thinks about is the wall having some type of contraption." Her eyes flamed. "Now go before I change my mind and have Hsu Xiao kill you all."

Annja gripped the sword. "That would be a grave mistake."

Vanya nodded at Tuk. "He gets ten minutes. No more. If he's not back on the other side by then, it will be his own fault."

Annja looked at Tuk. "Run and don't stop for anything. Understand?"

"I understand." He smiled. "Goodbye, Annja."

"Seeing you," she said.

Tuk dashed back into the temple corridor and vanished from view. Vanya calmly glanced at her watch and then back at Annja. "Ten minutes from now. Are we agreed on that?"

"Sure."

Hsu Xiao stayed stock-still. Annja could sense her desire to rush into the temple and strike Tuk down before he could get clear. "I think your dog wants off her leash," Annja said.

Vanya smiled. "She does. Very much so, in fact. But she's a good girl and she'll do what I say. Besides, there will be time enough for her to kill Tuk once we're done with you. Who knows, perhaps she'll even use your sword to do it."

"She'll have to get the sword away from me first," Annja said. "And the truth of the matter is, I don't think she'll be able to."

"I suppose Guge told you our theory?"

"He did."

Vanya shook her head. "He always did talk too much. I should have had him killed years ago."

"I'll tell you the same thing I told him," Annja said. "It's not going to work."

"How do you know?"

Annja shrugged. "Well, considering it's my sword now and I'm the one who's been living with it for years, I think I have a better insight into how the sword behaves than you do."

"That may be true for some things, but one might also

argue that you lack the perspective to see a possible means to separate the two of you."

Annja nodded. "I'll give you that. But what happens if this grand old theory of yours turns out to be one big mistake? What then? I'll be dead and you'll lose the only chance you have of getting the sword."

Vanya crossed her arms. "That's a chance we're willing to take."

"Wonderful," Annja said. "See, if I were you, I'd keep me alive and just try different ways to get the sword."

"You're too powerful to keep alive, Annja. Surely you must understand that. If you die giving us the sword or if you don't give us the sword, either way you will at least be dead and gone and no longer a threat."

"I find it difficult to believe that you consider me such a big danger to you or to your government."

Vanya sniffed. "What makes you think I give a damn about my government and all it stands for? Hasn't anyone ever told you that all disputes in the world boil down to the smallest common denominator? And that denominator is money and power. That's it. Show me any despot, any religious zealot, any tyrant—they all want the same things. Money and power make the world go around."

"And that's all you want?" Annja said.

Vanya checked her watch. "Five minutes, Annja. Five minutes to go."

"Answer the question. Is that why you've done everything here? So you can set yourself up as some sort of power mogul?"

Vanya sat on the low stone wall closest to them and stretched her arms. "I have existed in the inner circles of male dominance in China. As a woman, I've been told I'd never get anywhere of import and yet I rose to a position of great power within the intelligence service. And I've been able to keep an eye out for other promising women so I can help them along, school them in the ways in which we will take power, and then keep them by my side when I need them."

Annja glanced at Hsu Xiao. "I assume she's talking about you."

Hsu Xiao gave a curt nod.

Vanya laughed. "Hsu Xiao wants nothing more than to face you in mortal combat, Annja. Do you know that?"

"Well, I can respect that," Annja said. "At least she's not a coward like so many others who just want the fruit without doing any of the work."

"But I can't afford to lose her to that blade of yours. Not when I have so many plans for it."

"What kind of plans?"

"China's government needs some shaking up for one."

"You're going to rule China? Good luck."

Vanya shrugged. "Well, what would you have me do? Seize power from a nonnuclear power? What a waste that would be. Once Hsu Xiao has the sword, I shall be able to dispatch anyone who stands in my way."

"Seems to me you could do that now if you choose."

Vanya shook her head. "No. Hsu Xiao is incredibly powerful, yes. But with the sword, none shall be able to stand against her."

Annja frowned. "It's not a shield of invulnerability, you know. I can die just as easily with the sword as I can without it."

"Rubbish," Vanya said. "We know the sword grants you a much higher pain threshold and endurance."

"Yeah, it seems to. But it doesn't mean I can't die. If your friend Hsu Xiao here gets a face full of lead, no blade on earth is going to stop her from taking a ride down the River Styx."

Vanya smiled. "Perhaps. But with the sword, she will be much more potent than any of my enemies."

Annja grinned. "So that's it, isn't it. You've got a foe already who is too powerful. What's he got, someone even better than Hsu Xiao? Is that why you haven't moved on him yet?"

Vanya checked her watch. "You've got one minute, Annja."

Annja nodded. She glanced at the temple corridor and hoped that Tuk had made his way back to the cave. That he was on the phone with Garin right now, calling in the cavalry.

"So once you dispatch all your opponents, what then?" Annja asked.

"I will assume leadership of China and help guide her into the new millennium the way she should be. I'll be the new Jade Empress."

"Fruitcake, more likely. What makes you think that anyone will abide by you being the new ruler of China?"

"Because I will kill anyone who does not."

"And what about the rest of the world?"

"What about it?"

"I hardly think they're just going to roll over and say, 'Great,' when you come into power."

Vanya nodded. "That is true. I had been giving that some thought." She smiled. "A small demonstration of my power may be necessary to prove how serious I am."

"Small demonstration? Like what? You're going to wipe out Tibet?"

Vanya shook her head. "That's far too small scale for my liking. If I do that no one will even pay attention. No, I need something bigger. Something more along the lines of shock and awe."

Annja frowned as she realized what Vanya would target. "Taiwan."

Vanya shrugged. "It's been asking for it for years. They're such upstarts and it's really like a forgotten province, anyway. There's absolutely no way I could tolerate such dissent in my kingdom."

"Dual purpose," Annja said. "You show the rest of the world you mean business and you show your citizens their dissent won't be tolerated."

"I believe it's what we call a win-win," Vanya said. "And speaking of which, your final minute is now up."

"Is it?"

Vanya nodded. "Yes. It's time for you to lower your sword, Annja. You belong to me now."

31

Tuk raced along the corridor as fast as his legs, grinding like pistons beneath his body, would carry him. He made it back to the doorway and then found the secret exit to the spiral stone staircase leading up. The air bit at him; the cold temperatures were a distinct difference from the balmy weather he'd just enjoyed.

As he neared the top of the stairs, he looked up and saw the ceiling and what would be a trapdoor in the floor of the cave. It seemed perfectly flush and he supposed it would look exactly the same form the other side.

He reached up and undid the locking mechanism, a series of slide bolts that would discourage entry even if by some miracle the trapdoor was discovered.

Tuk braced himself on the stairs and shoved up at the trapdoor with all the strength he had. The weight was enormous and he soon realized that the trapdoor was actually made out of the stone of the mountain itself. For all intents and purposes, Tuk was trying to move a mountain to gain his freedom.

He glanced back down the staircase, half expecting to see the shadowy wisp of Hsu Xiao coming after him. Tuk had no illusions about whether he would live or die. His survival depended on gaining his freedom to call Garin.

Tuk shoved again, but the stone didn't budge. He took a huge breath and shoved once more, but the stone did not seem to want to give in the slightest. Tuk brought his arms back down and rested them for a moment.

He hadn't expected the weight to be so incredible.

He frowned and looked back up at the series of bolt locks. He counted them off and then to his horror saw that he'd missed two corner locking mechanisms that were of a different type than the simple slide bolts.

They weren't taking any chances with this door being discovered, he thought.

Tuk immediately focused his attention to the two locks. They looked like dead bolt locks, but with a simple turning mechanism. He twisted the first knob and heard the satisfying sound of the bolt sliding away with a solid thunk. He quickly did the same to the other lock and then brought his arms back down to rest again.

He'd never known that working overhead could so rapidly tax his arm muscles like this. He took a series of deep breaths and then launched himself right at the trapdoor, hoping that it would move.

He impacted and then he drove the door back and up.

A rush of cold air slapped him in the face and Tuk had an instant shiver. The wind swept in from the cave opening, but he was back.

Back on the other side.

He scrambled out of the staircase, but as he did, the little cell phone tumbled out of his pocket and fell over and over again back down the stairs, coming apart at the bottom. Tuk gasped as he saw the little phone split into two pieces.

"No!"

He scrambled down the stairs.

At the bottom of the stairs, he scooped up the components and then raced back up. Better to be on this side, and if Hsu Xiao's face suddenly appeared, at least he could slam the rock down on her head.

Tuk examined the components in his hand. Was the phone broken? Would it even work again if he was somehow able to put it back together?

He looked at the pieces and then frowned. There didn't appear to be anything broken. Perhaps it was just the battery that had come away.

He quickly slapped the battery back into place and then powered the phone up. For a few tense seconds he waited and then he nearly shouted with joy as the screen illuminated and Tuk saw that he had reception.

He pressed the number two. After about thirty seconds, the phone on the other end rang.

"Tuk?"

"Garin!"

"Where are you?"

"There's not much time. Annja's going to have to give up her sword if you don't hurry and get here."

"Tell me where you are."

"We're in the cave near the crash site. The place I told you where we found shelter. From the outside it looks like a small crack but you should be able to just fit inside."

"Tuk, we found that place. We searched it inside and out and couldn't find a thing. Are you sure that's the location?"

"It is! Listen to me! Once inside, there's a trapdoor in the floor of the cave that leads down a staircase and back over to the other side where we just were. But you've got to hurry."

"I've got the rotors turning now on the chopper. Hang in there. I should be there within twenty minutes."

"That will be twenty minutes too late! Annja made a deal to surrender if I was set free."

"Why on earth did she do that?"

Tuk sighed. "I don't know."

"Tuk, she can't surrender that sword. If she is able to give it away and it goes to someone villainous like these people seem to be, then the entire balance of good and evil in the universe will be thrown out of whack. She must not give up her sword. She's got to hold on to it at all costs!"

"But what am I supposed to do?"

"I don't know, but you've got to stall them somehow. I need time to get there."

"I'll do what I can," said Tuk. "But you've got to hurry."

He slapped the phone shut and paused on the floor of the cave. The last thing he wanted to do was go anywhere near Hsu Xiao or Vanya again. But Annja had given herself up so that Tuk could go free and reach Garin.

If she hadn't done that, he thought, I never would have gotten this far in the first place.

He started back down the staircase. Behind him, he left the trapdoor open. He hoped Garin and his men would find it as soon as they got to the cave.

If there was enough time.

As he descended, Tuk knew what he needed. He crept back down the hallway toward his prison cell and then turned at the juncture where he and Annja had crept up to the control room.

The smell that assailed his nostrils made him want to vomit, but he choked the surging bile in his throat and forced himself to enter the room. He lifted another AK from one of the dead guards and then took three extra magazines of ammunition.

As he was about to leave, he saw the computer terminal
ashing a message. Tuk frowned. He didn't read or understand
Chinese, but looked, anyway. Red flashing icons that made
im wonder what was going on.

Were they simply alarms going off? Did they know that
he trapdoor was now open to the other side?

Tuk used the mouse to try to navigate around and then
tarted clicking just for the sake of it.

The screen changed to something that looked like a chart
with varying levels fluctuating. He saw what he presumed
were danger points and noticed the fluctuating levels all hov-
red close to those marks.

"What is this place?" His voice echoed around the
oom.

"You don't want to know."

Tuk spun around and saw himself staring down the barrel
f a pistol.

"Mike?"

Mike didn't look very friendly. "Already embracing your
ue identity, I see. What did Vanya promise you if you came
ver to her side?"

Tuk shook his head. "Mike, I'm not with them. I swear
o you. I just escaped and called for some help. But Annja's
ack there with Vanya and her assassin, Hsu Xiao. And she's
iving herself up to them."

Mike looked shocked. "She's what?"

"It's true. They want the sword, so—"

"What sword?"

Tuk stopped. "Maybe I should let Annja explain that to
ou."

Mike thumbed the hammer back on the pistol. "Maybe
ou'd better explain it to me right now."

Tuk sighed. "Annja's got some sword she can conjure out
f thin air. I don't know what it is or what it does but it makes

her some kind of ferocious warrior. Vanya staged this enti
thing as a trap to lure Annja here."

Mike sneered. "This whole place is a trap."

"What do you mean by that?"

Mike nodded at the terminal. "You see those graphics?"

"Yes. But what do they say? I don't understand Chinese

"I do," Mike said. "And this whole installation is going
blow if we don't find a way to shut it down."

"Installation?"

Mike nodded. "It's a fraud. The whole thing. We're in
nuclear waste holding plant. The Chinese government bui
this Shangri-La facility over the waste plant. The immens
heat from the processing facility is the reason there's a tropic
landscape here when right on the other side of the mountai
it's arctic conditions."

Tuk shook his head. "How could they hide a place lik
this?"

"I don't know. We've heard rumors for years that the
were doing this but we never knew how to find them. Eve
our satellites couldn't pick them up. One theory is that th
atmospheric conditions surrounding the Himalayas make
almost impossible to see everything in detail."

Tuk looked at Mike. "Are you all right?"

"I'm fine. It just took me a while to discover what wa
really going on here. For a moment, I thought we might real
have stumbled upon the actual Shangri-La. But this is mos
definitely not it."

"So, what do we do now?" Tuk nodded at the pistol. "I
there any way you can put that thing down? It's making m
quite nervous."

Mike smiled. "You sure I can trust you, Tuk? I wouldn
want to have to kill you, but I will, if necessary."

Tuk held up his hands. "My plan was to come here, grab
weapon and then find Annja. She's going to need the help."

"So why did you stop?"

Tuk pointed at the computer. "This thing. The red flashing screen drew my attention."

"As well it should have," Mike said. "This place is entering critical condition."

Tuk frowned. "So, if that's the case, then where is everyone? What happened to all of the people who were here with us yesterday? The parade, the feast? Where are they?"

Mike frowned. "You don't want to know."

"I most certainly do."

Mike sighed. "Get out of the way." He pushed Tuk aside and sat down at the computer. He tapped a few keys on the keyboard and then shoved his chair back away from the screen and pointed.

"There."

Tuk leaned in close, at first unsure of what he was seeing. But then he recoiled in abject horror as the truth became apparent. Scores of bodies piled atop one another lay in a huge pile somewhere.

"Is that what I think it is?"

Mike nodded. "She killed them all. Witnesses, I guess. She kept just enough of her closest, trusted men alive to help her see it through. And then she had all of the bodies disposed of down in those waste tanks underneath this place."

"She dumped them into the nuclear waste?"

"Yeah, the installation is well-shielded—hence, the reason we can stay here and not get infected. But she dumped the bodies down into those tanks for another reason altogether."

"What reason is that?"

Mike's frown only deepened. "Isn't it obvious? Those corpses will upset the balance of the facility. It wasn't designed to handle bodies, only sludge. Those hundreds of dead bodies have thrown off the installation and it's now approaching a disaster."

"You mean?"

Mike nodded. "This entire installation is going to explode in about thirty minutes."

32

Annja smiled at Vanya. "You know as well as I do that I cannot give up and surrender myself to you."

Vanya frowned. "You're breaking your word? You promised you would surrender if we let the little man go."

"Yeah," Annja said. "I lied about that."

"Then you leave me no choice," Vanya said. She gave a scarcely perceptible nod and Hsu Xiao immediately stepped forward.

Annja had the sword in her hand a split second later. She grinned at Vanya. "Are you sure you're comfortable with the idea of me killing your best and brightest here? Once I'm done with her, there's not going to be anyone left who will be able to stop me from killing you."

Vanya sniffed. "As if it will even get to that point. Hsu Xiao will make quick work of you. I trained her myself."

Annja frowned. Did that mean that Vanya was an elite killer as well?

There was no time to think about it because Hsu Xiao

didn't wait. She launched her offensive immediately, rushing in at Annja, trying to close down the distance between them.

Annja knew the tactic. With her sword, her optimal range was greater than Hsu Xiao's. The Chinese assassin needed to be in close to wreak havoc with her claws. And Annja needed to keep her at least six feet away.

Annja dodged the initial attack and cut backward as Hsu Xiao's body shot past. But Hsu Xiao knew what to expect and used her claws to block the sword cut. Then she swept the sword blade up and slashed in at Annja's exposed right shoulder.

Annja felt the claws cut deep into her flesh and grunted back the pain. She felt hot blood cascade down her shoulder. A little deeper, she thought, and those damned claws would have severed muscle.

And that's exactly what Hsu Xiao seemed to be hoping for. If she could take away Annja's ability to hold the sword she wouldn't have to worry about it.

Hsu Xiao launched a series of kicks at Annja's midsection.

Annja stabbed straight out and the point of her sword nicked a line along Hsu Xiao's lead leg, ripping the assassin's pants and shredding the top of her thigh. Hsu Xiao let no sound escape her lips and retracted her leg out of range.

But Annja pressed the attack; coming up and lifting the blade high into the air, she chopped down at Hsu Xiao. She saw the momentary spark of fear in her eyes and Annja drove in hard, cutting down.

But then Hsu Xiao rolled away, got to her feet and flicked her wrist. Annja snapped her blade up in front of her, slicing this way and that. She heard the half dozen clangs as the throwing spikes all met the flat of her sword and fell harmlessly to the ground.

Hsu Xiao leaped onto the stone wall and waited for Annja to circle. Then she jumped from the wall to the ground, rolled and came up under Annja's blade as she attempted to cut down. Hsu Xiao raked her claws across Annja's midsection.

Annja felt like a razor had just passed over her belly and she let out a gasping breath. Hsu Xiao rolled away again, just out of range. Annja put one hand against her stomach and it came away wet, red and sticky.

She's going to slice me apart, Annja thought. She dropped back and waited for Hsu Xiao to come at her again. But Hsu Xiao only smiled. There was no way she was going to be fooled that easily.

Annja circled the assassin slowly. Vanya had backed away—content, it seemed, to let her prodigy take care of business. Annja felt herself growing annoyed with Vanya all the more because of it.

Annja's foot rolled over one of the throwing spikes and she knelt down to grab it. At that moment Hsu Xiao unleashed another volley and one of the spikes embedded itself in the top of Annja's left foot.

Annja grunted. She reached down and yanked it free. A line of blood spilled from the hand-forged iron spike and splattered the ground. She threw the spike back at Hsu Xiao, who just reached out and plucked the spike from the air with hardly any effort. Annja was amazed and frustrated. She's playing with me. Treating me like I'm only a nuisance.

Annja waved her on. "Come on. Let's do this."

Hsu Xiao danced closer and Annja studied her footwork. It seemed like a combination of a drunken style of Kung fu that Annja had once seen combined with a rare version known as Dragon. Her drunken style seemed to be the setup and then Hsu Xiao used the Dragon techniques to close the deal.

Annja knew that Dragon was a truly formidable system.

If Hsu Xiao knew Dragon and knew it well, then Annja was definitely going to have her work cut out for her.

Hsu Xiao smiled and her teeth showed for the first time. "I am enjoying myself, Annja Creed. Are you?"

"Having a great time, thanks. How's that cut on your leg?"

"It is nothing of consequence. But you seem a great deal more troubled by the three injuries you are suffering from."

"Hardly worth my time," Annja said.

"She will destroy you, Annja Creed," Vanya said. "But it doesn't have to be this way."

"Oh? What's my alternative? Give up and die, anyway? No, thanks. I'll go down fighting if I go down at all," Annja said.

Vanya called off Hsu Xiao and the Chinese assassin backed away, always obedient to her mistress.

"Put your sword down, Annja."

Annja frowned. "No way."

Vanya stepped closer. "It doesn't have to be the end. Perhaps there is another alternative I didn't consider until just a moment ago."

"And what's that?"

"Join us."

Annja heard the words and broke into a grin. Her shoulder throbbed and the injury to her foot ached. Her stomach didn't feel much better. "Join you? For what? So we can all rule China together?"

"If you wish, yes."

"I've already got a country to call my own," Annja said. "And I don't feel the need to take over another nation."

"I'm giving you the opportunity to be a part of something amazing here. Use your sword for us and what we wish to accomplish."

Annja shook her head. "More delusions of grandeur. There's no way your plan is going to work, Vanya."

"It will work. And you'll see that if you join us. I promise to make you a very wealthy woman. Imagine that. Why, you could even afford to get the very best medical care for your friend Mike."

Annja frowned. "Mike's condition is inoperable. The doctors said they couldn't operate for fear of Mike dying."

"Western doctors claim that," Vanya said. "You would be amazed at the advances that we've made in China. A lot can happen when you don't have to answer to a huge government bureaucracy."

"Yeah, what kind of advances?"

"The ability to slow the growth of cancer cells. In some cases, we have been able to permanently arrest cancer growth. If Mike's tumor never gets any larger, he'll be able to live out the full measure of his life in peace and prosperity. And you can make that happen."

"Just by joining my sword to your cause."

"Exactly."

"And what would I have to do?"

"Remove any troubling people from our path. Much the way Hsu Xiao does for me right now."

"So you'd have two assassins instead of just one."

"The more, the merrier. Isn't that the saying in the West? With two of you by my side, we can truly take over anything that we want. And we can rule the world as a triumvirate of power."

"I told you before that the sword doesn't make me invulnerable. You've seen yourself how Hsu Xiao was able to injure me."

"She is able to do that because she is the best at what she does. I trained her to be that way." Vanya shrugged. "But others? They would fall before you like the long grass before a harvesting scythe."

"How poetic," Annja said.

Vanya smiled. "Stow your sarcasm and join our cause, Annja. We have room in our organization for another powerful woman. Join us and see what the future may hold for you."

Annja looked at Hsu Xiao. "And how do you feel about that job offer? You cool with Vanya offering me a place next to you?"

Hsu Xiao smiled. "Whatever my mistress wishes, it is my duty to obey."

Annja frowned. "That's not exactly the warm and cuddly answer I was looking for."

Vanya waved her hand. "Hsu Xiao will do whatever she is told. If that means accepting you into our ranks, then she will do so gladly. I did not raise her to dispute my desires."

Annja nodded. "See? That's kind of what I have a problem with. Maybe it's an authority-figure thing. I just can't seem to get over this idea that following orders blindly without engaging the ol' noggin is a good way to go for me."

"It's the only way for you now, Annja. If you don't agree, then you're leaving me no choice in the matter."

"Oh, I don't know about that," Annja said. "Seems to me that Hsu Xiao and I could team up and just cut you out of the picture entirely. Why share something three ways when a partnership is so much more powerful?"

Vanya shook her head. "You're crazy. Hsu Xiao would never throw her loyalty from me to you. I've done too much to help her. I've taken care of her family—all of her brothers and sisters enjoy a wonderful standard of living in China's new economy thanks to me and the power I exert on their behalf."

"And I'm sure she's grateful for that," Annja said. "But

really, no one likes being under anyone's control for too long, do they?"

If Hsu Xiao had any reaction to Annja's words, she wasn't showing it. Vanya glanced at her and then back at Annja. "You're wasting your time."

"Am I?"

"Hsu Xiao will not turn against me. We've come too far together to throw it all away just because you talk a good game."

"Seems to me I'm talking the same game you're trying on me," Annja said. "So who's to say who is better at it than the other."

Vanya looked at her watch. "We're running out of time, Annja. I need your decision."

"What's the hurry?"

Vanya smiled. "Let's just say that my power grab relies on something very big and terrible happening so as to start the cracks of unbalance back in Beijing."

"What the hell does that mean? What have you got planned?"

"You no doubt realized that there were very few people still around last night?"

Annja nodded. The place had seemed deserted. "Yeah, I noticed all right. What about it?"

"They're all dead."

"You killed them?"

Vanya shrugged. "They had fulfilled their requirements. Each one of them was contracted to work for a certain amount of time and then they were to be released in order to go back to China proper."

"All that to sell us on the idea that this was Shangri-La?"

"You still don't get it, do you? This isn't Shangri-La at all. I told you that."

"I know that. So what is it?"

Vanya stared at Annja. "Are you going to join us or not?"

"I don't think so."

Vanya frowned. "That's truly unfortunate. Very well, then. You leave me no choice but to finish what we've already started." She glanced at Hsu Xiao. "Kill her."

33

Tuk led Mike back down the corridor. Each man was armed and Tuk felt better about Annja's chances now that there was definitely help on the way. And hopefully, Garin would find his way into the cave and bring reinforcements.

But he knew they couldn't rely on that. Tuk raced along the corridor and then drew up short as they approached the room with the giant Buddha statues. He pointed out the explosives to Mike.

"Vanya has the entire room wired to go up at any time. It's what she used to get us to come out into the open."

Mike inspected one of the bundles and shook his head. "This is serious military-grade stuff. How did she ever get her hands on it?"

"I don't know, but Vanya is certainly not all that she seemed last night. She's much more dangerous."

"I'd guess so, judging from how these were positioned. She had to have help from the military in order to do this."

Tuk pointed. "We're almost there."

Mike nodded. "All right, how do we play this? Straight-up assault or do we hold back and make them think we're more than we actually are?"

Tuk frowned. "I don't know much about military tactics, Mike. Your guess is as good as mine, if not better."

Mike checked the status of his gun and nodded. "I say we just shoot them both and be done with it. No sense letting them hang around any longer than necessary. And considering what Vanya is trying to pull here, it'd be better if she was dead."

Tuk held up his hand. "Wait, shouldn't we keep her alive so she can stop the installation from exploding?"

"I don't know if she even could," Mike said. "Short of fishing those bodies out of the treatment facility—which would mean exposing ourselves to immense radiation—there's nothing we can do. And when the treatment facility goes, everything else is going boom. This is the last place we want to be."

"I see." Tuk frowned. The idea of a nuclear waste treatment plant exploding made his heart ache with the thought of what would happen to the surrounding region.

"I know what you're thinking," Mike said. "But it can't be helped. If we had a team who knew what they were doing and had equipment, then maybe. But we don't have any of that. And we'd die trying."

"I know," Tuk said. "It just seems like it's going to result in a terrible environmental catastrophe."

"It will," Mike said. "Absolutely. But we need to find Annja and then get the hell out of here or no one is going to be alive to care about the cleanup. And we have to ensure this kind of thing doesn't happen again somewhere else."

"All right." Tuk made sure his weapon was ready. "Let's go and get this done before my heart goes soft."

"Just remember what Vanya's plans will do to your country and use that to fire yourself up," Mike said.

Tuk nodded. "I will."

Mike stepped forward and then stopped. His voice was a harsh whisper. "Tuk."

"Yes?"

"Don't…move…a muscle.…"

"What's the matter?"

Mike pointed at the floor. "There's a trip wire and my foot is resting against it. If I move anything, this whole room will blow up."

"Are you sure?"

"Trust me. Look at the wire and tell me what's it's connected to. And hurry up about it."

Tuk carefully followed the line of almost invisible wire across the room to where a large bundle of explosives sat wedged in with a claymore mine. He read the lettering *front toward enemy* and then retreated back to Mike. He'd seen them before in his intelligence days.

"Claymore and an explosive package wedged in with it. The claymore is American."

Mike frowned. "It is?"

"Yes."

Mike nodded. "All right. I'm going to ease my foot back. But before that, I want you to go into the corridor we just came from. If I do this wrong, one of us has to stay alive and help Annja. Can you do that for me?"

"Sure. I just can't figure out where this could have come from. I ran down this corridor only a few minutes ago in order to get to the trapdoor."

"It might well have been meant for you," Mike said. "Vanya's men could have easily laid this trap in the hope you would hit it on the way out. Did Vanya seem almost willing to let you go earlier?"

Tuk frowned. "Actually, yes. She didn't put up nearly the fight I thought she would have."

"That was probably part of her plan. With you blown up, the surprise would have enabled her to overpower Annja. Only the way you ran or walked must have carried you right over the trip wire."

"So I missed being blown up by luck?"

Mike smiled. "I could use a little bit of that luck right now, my friend." He nodded at the corridor. "Now go and let me get this done. One way or another I've got to get free of this or else we'll die."

Tuk retreated to the corridor and wedged himself in against the wall. If Mike was unsuccessful, the explosion would no doubt cause some serious damage to the facility, especially given how much explosive was in that room.

Tuk shook his head. How had he managed to get himself wrapped up in all of this, anyway? All because some stranger named Garin had hired him to look after Annja and make sure she was safe.

Tuk sighed. He didn't think he was doing such a wonderful job.

Mike's face appeared around the corner. "Okay. I think we're all set now."

Tuk let out a breath. "Thank God. I thought the entire room was going to explode if you didn't manage it."

Mike nodded. "I got myself free and then replaced the pin in the claymore so it wouldn't go off. I did a quick check of the room to make sure there weren't any other surprises lying in wait for us. It's clear."

"They probably didn't have time to set anything else up," Tuk said. "And then Annja killed them, anyway."

Mike smiled. "She did, did she?"

"Oh, yes."

"She's a marvel that one." Mike gestured with his gun.

"Now come on, let's get out there and see what we can do to help."

Tuk led them back to the statue room and then toward the doorway. He could hear voices. And he gestured for Mike to get low.

Tuk looked out and saw Annja with her sword in her hands. Across from her stood Hsu Xiao and Vanya. Tuk frowned and looked at Mike.

"Annja's injured."

Mike nodded. "I can see that. But how badly? Do you think she can still fight?"

"You've known her longer than I have," Tuk said. "But if I had to place a bet on whether or not she could, I'd definitely say yes."

"So would I."

"Look at Hsu Xiao's leg. It seems like Annja managed to get something in on her, too."

Mike chuckled quietly. "Good, that means she'll be easier to take care of."

Tuk looked at him. "I don't know. She scares the hell out of me."

"Nothing to it. She'll die as fast as anyone else once she's got enough bullets in her."

"Well, do you mind shooting her, then? I'd rather not have to deal with her."

"Fine."

Tuk leaned back and looked at Mike. "Are you ready?"

"Time's ticking, my friend. Let's get this done."

Tuk got to his feet and readied the assault rifle. Everything was set to go and he flicked the selector switch to semiautomatic. Perhaps, he thought, if he got the drop on Vanya quickly, he wouldn't have to shoot her. That would be a good thing. Maybe there was a way to stop the facility from exploding. Maybe Vanya knew what to do.

"Tuk!"

Tuk looked at Mike. "Sorry."

"Come on, man, let's get this done. I'll go after Hsu Xiao and you take down Vanya. Don't stop for anything until we have them both down and dead, okay?"

"Mike, what if Vanya knows how to stop the facility from exploding?"

Mike shook his head. "Listen to me, Tuk. That treatment installation is not going to tolerate the infusion of scores of bodies. It wasn't designed for that. Vanya knows that and that's exactly why she's done what she's done. She wants this place to blow up. She's got no interest in saving it, and if you think she does, you're wrong." Mike leaned closer to Tuk. "Now listen to me. I know this isn't what you signed on for, but we've got to do something here or else we're all going to die. Do you understand?"

Tuk nodded. "Yes. I understand. Sorry."

"I'm not a killer, either, Tuk. This isn't something that I do every day. But at the same time, I know that these people are responsible for unleashing some truly bad stuff on the world. And I think it's fairly safe to say that they deserve to be punished for their crimes."

"I agree with you, Mike. It's just that, in all my years of work, I was always beyond that type of work. And I never minded being there."

"I'm afraid there's no one else who can do what needs to happen. Two targets. Two of us. It's the only way to make sure we're successful," Mike said.

"All right. I'm sorry."

"Forget about it. Let's just get this done."

Tuk moved up and took his position. "I'm ready."

Mike brought his gun up into his shoulder and sighted. "On three, okay?"

"Okay."

"One…"

Tuk took a series of deep breaths. His heart pounded against the inside of his chest like a hammer going a thousand times a minute.

"Two…"

Tuk steeled himself. He let his trigger finger come to rest just outside the trigger guard. He brought the weapon up so he had a clear sight picture. He settled the sights on Vanya. Mike was right, he decided. Better to finish this and then get the hell out of here. No sense dying for no reason. And at least they'd be able to tell the world what happened so it didn't occur again elsewhere.

Tuk heard Mike start to say "three" but the word died on his lips as they suddenly heard another voice from somewhere behind them.

"Stop."

It wasn't a shout. It just a simple command. Softly spoken. But most definitely a stern command.

Tuk frowned. Something about that voice reminded him of someone.

"Put your weapons down or we will shoot you where you stand."

"Mike?" Tuk whispered.

"Better do it, Tuk. There's a gun barrel aimed at the base of my skull right now and I don't think these guys are fooling around."

Tuk lowered his weapon.

"Very good. Now both of you turn around very slowly. If either of you moves too fast, we will shoot."

Tuk gulped and then turned around slowly. Mike was in front of him but he heard the surprise in Mike's voice. "You."

"Move aside so I can see the man behind you, Mike."

Mike moved and Tuk was startled. Three men stood there.

He recognized the sneering smiles on the faces of Burton and Kurtz.

And in the middle, his eyes hidden behind a huge pair of sunglasses, stood Mr. Tsing. He held a silenced pistol in his hand and gestured with it. "Step away from the doorway. We wouldn't want to interrupt the party out there too soon, now, would we?"

Mike kept his hands up. "What's this all about Tsing?"

"It's about me making sure my investment doesn't run away from me."

"I'm not running."

Tsing smiled. "I must say you've done a fantastic job, Mike. I almost didn't expect you to find it. But you have. And I'm ready to take it over for my very own paradise."

Mike shook his head. "I don't think you want to do that. This isn't Shangri-La at all. It's a nuclear waste treatment facility disguised by the Chinese as a palatial tropical paradise."

Tsing laughed. "Don't be ridiculous."

"I wish I was," Mike said. "But the woman who created this entire mess is standing right outside. You can ask her if you want."

Tsing eyed Mike but then frowned as he cast a glance at the doorway. "Perhaps I shall."

34

"No one move, please."

Annja looked up and gasped as she heard the voice and saw Mr. Tsing striding out into the open pavilion. He paused, looked up at the sky and seemed vaguely annoyed that the sun was out. But he merely adjusted his sunglasses and kept walking ahead.

Behind him came Tuk and—Mike! Annja was so happy she almost forgot to stay still. Then, behind Tuk and Mike came Tsing's two thugs, Burton and Kurtz. The automatic rifles they held didn't look the least bit friendly.

Tsing directed Tuk and Mike to one side with Kurtz covering them. He pointed at Burton. "Stand there and cover everyone else, but particularly that woman there." This last statement was directed at Hsu Xiao. "If anyone moves, kill her first."

Hsu Xiao glared at Tsing. "I should have killed you when I had the chance."

"Well, it's not as though you didn't try, my dear. After

all, that nasty little neurotoxin you put into my glass was something else. A rather spectacular little drug, isn't it? Unfortunately, I simply wasn't feeling like a drink, so after you left, I happened to pour it into the large fern in the study. Imagine my surprise when the damned thing toppled and the fronds turned that horrible shade of brown." He smiled. "Of course, by then you had already departed Katmandu for places unknown—until now. We scoured the city for you, of course. I'm not exactly fond of people who attempt to poison me or want to see me shuffle off this mortal coil."

Hsu Xiao said nothing, but Annja could feel the rage boiling off of her. She wanted to strike Tsing down badly.

Vanya must have sensed it, too, because she spoke quietly in Chinese to Hsu Xiao and it seemed to at least calm her down somewhat.

Tsing smiled. "I'll bet you really want to have a go at me right now, don't you? Make up for all those times I forced myself upon you? All the times you pleaded with me to stop because you didn't like it and yet I continued because you were mine. All along it must have driven you nearly insane not being able to slice my throat with those ridiculous claws of yours. But you hadn't yet found out what you needed to know, had you?"

Hsu Xiao said nothing.

Tsing leaned back against the wall and looked at Annja. "You see, Hsu Xiao was a plant. She needed to know if I had any inkling of the location of this place. It was imperative that I didn't, I imagine. Because if I'd caught wind of it, then I could have taken steps to ensure that that woman there," he said, pointing at Vanya, "couldn't go ahead with her plans."

Annja frowned. "Who exactly are you, Mr. Tsing?"

He smiled. "Me? Why I'm just your average Chinese businessman. That's all. Nothing special about me."

Vanya laughed. "Tsing is the resident Chinese intelligence

officer in charge of Katmandu. It is his responsibility to report on anything that might jeopardize the control China has over Tibet from this side of the border."

Tsing shook his head. "Now, really, was it necessary for you to reveal that? I believe she might have readily accepted my other explanation, but no, you had to go and ruin it. Shame."

"Annja is too intelligent to fall for that. It doesn't add up."

Tsing smiled at Annja. "Vanya is upset because I report to the very people she would no doubt like to see removed from power—one way or another. And it was my job to make sure our operations in the area were safe and secure."

He got up and walked around the courtyard. "Imagine my surprise then when the transponder we placed in the plane we loaned you and Mike started beeping from this very mountain. It was rather amusing, actually. And at first I couldn't believe it. You see, I'd seen the map, and never imagined that you would find yourselves here rather than the exact position the map shows. But then the universe is a strange thing, isn't it? And whether through luck or serendipity or what have you, you and Mike, and even that little insignificant speck of dust called Tuk, found yourselves here."

Annja saw fury blaze across Tuk's face. "So you knew about this place all along?" she said.

Tsing smiled. "My dear, I helped build this place. It is here because I sought out a special location for us to conceal our activities. My government has been trying for years to come up with a means to dispose of certain elements of our waste. We've tried all manner of things and nothing worked."

"So you came here."

"We came here because one of our scientists had an idea. He said that if we could harness the heat from the waste and channel is just so, we could turn a frozen landscape into a

tropical one. The idea was a bit far-fetched but it grew to gain
support and the initiative was launched several years back.
It was incredibly expensive, but we thought that if we could
achieve what the scientist claimed, we might actually turn
this place into a tourist spot."

Annja's eyebrows shot up as high as they could go. "You
wanted to bring tourists here atop a pile of nuclear waste?"

Tsing chuckled. "I know it seems crazy, but really, look
around. You must admit that we did an amazing job building
it. Look at the incredible statues. It's all very convincing. Even
the fruit trees are real."

Annja felt sick at the thought that she'd eaten a peach off
of one of them a few hours earlier. Had she known about the
nuclear waste, she wouldn't have been so gung-ho about it.

"The resort itself was obviously designed to help us offset
our costs. And we know the lure of Shangri-La is so great
that we would draw hundreds of thousands every year. But
more importantly, if the technology worked, then we would
put it to use in certain other areas of our country where the
land is less than optimal for growing food."

"This is insane," Annja said. "You're talking about burying
nuclear waste in the ground. The consequences of that would
kill thousands."

Tsing held up his hand. "We are talking about burying
it, but not in the manner you think. We don't just lob it into
the soil and be done with it. We plant a containment device
that not only keeps the waste from leeching into the soil,
but generates and channels incredible energy. Not only does
it enable the soil to grow warmer and more fertile, but we
also thought we could siphon off some of the heat to help
keep houses warm. Imagine being free of oil as a heating
implement. The savings alone in that field would amount to
hundreds of billions of dollars."

"But at what cost?" Annja asked.

Tsing smiled. "Well, there's the rub, as you say. We needed workers to handle it and we would have to swear them to secrecy. The only way to guarantee that they didn't talk was to move their families in with them. They would work at the resort and reap the benefits." He frowned. "Speaking of which, where are all the workers?"

Mike cleared his throat. "They're dead."

Tsing whirled around. "Dead? How? There were six hundred of them stationed here. How did they die?"

Mike pointed at Vanya. "She had them killed."

Tsing turned back on Vanya. "You did what? You killed them? My God, woman, there were children with their parents here."

"Not any longer," Mike said. "Every last one of them is dead."

Tsing leaned against the wall. "This is not the news I was hoping to hear."

Annja shook her head. "I find it difficult believing you, considering you threw a man off the roof the night you met with us."

Tsing sniffed. "The man I threw off the roof worked for Vanya. He was attempting to penetrate my organization. When we got wind of it, we took care of matters. He was an interloper. Had I known I had not one but two such traitors in my midst, I surely would have delighted in taking care of the other one, as well."

Hsu Xiao spit in his direction. "You make me sick."

Tsing laughed. "Yes, well, funny how times change, isn't it? I can vividly recall you begging me to do some very interesting things to you. Such a dirty little girl you are." He glanced at Vanya. "I'm assuming you trained her to do that, as well."

Vanya glared at him. "Hsu Xiao is a true servant of the people."

"Yes, whatever. Save me the propaganda speeches, would you? It seems to me that we have a few things to clear up here."

Annja smiled. "This ought to be good."

Tsing looked at Mike. "Where are the bodies of the workers? They will need a proper burial and my superiors will need to be informed."

Mike shook his head. "Well, then you've got a serious problem."

"Why is that?"

"Because Einstein over there had the bodies thrown into the treatment facility beneath us."

Annja thought she saw the color drain from Tsing's face. "Please tell me that you're lying."

"I wish I was, but it's the truth. Ask Tuk and he'll confirm it."

Tsing whirled around and stared at Tuk. "Is it true?"

Tuk, despite his obvious hatred, nodded. "I saw the bodies on the security cameras inside the mountain."

Tsing turned around and looked back at Vanya. "You did this?"

Vanya smiled. "I did."

"You know what this will do?"

"Of course."

Mike nodded. "Yeah, see, that's the other problem. By my watch, if I was reading those levels right back in the computer room, we've got maybe ten minutes before this place starts to melt right into the earth or blow up. Either way, it's not going to be a good thing."

Tsing frowned. "I assume there's no way to stop it?"

Vanya laughed. "Perhaps if you were to go down into the treatment facility and pull every last body from it, it might help ease the tension."

"You know as well as I do that we cannot enter that facility without the proper equipment," Tsing shouted.

Mike cleared his throat. "Then it might be a good time to tie up your loose ends and get the hell out of Dodge. I certainly don't want to hang around here any longer than absolutely necessary."

Tsing walked over to Burton. He whispered something in his ear and Burton nodded.

The air exploded with two shots that tore into Vanya's chest. The 7.62 mm rounds ripped her open and she dropped to the ground. Blood pumped out onto the stone floor and Tsing regarded her as if she had been a mere nuisance to him.

"She should have endured far greater pain and misery before I released her to death." He pointed at Hsu Xiao. "You will suffer for her crimes back in Beijing, I assure you."

"There is nothing they can do to me that would be worse than the horror of having your seed inside of me," she said.

Tsing laughed. "No, you see, that's where you're wrong. There is a great deal they can do to you that will make you wonder how much better it would be to reside in hell. The men in Beijing are masters of what they do. And they exist for the suffering of people like you who would see our state undermined for the petty purposes of personal grandeur."

Hsu Xiao fell silent.

Annja looked at Burton and Kurtz. They hadn't moved or said anything since Tsing's last order.

Annja spoke up. "So, I guess now would be a good time to leave?"

Tsing shook his head. "I'm afraid not. The last thing I can afford is to have you or anyone else left alive who can tell the world what has happened here."

"The world's going to find out, anyway, when this place blows up," she said.

Tsing shrugged. "They might think they know, but there will be no proof to find. All of the contractors involved in the construction of this facility have already been killed and their remains scattered. There are no notes of the construction that took place. In short, there's really nothing around that would ever tie the Chinese government to the horrible human tragedy about to befall this place."

"Someone will find out."

Tsing shook his head. "I doubt that very much."

"So, you're going to kill us?"

Tsing smiled. "Well, what would you do in my place, Annja? Let you all live and go free? Come on now, you're not that naive and neither is your friend Mike. Even Tuk there knows that he can't walk away from this one."

Tsing smiled once more and then turned to Kurtz. "Shoot them."

35

But even as Kurtz and Burton both moved to carry out the order, Annja and Hsu Xiao moved at the exact same time. Hsu Xiao unleashed a volley of throwing spikes and Annja had her sword in hand in an instant, cutting down at Kurtz's exposed arm.

Hsu Xiao's spikes bit into Burton's neck, jutting out of his larynx at odd angles. Burton's weapon swung up, wildly spraying rounds across the pavilion. Hsu Xiao had to dive and roll to avoid being struck by any of them.

Annja's blade sliced Kurtz's arm and his trigger hand fell slack, blood spouting and spraying the surrounding area. Kurtz screamed and tried to swing back to punch at Annja, but she sank down and then stabbed right up into Kurtz's exposed midsection. Her blade sliced Kurtz's heart in two.

Kurtz grabbed at Annja's blade and then fell back and off it as Annja got to her feet.

Across the way, Burton clawed at the spikes in his neck, gurgling on the blood that filled his lungs. His fingers scraped at the spikes and then he slumped over and fell, ramming the weapons deeper into his neck.

It happened so quickly that Tsing barely had time to comprehend it. In seconds he'd gone from a position of power to suddenly being drastically outnumbered.

Annja meanwhile had a more immediate threat. Hsu Xiao had gotten off the ground and now stalked her.

"It doesn't have to end this way," Annja said.

Hsu Xiao smiled. "I exist to deal out death."

"You can change."

Hsu Xiao cast a quick glance at Vanya's corpse and then shook her head. "No. I can't. And what would I do without my mistress? I live to serve her whims and I have carried out my orders faithfully, even when they entailed doing horrible things that no one should have to endure."

"You've served her honorably, no doubt," Annja said. "But let it go now. Think of your family."

"My family doesn't know I exist," said Hsu Xiao. "Vanya raised me from the time I was taken out of the nursery. My mother had triplets and was told only two survived. I was raised in secret to be a tool for her ambitions."

"Go home, then," Annja said. "Find your family. Tell them who you are."

Hsu Xiao shook her head. "I will never be permitted to live. I know too much and my connection to Vanya means I will be branded an enemy of the state. My life is forfeit."

Tsing sneered. "She's right. And once I get back I will see to it that she and her entire family are put to death."

Annja was about to say something when Tuk kicked Tsing's legs out from behind him and then clocked him on the head. Tsing sank to the stone floor unconscious. Tuk frowned. "He talks too much."

Annja kept her eyes on Hsu Xiao. "What if Tsing doesn't survive? There would be no one left to tell the government what happened here. You could make up any story you wish and they would never know."

Hsu Xiao shook her head. "It's not possible. I know what my future holds and I know what I have to do."

"But—"

As Annja started to protest, Hsu Xiao was already rushing at her. She cut and slashed and hacked at Annja, driving her back toward the grand staircase. Annja struggled to endure the assault, surprised that despite Hsu Xiao's injury she was still incredibly strong.

"Dammit, it doesn't have to be like this!"

Hsu Xiao smiled. "It does. I will die, Annja Creed, but first I will see to it that you die, as well. My mistress would have wanted it that way."

Annja felt the stairs beneath her feet and fell away, tumbling down them. The treads bit into her spine as she rolled. Annja willed the sword away before it toppled from her hands. She concentrated on tightening up into a ball as much as possible. If she could just minimize the impact to her body, when she came to rest at the bottom, she'd be okay.

But she hadn't counted on the steps being so sharp. The treads cut at her and she knew she was bleeding everywhere. When the bottom rushed up to greet her at long last, Annja unfolded with blood running from her arms, legs, back and head.

Hsu Xiao followed her down the stairs and landed gracefully at the bottom none the worse for wear.

Annja summoned the sword to her hands. "You mean to end this?" she asked.

Hsu Xiao nodded.

"Then let's do it." Annja frowned.

Hsu Xiao ran at her and Annja cut up, trying to take the offensive. But Hsu Xiao came in close and knee-locked Annja.

Driving her own knee against Annja's, she swept Annja's leg out and she collapsed onto the ground.

Annja pivoted and backfisted Hsu Xiao in the stomach. Hsu Xiao grunted and staggered away.

Annja got to her feet and brought the sword up in front of her, charging forward to cut down again and again at Hsu Xiao's exposed body. But as she brought her last cut straight down, Hsu Xiao brought her claws together and stopped the blade.

Annja was shocked. She'd never known anything that could stand up to a direct cut from her sword. It was then she realized that Hsu Xiao didn't have regular fingernails at all. She had metal claws like some movie character.

Worse, her claws had edges everywhere instead of just on one side.

Hsu Xiao flicked them at Annja and she felt one of them score a line across her face.

Blood streamed down her cheek.

Hsu Xiao pushed off against the sword blade and then kicked Annja again in the stomach. Annja rolled over backward, keeping a hold on the sword, but also smarting from the impact of the kick.

Annja immediately lashed out with her own kick and Hsu Xiao blocked it by bringing her leg up so it bent at the knee. Annja felt the kick slide off, but used the momentum to try to close some of the distance.

She did so and shot an elbow into Hsu Xiao's midsection. The assassin grunted and then thrust her hand at Annja's trachea. The shot scored a hit and Annja felt herself gagging and choking at the same time. She willed her throat to stop convulsing and prayed it wouldn't swell up.

Hsu Xiao raked her claws back and tried to catch Annja, but Annja had already started to duck and the claws only sliced through where her hair had been seconds earlier.

Annja pivoted on the ground and tried to sweep Hsu Xiao's legs out from under her, but the woman leaped into the air and then came down, aiming her heels at Annja's exposed knee. Annja saw the attack coming and, at the last possible second, curled her leg to avoid the incapacitating blow.

Hsu Xiao cut down and Annja barely had enough time to bring the sword up to block the shots. Hsu Xiao's claws clattered off the steel of the blade and Annja tried a halfhearted stab at Hsu Xiao's midsection.

Sweat poured off both of them. All of Annja's injuries stung from the sweat and salt rubbing with the blood and exposed skin. Hsu Xiao seemed to be running on fumes but her attacks never wavered.

She came at Annja, slashing with her claws at Annja's abdomen once more. Annja pivoted out of the way and used the pommel of the sword to backhand Hsu Xiao by the temple. She struck but the pommel only grazed Hsu Xiao. The assassin tumbled past and tucked herself into a roll.

Annja chased and cut down but then Hsu Xiao stopped herself and shot a donkey kick into Annja's body, catching Annja under the ribs. Annja felt the two previously injured ribs crack again and she cried out in pain.

Hsu Xiao recovered and then lunged at Annja, her claws already unfurling and aiming right at Annja's face. Annja ducked back and the claws arced through the space where her head had just been.

Annja brought the sword up and tried to once again stab into Hsu Xiao's midsection, but the assassin merely spun and the blade cut nothing but air.

This is getting ridiculous, Annja thought. I need to find a way to finish this thing once and for all. I haven't got much energy left and time is running out.

By Annja's estimate, they had perhaps five minutes until the entire installation blew up.

She had to end this battle.

Hsu Xiao delivered two sharp hand strikes to Annja's collarbones and Annja felt the jarring impact like it was a concussion grenade. She slumped with the strikes and Hsu Xiao followed up by kneeing Annja in the face.

Annja heard her nose crack and a fresh river of blood flowed down her face.

"You're finished, Annja Creed," Hsu Xiao said through clenched teeth. "Give up now and I will kill you painlessly."

"I don't know how to give up," Annja said. She cut back at Hsu Xiao and, this time, the point of her sword caught the lithe assassin near the ribs. Annja twisted the blade but Hsu Xiao had corrected her position and the blade cut no more.

Hsu Xiao danced away but Annja could see that she'd struck a solid cut. Blood was spreading on Hsu Xiao's shirt.

Annja pressed the attack, cutting out from the side, trying to cleave Hsu Xiao in two with the blow. Hsu Xiao ducked the blow and then tripped Annja as she passed.

Annja sprawled onto the ground and the sword clattered away.

In an instant, Hsu Xiao was atop Annja. Annja flipped over and faced Hsu Xiao. The Chinese assassin raked at Annja's face again and again.

Annja blocked the strikes and punched up into Hsu Xiao's face, scoring a direct hit on her nose. Hsu Xiao's face opened up and blood covered them both.

Annja kicked her hips up, trying to dislodge Hsu Xiao but the woman would not allow herself to be bucked off. Instead, she brought one of her claws under Annja's ear, nearly nicking it off in the melee.

Annja grimaced and used her elbows again to strike at Hsu Xiao's temple. She scored once and Hsu Xiao rolled clear.

Annja got to her feet, wobbling from the loss of blood.

Hsu Xiao also seemed unsteady, but her claws still gleamed in places that weren't covered with Annja's blood.

"It doesn't have to be this way," Annja said.

Hsu Xiao smirked. "You're begging for mercy now? I wouldn't have thought you were the type."

"I'm not," Annja said. "I'm giving you the chance to give up and stay alive."

Hsu Xiao shook her head. "We're too far into this. It has to end here and now."

Annja shook her head. "I don't want to have to kill you."

Hsu Xiao shrugged. "Then you're in trouble. Because I desperately want to kill you."

Annja frowned. "So be it."

Hsu Xiao rushed at Annja and Annja summoned the sword into her hands. The distance was almost too tight, but Annja managed to wedge the blade up and in so the point was aimed right at Hsu Xiao's heart as she came screaming back in one last time.

The tip of the sword slid into her chest and through her heart.

Instantly all the strength drained from the assassin's body and Hsu Xiao collapsed against Annja's chest, the blade jutting out through her back.

For a moment, Annja could have sworn she felt the pulsing tremor of two heartbeats. But then she realized it was only her own, echoing back from the body of her rival.

36

Annja rolled out from under Hsu Xiao and stared at the lifeless body of an enemy who had very nearly killed her. The sword hung heavy in her right hand and she closed her eyes and returned it to the otherwhere.

When she opened her eyes again, Hsu Xiao's stared into hers and, for just a moment, a spasm of fear rolled through Annja's stomach, but she looked again and knew that Hsu Xiao's lifeless cold orbs would never again hold life in them.

Her body ached and she struggled to get to her feet. She was weak from the loss of blood. Annja said a silent prayer of thanks for the skill and help in defeating Hsu Xiao and then she started to climb the stairs.

"Annja!"

Tuk raced down and helped her stagger up the stone steps. Annja kept her eyes focused on the walk ahead, but each step seemed to exacerbate the intense pain she felt riddling her body.

At the top of the stairs, she saw that Mike had a gun trained on the now-conscious Tsing. Tsing looked at her and smiled. "I see you persevered over a very adept enemy."

"She was incredibly skilled," Annja said. And then she felt her world tumble sideways. Tuk was there to catch her and he lowered her to the stone floor, wiping some of the sweat and blood away from her eyes.

"So what happens now?" asked Tsing. "Do you all go home riding off into the proverbial sunset? And what about me?"

Annja frowned and glanced at Mike, who had the gun trained on Tsing and looked as though he wanted to use it. "What do you think, Mike?"

"Damned if I know, Annja. A big part of me wants to shoot this guy and be done with him. But I've never murdered a man in cold blood before. Even someone like this turd, who clearly deserves it."

Annja tried to smile but groaned instead. Next to her, Tuk nursed some of her wounds.

"You're lucky to be alive," Tuk said quietly. "I've never seen a fight like that."

"I've never had a fight like that," Annja said. "And for a while there, I thought I was actually going to die."

Tuk grinned. "It looked that way. I wasn't sure what we were going to do if Hsu Xiao beat you and came running back up those steps. Mike and I were simply going to shoot her down with as many bullets as possible. It didn't look like anything could stop her."

"I wasn't sure anything could," Annja said. "But she made a mistake and I saw it. Sometimes, that's all it is. There's nothing amazing or significant about the victory. It's just a small thing that reveals itself in a blink in the action. You either take the opportunity or you lose it and die."

"And you took it."

"Fortunately," Annja said. "But I almost missed it. And if

I had, that would be me down there at the foot of those stairs instead of her."

"She was terrifying and incredible," Tuk said. "I know it seems silly, but I almost respected her for her ability."

"It's not silly," Annja said. "She should be respected. God knows I sure as hell do. I've faced a lot of foes and I remember only a few of the highly skilled ones. Hsu Xiao goes to the top of the list as far as I'm concerned."

Tsing cleared his throat. "I hate to break up this precious bonding moment and all, but according to your friend Mike, we only have two minutes to make our escape."

Annja looked up at Mike. "Is that true?"

Mike nodded gravely. "I'm afraid it is."

Annja glanced at Tuk. "Help me to my feet, would you?"

"Sure." Tuk got behind Annja and helped her up.

Annja wobbled once but then took a breath and got her heart beating steadily. "All right, let's go."

Tsing stood. "What about me?"

Annja looked at him. "What about you?"

"You're not going to kill me?"

"Tsing, I don't give a damn about you right now. All I care about is getting the hell out of here. You can come with us or you can stay. But no one's going to help you. You live or die by your own hand. Not mine or anyone else's."

Mike led the way toward the corridor and Tuk and Annja followed. From deep below them, there came a rumbling sound. All of them paused and then Mike waved them on.

"It's starting! We have to run!"

Tsing shoved Tuk out of the way. "Let me through, you pathetic people!" He dashed for the corridor ahead of them and disappeared from view.

Mike leveled the gun on him but Annja called out, "No!"

Mike stopped. "Why?"

"Let him go. If he gets himself out of this, we'll worry about him on the other side."

"You're being merciful," Tuk said.

Annja shook her head. "No, it's just I don't care about him anymore."

Another rumble caused the stone floor to shake and start to break apart. It was like being in the middle of an earthquake. From above, rocks and stones tumbled loose and cascaded down.

"Get inside the temple!" Mike shouted. "It's all going to come down around us!"

Tuk helped get Annja into the corridor. Behind them, the pavilion started to cave in and the floor buckled. As they ran past the statues, the closest one toppled over and then there was a terrific explosion.

Annja felt herself knocked clear off her feet and she crumbled to the floor as bits of stone came showering down around them.

"Annja!"

She felt Tuk's hand clutch at her own. He pulled her free of the debris, masonry dust caking his face. He coughed and brought her to her feet.

Annja tried to breathe but coughed on the dusty air, too.

"We've got to keep moving!" Mike said.

Annja could barely see Mike in front of them. He was struggling to stay upright and Annja realized that the floor was slanting. Like being on a listing ship, the entire surface was heaving as the facility beneath them started to explode and crumble in upon itself.

Another tremor rocked the temple and more rocks and stone came flying at them. Tuk steered Annja around some of the larger boulders.

From someplace ahead of them they heard a scream.

They hurried on and found Mike standing over Tsing. A

large section of stone lay atop Tsing's body, but he was still conscious.

"Hurry! You've got to get this off of me!" he pleaded.

Mike looked at Annja and shook his head. "There's no way we can lift it. It must weight a ton or more."

Tsing's face showed terror. "No! You cannot leave me here to die. You've got to help me!"

"We're out of time, Annja," Mike said.

Annja looked down at Tsing. "I told you that you were free to help yourself. But by your own hand. Not by ours."

"But surely you don't mean that! Help me, Annja Creed! Help me!"

Annja looked at Tuk. "Let's get the hell out of here."

Tuk nodded and they pressed on. Behind them they could still hear Tsing crying for help. "Don't leave me!"

Another rumble sounded and the room behind them crumpled and caved in, drowning out any more of Tsing's pleas for mercy or help.

Dust clouds followed them as they pressed toward the prison cell that had held Tuk. And then the doorway to freedom stood before them at long last.

Mike reached it first and waved them through. "Come on! We're almost there!"

Annja pushed Tuk ahead of her. "I'll make it. Just get yourself out."

Tuk looked at her once and then rushed ahead. Annja smiled and knew he'd survive. She urged her feet to keep moving.

Another tremor rocked the room she stood in and then she heard an incredible sound of something being torn wide-open. The floor behind her started to yawn and a gaping hole erupted beneath her feet.

"Annja!"

She turned back and saw Mike waving her on. Tuk creamed for her to jump.

Annja saw the fissure growing wider and she knew she vould have one chance to make the jump.

As the fissure spread, Annja dug deep and felt her heart hundering in her chest as the last bits of her adrenaline gave ier a sudden turbo boost of power. She leaped through the air is the floor fell away, finally reaching out for the doorway.

Her hands found the doorjamb of stone and she felt the loor give way beneath her. She found herself dangling in open space as the stone fell into a seething mass of angry greens and yellows a hundred feet below.

All of the nuclear waste that had been stored in the facility vas churning like a boiling cesspool of hell.

Annja felt her grip slipping.

She had no more strength anywhere in her body.

And just as she was about to lose it all—just as she was about to topple backward and fall into the swirling nuclear nists—she felt two hands clutch her and pull her through the loorway.

She fell into Tuk and Mike and they dragged her toward he staircase.

More explosions thundered around them as they clambered up the stairs toward the trapdoor.

Mike made it through the trapdoor first. Annja felt herself ifted up and then Tuk's face appeared behind her.

"Quickly, Tuk, shut the door," Mike said.

Annja managed to pull herself clear and then she heard Tuk slamming the stone trapdoor behind them.

Cold winds pounded them as the cave itself started to rumble.

"It's not safe here!" Mike said. "The whole mountain is going to give way."

"Outside!" yelled Tuk. "We've got to get outside!"

Mike and Tuk eased Annja through the opening in the cave and then followed her out. Blinding sunlight greeted her and the numbing cold bit at every pore of her body. Annja felt pain like she'd never experienced before in her life. Every fiber of her soul seemed like it was on fire.

She bled and sweated and froze as the mountain rumbled around her like an angry volcano.

"This way!"

Mike pointed down the slope toward the crash site of the plane. Tuk helped Annja up. "We've got to keep going!"

Annja shook her head. "I can't."

"You must! Don't give up on me now, Annja Creed!"

Mike came back and tried to scoop Annja up in his arms. He took two steps forward and then fell into the snow. It was too deep and he was still too weak himself to carry Annja.

"You've got to walk! We'll help you!"

Miniavalanches started breaking loose from the ice sheet and tons of snow and ice started rocketing down from the peak toward them.

"Run!"

Annja felt like her legs were lead but she pushed herself further than she ever had before. She had to get down the slope.

Tuk ran along beside her, his legs still pumping like mad pistons.

Mike's big arms tried to lift Annja along when he could and the three of them kept stumbling along.

"Look out!"

A snow boulder rumbled past them, barely missing them all by mere inches. They kept trying to run through the waist deep snows back toward the plane.

Annja wanted to tell Tuk to use his cell phone, but if she did he would have stopped and that would have been the end of them all. They had to keep moving. They had to make it back down the mountain.

And then Annja heard an incredible sound amid the thundering rumbles and cracks of rocks tumbling loose from their millennia-old perches.

A helicopter.

At first she thought she was imagining it, but then she saw the chopper appear overhead, its rotors beating the sky around it.

"It's Garin!" shouted Tuk. "He's found us!"

Annja tried to smile, but only took two more steps toward the helicopter before she tumbled and fell facefirst into the white snow.

37

A gray, cloying mist surrounded Annja as she floated with no sense of time or space. She could feel her strength returning slowly, and yet a big part of her had no desire to relinquish the peace she felt in this strange limbo world. It was easier here, she thought, than to have to go back to the real world.

But something needled at her persistently, poking its way into her dreamworld consciousness. It refused to leave her alone. And finally, after trying to ignore it for a long while, Annja succumbed.

"Annja!"

She heard the voices calling her, but resisted opening her eyes until the very last moment, hoping against hope that this was all part of a dream. That when she opened her eyes, it would be dark outside, she'd stare at the clock and see it was only three in the morning, heave a grateful sigh and then roll over to go back to sleep.

"Annja!"

Not this time.

She groaned and opened her eyes. The first thing she saw was Tuk's face roughly an inch from hers.

She nearly jerked herself right out of bed. "Tuk! Jeez, give a woman some room, would you?"

Tuk pulled back, his eyes moist with tears. "Oh, thank God you're back. The doctors, they said you were going to be fine, but I worried. I've never seen anyone take the abuse you took and live to tell the tale. I was worried. I sure was. But you're back now. Everything's great."

Annja pushed herself to sit up in the bed.

Tuk smiled, wiping his tears. "I've been keeping a watch over you every day just to make sure the doctors don't screw up."

Annja laughed. "Second-guessing all of their decisions? That must make you the most popular person in the hospital right now." Annja glanced around. The walls were the standard antiseptic hospital white that she hated. Something about being in the hospital always made her feel sick. "Where am I, anyway?"

"Katmandu. Garin and his crew brought you straight here. We didn't even land in Jomsom to refuel, just flew straight in. He was well and truly worried, that one was. But he kept saying to us that if anyone could survive, it would be you. Seems as though he's quite fond of you."

"Oh, really? That would be news to me." Annja saw the vase of fresh flowers on the nightstand. "Are those from you?"

Tuk shook his head. "No. Those are from Garin. He said it was important to make sure you saw them when you woke up. Something about how flowers always bring us back to the goodness of God's earth. Some religious thing or something. I don't know."

Annja looked at the flowers. They were fresh orchids and

she wondered where he might have had them flown in from. They were beautiful.

"So, where is everyone?" she asked.

"Garin's gone to get something to eat, but I think he was really more interested in chasing down the nurse who was in here a few minutes back."

"That sounds just about right," Annja said.

"Mike is upstairs having a second opinion about his head."

"What do you mean?"

"He says he hasn't had any headaches since we got out of that place. He wanted to know what was going on."

Annja frowned. "Are they even set up for that kind of diagnosis here? I mean, no offense, but third-world medical care isn't always the best."

Tuk frowned. "Well, they do a pretty good job here. I've been very impressed with the care you've received."

"Well, thank you. It's nice to know someone is looking out for my best interests."

"Absolutely. If you hadn't saved my life, I wouldn't even be here right now."

Annja shook her head. "It's you who should be thanked, Tuk. If Garin hadn't hired you to watch over me, none of us would have reached this point. I'm indebted to you for the rest of my life—however long that happens to be."

"Just doing my job."

"And you did a damned good job of it," Annja said.

Tuk eased himself off the corner of the bed and set about smoothing the wrinkles in the sheets he'd left behind. "Well, my days of working are now at an end, so it's nice I was able to go out on such a high note."

"You're retiring?"

"Garin paid me handsomely for all my hard work. I've got more than enough to retire to the countryside and get a small place. I can sleep as long as I want, eat when I want and never have to worry about anything until I get bored."

"Well, if you ever do get bored, you're welcome to look me up. I'm sure I can find some sort of excitement for you to get mixed up in. Seems I attract the stuff like nobody's business."

Tuk nodded. "Yes, well, thanks for the offer, but I don't know if I should. Things get more dangerous around you than I'm comfortable with. I mean, a little danger is fine, but fully automatic weapons, assassins and nuclear waste are too much for me."

"You're not the only one."

"Yes, but you know how to deal with it. I don't. I'm not some globe-trotting superhero who can take down enemies and save the world."

"Neither am I, Tuk," Annja said. "I try to get out of bed in the morning and see where the day takes me. I've got this part of me I'm trying to make sense of. Some kind of destiny that I can't always come to terms with, and yet I've got to. The danger, the near-death experiences, they're all a part of it. But I don't ever look in the mirror and think that I'm something amazing. The day I do that, I think will probably be my last."

"You're modest, too, aren't you?" Tuk asked.

"I don't know about that," Annja said. "I'm just me."

Tuk nodded. "Well, I've got to head out. I'm going to see about a house up the hills."

"Hills?"

Tuk shrugged. "Mountains, I guess you'd call them."

"You're buying there even with all of that snow?"

"I love the snow," Tuk said. "It's just dying in it that I can't stand."

Annja grabbed him and gave him a hug. "Anytime you want to come to the States, give me a call and we'll hang out. You're a good man, Tuk, and I'm happy to have known you."

Tuk pulled back and brushed his hands across his eyes. "You're going to make me cry. Stop that." He blinked back tears and smiled at her. "I'm happy to have made your acquaintance, too, Annja Creed. You really are an amazing woman."

"Thank you."

Tuk waved at her one last time and then ducked out of the door quickly. Annja listened to it hiss shut and closed her eyes.

She thought about it for a few minutes and decided that if she could just lie in this reasonably comfortable bed for about a month, she might honestly start feeling pretty good again.

She could sleep the days away and just concentrate on getting herself back to normal. She stretched her limbs and felt her muscles expand and then contract. A yawn came over her and she sank back into the bed, allowing her spine to lengthen, and she heard a few muffled pops as it relaxed even more.

The phone on the bedside table rang. Annja opened her eyes and stared at it. "So much for peace and quiet."

She reached for the phone and picked it up. "Hello?"

"Annja? It's Doug."

Annja groaned. Doug Morrell was her producer on *Chasing History's Monsters*. "Doug, what are you doing calling me here? Did you hear that I was close to death?"

"Of course I did. But since you answered the phone, it can't be all that bad, can it?"

"I suppose not. I haven't seen the doctors yet, though—"

"Well, there's no time. Listen, I need you to get to Scotland. A whole rash of new Nessie sightings have just sparked up over there. We're talking some crazy stuff. People running into the monster on boats, cars and someone even claims they stumbled upon it on a path in the woods."

"Sounds delightful. Why don't you send Miss Lose-My-Top on this one so I can take a much-needed vacation?"

"Annja, your vacations are what tend to get you into trouble in the first place. Need I remind you that this trip to Nepal was supposedly a vacation? And we nearly lost you! No way. I need you back to work as soon as humanly possible."

"I'll ask my doctors how soon I can get out of here. Is that satisfactory to you, Doug?"

"As long as they say you can leave tomorrow, then, yeah, absolutely."

"I'll be sure to tell them that."

"Call me when you're released." The phone disconnected and Annja slumped back into the bed.

The Loch Ness Monster? Again? Hadn't she already run that story down before? And yet here it was again.

Annja took a series of deep breaths and willed herself to relax. Doug could wait if need be. She wasn't in a hurry to go anywhere or do anything until she had rested enough to truly regain her strength.

There were only a few times when she'd felt as totally drained as she had back on the mountain. And each of those times had meant a longer than normal recovery time for her.

No, someone else could run down the Loch Ness story if Doug wanted it so badly. Annja wasn't sure what she wanted to do, but traipsing through a cold lake district in Scotland.

A trip to a spa would fit the bill nicely, though, she thought. A long series of massages, hot baths, aromatherapy and good meals. Now that might be something worth looking into.

She wondered if Garin had succeeded in chasing down the nurse he was apparently after. Annja frowned. Here she was, lying near death in a hospital, and all he could think about was another notch on his bedpost.

Way to show me that you care, Garin, she thought. Thank God Tuk was here.

She thought about Mike. What did it mean that his head didn't hurt him anymore? Was there a chance that his tumor was in remission? Could it mean that he would have more years of his life to live out rather than some quick death sentence?

Annja hoped it would mean he'd be able to enjoy his life again. Although she wondered how the cancer could have gone into remission. Was it due to something they'd been exposed to back at the facility? Did radiation exposure kill cancer cells? Annja wasn't sure how the whole chemotherapy thing worked, but if Mike had explored the facility and possibly gotten himself some exposure to radiation, then maybe that had affected his tumor.

So, some good comes out of all of this, after all, she thought.

She took another deep breath and exhaled slowly, willing herself to fall asleep. She felt certain that at any moment Garin would no doubt burst through the door and disturb her peaceful atmosphere.

The door hissed open. "You have the worst timing," she said.

She opened her eyes.

But Garin wasn't standing there. A Nepali nurse had come in and stood next to her bed, smiling at her.

"Oh," Annja said. "Sorry, I thought you were somebody else."

The nurse nodded and Annja looked at her again. It couldn't be. Not her.

"You're dead," she started to say.

But then the nurse's hand clamped down over Annja's nose and mouth, trying to smother her.

38

Annja struggled to free herself from the crushing weight of Vanya's body as she tried to smother Annja. Vanya dropped an elbow into Annja's midsection and the impact made Annja gasp for breath even more.

Annja swung her arms up and clapped Vanya around the side of the head, trying to rupture her eardrums. But the older woman ducked the blow and Annja's hands only smacked Vanya on the side of the head.

Vanya climbed atop Annja and tried to choke her. Annja gagged and kept fighting, aware that she was rapidly losing consciousness. All of her strength seemed to have left her.

Vanya's voice was a sinister whisper in her ear. "You've ruined my plans, Annja Creed. I can never go home again and it's all because of you."

Annja kicked her hips up and dislodged Vanya, who fell to the floor. Annja scrambled to her feet on the other side of the bed. She ripped out her IV line and grimaced as pain shot through her body.

"I saw you die. Tsing's man shot you three times in the chest."

Vanya got to her feet slowly. "Another little bit of make-believe. I didn't get as far as I have in this life by being too stupid to wear a bulletproof vest with a layer of fake blood over it for just that purpose."

"You wear that everywhere?"

"Whenever there's danger to me, yes."

"But the facility exploded. You should have died there with Tsing and your assassin, Hsu Xiao."

Vanya's gaze was searing. "You killed my most illustrious pupil. Yet another reason to come after you. And as for not escaping, there is always more than one exit in anything I get involved with. As soon as you all fled, I got up and ran. I was back in Katmandu before you."

Vanya circled the bed. Annja backed up, aware now that the woman had a scalpel in her hand.

Annja frowned. "Why not just shoot me?"

Vanya shook her head. "Metal detectors downstairs. I wouldn't have gotten it through." She hefted the scalpel. "But a little blade, well, they're easy to find in a place like this."

Annja felt the wall behind her. She tried to summon the sword, but couldn't visualize the blade properly. Her sword wasn't there.

Vanya smiled. "What's the matter, dear? Having trouble conjuring your special sword?"

Annja frowned and tried again, aware that Vanya was edging closer to her. Annja could just make out a fuzzy image of the sword, but it didn't seem to be enough to get it to materialize in her hands.

So she lunged, and threw the pitcher of water from the nightstand at Vanya. But Vanya, surprisingly nimble for her age, ducked the container and moved even closer.

"Not to worry, Annja," she said. "I'll sever your windpipe

so you get to die choking on your own blood. I figure it's the least I can do, considering how you treated Hsu Xiao."

"I gave Hsu Xiao the chance to walk away," Annja said. "She chose to end her life by fighting me."

"If you had joined us, we could all be in power right now. The fallout from the facility explosion would have enabled us to seize power, Annja. Instead, all of my dreams have been laid to waste because of you and that sword of yours. Ever since I heard of it, I've been obsessed with having it. And now you can't even bring it out to kill me."

Annja looked around frantically. There was precious little she could use to fend off Vanya.

"Help me!" she screamed.

"They'll never get here in time," Vanya said.

Annja made a lunge for the red distress call button and punched it hard.

But Vanya kept laughing. "They won't come. I unhooked the receiver at the nurse's station. We're all alone, Annja. And now I can finally finish what I started."

She slashed at Annja's throat. Annja ducked and then kicked up at Vanya's kneecap. The kick landed square and Vanya grunted as the heel landed flush. But her leg didn't buckle.

"That works better if the leg is straightened," Vanya said. Then she punched Annja across the jaw.

The blow sent Annja reeling. She toppled over the bed, landing on her feet near the door. She made a run for it, but the door was locked.

"I've got the key right here," said Vanya. "You're welcome to try and take it from me."

Annja tried to summon the sword again. It was a little more clear, but she still couldn't see clearly enough to bring it out.

Vanya edged closer again and, this time, when she slashed,

the edge of the scalpel bit into Annja's forearm, scoring a line from the wrist to the elbow. Annja glanced down and saw a flap of skin hanging loose. Blood poured from the wound and spilled across the sheets and the floor.

Annja slid back toward the wall, gripping her arm. Vanya came closer. "I'll make it quick," she said.

Annja lashed out with another kick and landed it square in Vanya's stomach. Vanya doubled over and backed away.

I've got to get the sword, Annja thought.

But then Vanya was coming at her again, cutting and slashing with the scalpel.

Annja fell back under the assault, and when she tried to check Vanya's advance, Vanya grabbed her wounded arm and Annja screamed. Vanya's nails sank into the exposed muscle and tendons and crushed them under her grip.

The pain nearly caused Annja to pass out.

But she used all of her strength to throw Vanya back across the room. The woman slammed into the wall opposite the bed and fell to the floor. But she immediately scrambled to her feet and came running again.

"You're not going to make it out of here alive, Annja Creed," she shouted as she cut down with the scalpel. This time, it stuck into the exposed bone in Annja's forearm.

Annja screamed again and tore her arm away from Vanya's grasp, the scalpel jutting out at an awful angle. Annja glanced down at the blade and yanked it free. Then she stalked Vanya.

But Vanya pulled out another scalpel and the two of them circled.

Vanya feinted and came in with a straight stab. Annja sidestepped the thrust and slashed across the top of Vanya's forearm, drawing blood for the first time.

Vanya let out a shriek and then retreated, but still kept her blade in front of her.

Annja, woozy from the injuries, advanced but slowed down.

Vanya backslashed at Annja, who checked the blow and then stabbed into Vanya's stomach with the scalpel. The cut was superficial, but Vanya staggered back, clutching at her abdomen.

Vanya suddenly flew at Annja and the rush of energy toppled them back over the bed. The nightstand yielded to their body weight, splintering and breaking into pieces.

Jagged bits of wood scattered about them and Vanya raised herself up, grabbing one of the coarse pieces. She brought it down on Annja's head.

Annja felt the impact and nearly lost consciousness. But she fought back against the rising tide of blackness, punching at Vanya and scoring a direct hit on the older woman's face.

Vanya's nose cracked and a stream of blood shot out, staining an already slick floor.

Annja tried to stand but her head throbbed. I can't take much more of this, she thought.

For a moment, her vision wavered and then Annja sank to the floor. She closed her eyes and prayed that she would see the sword. She needed it now.

The sword materialized in her mind's eye. She grabbed it and opened her eyes just in time to see Vanya rushing at her with everything she had.

Annja slid back down against the wall, the sword held up in front of her.

Vanya's eyes locked onto the blade and then, with a scream, she slipped on the bloody floor and pitched onto the blade.

Annja felt a sickening lurch as Vanya's body hit the tip. There was a moment of tension and then Vanya's body slid down the blade, coming to rest on the floor at Annja's feet.

"You want the sword?" Annja said. "Now you've got it."

Annja slumped back against the wall and realized that the

world hurt a whole lot more than she'd ever been willing to admit.

The door to her room flew open.

"Annja!"

Annja raised a hand weakly. "Here."

Garin's bulk rushed in and Annja couldn't believe how happy she was to see him.

"Are you all right?" he asked.

"What are you saying? I look like crap?"

Garin eyed Vanya. "I wondered if anyone might try to make an attempt on your life. I went to find the nurse who was acting strangely."

"Tuk said you were checking her out."

"I was. But not in the way you think." He looked over Vanya's body. "She had some fight in her, didn't she?"

"Almost too much," Annja said.

Garin stepped outside and called for a doctor. When he came back in, he knelt by Annja and looked at her arm. "This is going to take a while to heal."

"Great."

"Just can't stay out of the fights, can you?" He smiled at her and, despite feeling like death, Annja grinned back.

She heard a commotion out in the hallway. "Doctors are coming," she said.

Garin nodded. "Yeah, and you might want to put that blade away before anyone sees it."

Annja nodded. "Good point." The sword vanished.

Garin helped her get back to the bed. Annja felt the incredible strength in his body and wished that she could borrow some of it so she didn't feel quite so small and weak as she did just then.

Garin hovered over her. "You're going to be fine, Annja. It takes more than this to keep you down."

Annja smiled. "If you say so."

The doctors and nurses rushed in. Their shouts echoed down the hallways as they called for police, more nurses and a cleanup crew. Garin hovered close by and Annja got the distinct impression he wasn't going to let her out of his sight for a good long time.

That was fine. Because if Vanya had any friends looking for revenge, there was no way that Annja was going to be able to fend them off.

Garin leaned over her as the doctors and nurses started tending to her wounds. "Hang in there," he said.

She smiled weakly. "What else would I do?"

Garin backed up as more nurses came in and shooed him away from Annja's bed. She let herself be tended to, not really feeling much pain anymore—not really feeling much of anything. Her mind drifted and floated all around the hospital room. She saw the doctors studying her wound intently while one prepared to sew her up. Nurses and attendants hauled Vanya's body away with a sense of bewilderment on their faces. They could see that Vanya had impaled herself on something, but what? And where was the weapon now?

Garin steered their questions away but Annja wasn't worried. She knew that he could field all their concerns and keep everyone quiet about anything he wanted to. And she felt better that he was in the room with her.

"I'm going to sleep now," she said quietly.

39

Annja opened her eyes to bright sunshine flooding her hospital room. One of the windows overlooked a courtyard and the scent of flowers hung in the air. She smiled and rose to take a shower.

She'd stayed in the hospital for just over a week, happy to take it easy for once. The doctors told her it would take a few more weeks for things to heal completely, but they had also told her she was strong enough to go home.

Annja's single bag lay on the bed and she rummaged through it, looking at the variety of clothes Garin had purchased to replace what she'd lost early on in the trip. She settled on jeans and a turtleneck sweater.

As she carefully pulled on the clothes and then brushed her hair, a knock sounded at the door.

Before she could respond Garin's face appeared around the corner. "Are you indecent?" he asked. He frowned when he saw she was already dressed. "Damn, I was hoping to time it better."

Annja smiled. "Really? You're resorting to a quick game of peekaboo? Is it that thrilling?"

"Depends on the woman," Garin said. "With you, peekaboo would definitely be a highlight."

"Keep dreaming, then," Annja said.

"I shall." Garin nodded at the bag. "Just about finished?"

"Yeah. Thanks for the clothes."

"Least I could do. After you nearly died on this adventure. I figured clothes shopping might not be high on the old priority list. Plus, there was the incredibly beautiful salesgirl—"

"Garin."

He held up his hands. "Sorry, just kidding. You know I have to reinforce my reputation any chance I get."

"Well, give it a rest, would you? It wears on me lately."

Garin sat by the window and watched her.

Annja finished packing her bag. "You know, there's one thing that's been bothering me about this whole thing."

"What's that?" Garin turned to peer out of the window.

"You."

He glanced at Annja. "Me? What about me?"

"Well, you hired Tuk to watch over me. But why? I mean, if you were so concerned about my safety, then why on earth didn't you just come here yourself and take care of the danger?"

"It's not always that easy, Annja."

"Baloney. I've never known you to back away from a fight. And now all of a sudden you start? It doesn't make sense."

Garin smiled. "I wasn't backing away from anything. But at the same time, I needed a low profile."

"Why?"

"Because I didn't know who was after you until Tuk started relaying information to me. And even then, it took me a while to piece things together. When he told me about Hsu Xiao,

I had to go back and search through my databases and ones I'm not supposed to have access to. Even then I was playing catch-up the entire way."

"I guess."

Garin stood in front of her. "Believe me, Annja, if there'd been a way for me to take this off of you, I would have. But I couldn't risk it without having concrete proof, and by then things were so far in motion already, I couldn't get to you in time. I had to rely on Tuk. And thank God he turned out to be as formidable as he was."

Annja looked at him. "Why do I get the feeling you're not telling me everything?"

Garin sighed. "You're so damned intuitive it drives me crazy. And honestly, I forget who I'm dealing with sometimes. You're not just a pretty face, are you?"

"I'm not a pretty face, right now," Annja said, smiling.

"I couldn't be here in Katmandu because I'm too well known. As it was, I took a great chance coming to hire Tuk."

"Who knows you?"

Garin shrugged. "The better question might be who doesn't know me?"

"Tsing?"

Garin nodded. "We did some work together a while back. He knew me very well and…let's just say that it didn't end well."

"In what way?"

"Let's suppose he told me that if I ever showed my face in Katmandu again, he'd have me drawn and quartered."

Annja smiled. "Sounds about right."

"When Tuk told me that Tsing was involved I kept an even lower profile. Specifically, I flew to India and stayed there until I knew what was going on. Once you were off to Jomsom and Mustang, something didn't feel right, so I flew back into the country, waiting for Tuk's phone call."

"But when it came," Annja said, "we'd already crashed."

"Exactly. By then, I didn't much care if Tsing knew I was back. I went to him, prepared to offer a truce until I could find you, but he'd already chased you up to Jomsom. Or actually, I think he was chasing Hsu Xiao because she tried to poison him."

"So, by the time all of this was happening, we were already at the fabled Shangri-La."

"Yes, well, that does sound better than nuclear waste facility masquerading as a mystical land."

Annja hefted her bag. "You ready to go?"

Garin rose. "Sure am."

They walked out of the hospital together and the weather was spectacular. Annja took a deep breath and exhaled. Her body felt good. Not perfect, but really good. And well on the mend.

She felt rested. Better than in a very long time. "I'm looking forward to going home," she said.

Garin smiled and handed her a plane ticket. "Here you go. It's first class."

"First class? What did I do to deserve this?"

"As if you didn't know."

Annja laughed. "What about you, Garin? Where are you off to now?"

"Ah, well, you know how it is. Lots of things to do and see. Lots of other activities to keep me busy."

Annja looked at him for a moment. "Maybe someday you'll stop doing whatever it is that you do."

"Maybe," Garin said. "And maybe someday you'll stop what you do, too."

"I don't know if I can. The sword seems to have my destiny all mapped out but damned if I can fathom it."

"We all have our destinies to play out, Annja," Garin said. "But play them out we will. And maybe when they're done and finished, we can actually live how we want to. You know, if you happen to believe in free will and all."

"Free will," Annja said. "That's quite a concept." She turned her gaze away.

"Looking for something?" Garin asked.

"I was hoping to see Mike. I haven't seen him since the mountain. He left me a message saying something about his brain tumor, but then it got cut off and I never learned what was going on."

"Maybe Mike's got his own destiny to play out, too." Garin smiled. "Remember, nothing's ever quite what it seems, is it?"

"What's that supposed to mean?"

Garin kissed her on the cheek. "Goodbye, Annja. I'll be seeing you around. We won't always be friends, but we won't always be enemies, either. Remember that the next time you want to kill me."

Annja looked at him for a long moment and then stood on her tiptoes to kiss him on his cheek. "You do the same."

"I shall."

She watched him walk away and vanish into the crowd. Annja never knew how such a large man could so easily disappear, but somehow he always did.

Annja looked around. She needed a taxi and then it was a trip to the airport followed by a long flight home. She wondered if they served ice cream sundaes on the plane?

A taxi sidled up next to her and she got in. "Airport, please."

"Why the hell do you want to go there?"

Annja looked up and then saw the face of the driver. "Mike!"

He grinned at her. "Hey, kid."

"What are you doing driving a cab?"

Mike nodded at her ticket. "You got time to take a ride? Maybe have a conversation about stuff?"

"My flight's not for hours yet. I've got some time."

"Good." Mike eased out into the traffic and they drove through the congested streets of Katmandu. Gradually, the city limits fell behind them and they passed into more rural areas. Annja looked out of her window and watched the children playing soccer and laughing and running through the streets.

"What's going on?" Annja asked.

"You'll see," he said.

He pulled over near the airfield where they'd been stowed aboard Tsing's plane and switched off the cab's engine. Then he got out of the car and leaned against the hood.

Annja followed him. "It's great to see you again, you big lug."

He hugged her and then set her back down. "Sorry, I haven't been around. I had to take care of some things."

Annja nodded. "I heard. Tuk said something about your cancer being in remission. That's wonderful news! Congratulations."

"Thanks. But it's not in remission."

"It's not?"

"No. It's gone. Completely."

Annja felt her heart leap. "Even better! Wow, how did that happen?"

Mike shrugged. "I don't want you to get mad at me, okay?"

Annja backed away. "What is it?"

"I never had it to begin with."

"What?"

Mike held up his hands. "Annja, hear me out—"

"You faked that? I was beside myself with grief for you and now you tell me it was all a lie? How dare you!"

"I had to lie, Annja."

"Why in the world did you have to lie?"

"Because that was part of my cover."

Annja frowned. "Cover? What cover? You're a teacher, Mike. You don't need a cover."

"The teacher thing is my cover. The brain cancer was another facet of it. Together, they helped sell me."

Annja shook her head. "Jesus Christ, don't tell me you're a spook."

"Guilty."

Annja sighed. "How the hell did that happen? The last I heard you were doing great at your job and you had a great career."

"I do have a great career. But it's doing something other than teaching. The Agency uses me for a variety of unorthodox assignments, and the rest of the time I'm a mild-mannered teacher. It works out very well."

"CIA?"

"Yes."

"You don't look like a case officer."

Mike smiled. "Not everyone who works for the CIA, works for the CIA, if you get my meaning."

"I don't."

"The Agency uses a whole network of independent contractors. It goes back many years. In this country there is a network of people who can be called upon at any time to step up and take on assignments best handled by someone other than official CIA officers, even those deep-cover guys. So the Agency uses us and we're sort of cutaway from the apparatus as a whole. It gives us better flexibility and more freedom to pursue what needs to be done without a whole bunch of hamstringing oversight."

"If you say so."

"Don't be upset with me, Annja. I feel bad enough that
had to get you involved in this. It's all my fault that this
happened to you and you got so banged up. But I needed you
to come along or I never would have been able to sell it to
Tsing."

"Sell what to Tsing?"

Mike sighed. "For a long time now, the Agency has suspected that the Chinese have been dumping nuclear waste
somewhere, but we never knew where. Some analysts thought
it was a safe bet that they were dumping it at sea, but we've
been watching for signs of that and never caught them doing
it. That left either space or they were burying it.

"Now the Chinese have a fairly admirable space program,
but they're not anywhere ready to start shipping rockets full
of waste to dump up there. So that left burying it."

"Would they really do that?"

"China's got more environmental waste than almost any
other country on the planet, including us, if you can believe
that."

"I don't know if I can."

Mike continued. "We'd heard rumors about a construction project that happened over near Mustang, but we never
had a solid lead to follow until a few weeks ago. One of the
contractors offered a map of the area on the black market."

"A map? That one you had that supposedly showed the
way to Shangri-La?"

"The same. Of course, Tsing tried to buy it back, but the
dealer said no way. We heard about it and the Agency figured
I would have the best chance of acquiring the map."

Annja shook her head. "Wait—why would Tsing need to
buy back a map to a place he already knew all about? Didn't
he help build it?"

"He sure did. But he wanted the map so he could make

sure it was off the market. He didn't need it per se, it was just his attempt to contain an information leak."

"But why go to him for the fifty thousand you needed to buy the map? Couldn't the Agency just front you the cash?"

Mike frowned. "No, Tsing was too well connected in Chinese Intelligence to ever believe that I had the capacity to finance the map purchase. If the Agency fronted me the money, Tsing would have known who I was immediately and just had me killed."

Annja sighed. "I'm still confused as to why Tsing ever brought us before him and told you that he was interested in finding Shangri-La. What was that all about?"

"The code name for the supposed location of the nuclear waste facility we had learned about was always Shangri-La. The contractor who put the map on the market called it that after what the Chinese planned to name the place."

"So, a dual-meaning sort of thing, huh?"

"To Tsing, I was just a history teacher looking for the fabled location of the real Shangri-La. In his mind, he was going to get the map back. In my mind, I was working to ascertain the exact location of a nuclear waste facility built and operated by the Chinese government. Three layers of duplicity, I guess you could say."

"And one very confused Annja Creed."

"Welcome to the intelligence world."

"No, thanks." Annja turned away. "What happened to the facility, anyway? I haven't seen any mention of it on the news."

"That's because there hasn't been any."

"How in the world could they possibly keep that a secret?"

Mike shrugged. "They had help."

"Who?"

"Uncle Sam."

"We helped them? Why the hell would we do such a thing? They damn near contaminated an entire country. The world deserves to know what happened."

"Things aren't that black and white anymore, Annja. The cold war's over and we live in a new world now. Enemies aren't always enemies. Friends aren't always friends. About the best we can manage now is a sort of gray relationship where hopefully we all get along and manage to keep the world spinning."

"So we helped them keep the lid on this?"

"More than that, we helped them clean it up."

"Clean it up?"

"Turns out their containment structure is pretty amazing. It kept most of the gloop inside where it needed to be. The Shangri-La structure atop the waste box simply fell in and vaporized or whatever."

"But all that radiation…?"

"Currently being piped to a new treatment facility. One we're helping the Chinese build so they do it right." Mike shrugged. "It ain't a perfect world, Annja, but it's pretty much the only one we've got."

"And what about me?" Annja asked.

"What about you?"

"I ate a peach off one of the trees in the land we were in. So am I going to get radiation poisoning?"

"Nope."

"You say that so positively."

"I am positive. You weren't exposed to any radiation. Nothing showed up on your tests."

"What tests?"

Mike smiled. "The ones you took while you were in the hospital."

"I don't remember those tests."

"Blood work, mostly," Mike said. "I had my friends check

you out to make sure there was no lasting damage to you. You'll be sore from your other injuries, but otherwise, you're good to go."

Annja frowned. "And what if I don't feel like keeping what happened here a secret? What if my conscience demands I tell people about it?"

Mike scowled. "Then I'd have no choice but to let my superiors know about that incredible sword of yours."

Annja stopped. "You're blackmailing me?"

"It's not blackmail, Annja. It's just an agreement. We help each other here. You don't get hassled by the government and you keep quiet about that thing you witnessed. Everybody makes out just perfectly."

"What about Tuk? He saw the same things I saw."

"Tuk's not a problem. He's being paid a handsome annuity to stay quiet. And he says he wouldn't say anything, anyway."

Annja stayed quiet for a moment. "All right."

Mike clapped his hands. "Great. Thanks, Annja."

"So, answer me this. How did the Chinese know about Tuk? And how did they find all those people to look like him? He really thought they were his long-lost tribe."

"Hsu Xiao reported Tuk to Vanya and they figured it out from there. As for the workers, they'd been carted in from a small village in southwestern China. Turns out everyone there is that size and no one really knows why. Who knows, maybe that's where Tuk is really from."

"I guess it doesn't matter now," Annja said. "Vanya killed them all."

Mike nodded. "One of the tragedies of this whole thing." He pointed at the cab. "We should get going."

Annja slid into the cab and rested her head back against the seat. The enormity of what Mike was asking her to do was something she would have to reconcile on her own time.

Mike started the engine and drove back out onto the street. "Look, I know it might take you a while to get through what I'm asking you to do, but I've got something that might take your mind off of that."

Annja almost laughed out loud. "And what, pray tell, is that?"

Mike tossed something into the backseat. Annja picked it up and saw that it was a laminated map. She unfolded it. After a moment, she looked back up. "Is this what I think it is?"

Mike nodded. "Yep."

Annja smiled. "I don't know if I should go looking for another Shangri-La so soon after this one."

"Annja, this is the real thing! Honest! I got this map from a friend of mine who swears the real Shangri-La is in the Kunlun Mountains. Hey, it's better than the Himalayas, right? Not nearly as cold there. Well, maybe it is cold there, too, but you know…"

Mike kept talking, but Annja just stared out the window. She was headed to the airport, that much was certain.

But beyond that, she had no idea.